Head snapping upright, Nick turned his murky gold eyes to me. "Why were you screaming?"

"Dude, I was fighting vampires. They're scary, and sometimes, there's screaming. It's like a reflex or something, okay? And then this big tiger showed up, except it wasn't a real tiger, but Logan."

"He saved you."

That stung. Man, did it sting. "For your information, I was holding my own. Even ashed two before it was all over, thank you very much. You and the boss think I'm totally helpless, and you can both kiss my ass for that. Now, I want some damn donuts."

Discord Jones

Arcane Solutions

Gayla Drummond

Katarr Kanticles Press

Katarr Kanticles Press
Texas, USA
Edited by Tonya Cannariato
Copyright © 2012 Gayla Drummond

ISBN-13: 978-0615597058 (Katarr Kanticles Press)
ISBN-10: 061559705X

Acknowledgments

I'm lucky enough to have found a wonderful group of friends online, who often put their own time and energy into my work by beta reading, critiquing stories and covers, editing, and helping to come up with items like city names.

Bex, Shutsumon, Carrie, Kate, Tonya, Jo, Rebecca Clare Smith and Damian all helped perfect the cover design for this book, as well as beta read and critiqued the story.

Kate, Tonya, and Jo helped to create the city's name of Santo Trueno the series is placed in.

And David, who puts up with my calling him 'House Hunney' online and my weird writerly habits.

Thanks, guys and dolls.

Arcane Solutions

One

"If Zoe's been turned, do you want me to bring her home or stake her?"

Just a regular Tuesday morning, meeting with clients concerning their under-aged vamp bait. At least for me: Discord Jones, psychic and private investigator, at your service.

Nothing like this was in the parameters for the couple sitting across from me at my desk. Mid-forty yuppies, dressed for success in power suits with hundred-dollar haircuts, they were the fidgety types, though I seemed to have stunned them still.

Their mouths dropped open, and their widened eyes stared at me. Mr. Mitchell glanced at his wife. "We...we haven't thought about that."

"You need to." I laced my fingers, and rested the ball of my hands on the desk to keep from reaching out to shake sense into the couple. No point alienating clients until after the check cleared. At this stage, I could afford to be kind. "A newly turned vampire isn't anything like those you may have seen wandering the streets at night. It takes them a while to learn to control their thirst, and frankly, most only manage to if an older vampire keeps them in line."

Her husband was staring at the file when I asked, "Did you bring a recent photo and something personal belonging to her?" Mrs. Mitchell nodded while pulling a framed 5x7 and plastic baggy from her purse. "If you'll just please put them on my desk."

She complied with my request, her forehead wrinkling a little. I offered a little explanation after blinking away the dazzle of her rings. "Psychic abilities aren't magic, and they don't always work—at least not immediately."

"Just find her." Mrs. Mitchell pressed her trembling lips firmly together. She loved her daughter, but there was some irritation and frustration mixed in that love, seeping through the tiny crack in my shield that I allowed for client meetings.

"I have a high success rate," I said gently. "But I'm not infallible. I'm not going to touch that necklace and be able to tell you she's at a certain address. I may not sense anything at all the first time I handle it."

"But you can bring her home?" Mrs. Mitchell had recovered a bit.

"Once I find her, yes. It will take a combination of my abilities and brute force, if she's been turned. However, before I bring her home, you two need to have some plans in place. She'll need to be confined, fed, and have someone on hand who can keep her from doing anything unpleasant." *Like munching on you.*

Both nodded. I moved on. "Do you have any reason to believe she was kidnapped, or are you certain she ran away?"

"She ran away." Mr. Mitchell answered, disgust coloring his expression and voice. "Zoe hasn't adjusted to the divorce or our marriage."

"We don't know that," his wife snapped, shooting him a glance that promised a night on the couch.

"How long ago was your divorce?"

"Four years ago. Zoe was twelve then. We married a year after it was final." She returned her attention to me, the straight seam of her lips defying me to ask the whereabouts of Zoe's father, notably his absence from this room now. Okay, then I'd be checking that out later. Taking a few more minutes to wrap things up, I assured the Mitchells that I'd keep them updated as often as possible. While showing them out, I noticed Kate's office door was open and caught a glimpse of a guy inside.

I'd felt enough glimmers of impatience and anger from Mr. Mitchell to make it clear that he really didn't give a damn if Zoe were found. As soon as the heavy glass door swung closed behind them and began to distort their receding images, I took a deep breath and let it out. Nope, not calm enough yet to handle the necklace. I needed a distraction and Kate's office offered a fine one.

"Hey." Leaning a shoulder against the doorframe, I looked the guy over. He was hot, in that younger Harrison Ford as Indiana Jones way. Dark brown hair, tanned skin, and dark chocolate eyes, which were returning my assessment with a slow up and down sweep. "Intro, please?"

"Jones, this is Nick Maxwell, new hire." Kate appeared bored. One of these days, I would find out who her mysterious boyfriend was. He had to be an ultra hottie because she never reacted to yummy eye candy, and this Nick guy was firmly entrenched in that particular category. "Maxwell, this is Discordia Jones, our resident psychic."

His lips quirked. "Hello. That's a hell of a name."

"Hey. Yeah, it was my mom's idea." Kate had left out what he was. Everyone at Arcane Solutions was something a little more than straight human. Like the witch currently wearing a faint sly smile while fluffing her deep purple hair with her electric blue nails. The message was clear: I was on my own in finding out. "So what's your specialty?"

A full-fledged grin appeared, striking gold sparks in his eyes. "Back watching and hunting."

Apparently human and it was daylight. I took a not-so-wild stab in the dark. "You're a shifter?"

"Wolf. Is that a problem?" His grin turned feral.

I shrugged and crossed my arms. "Not one I have."

Prejudice had received a surge of popularity since the Melding, with so many new species appearing. Shifters were a favorite target, forced to assume their animal shapes on full moon nights.

After all, the legends and movies had always painted them as uncontrolled, ravening, bloodthirsty beasts. The few I'd met since beginning to work at Arcane Solutions were anything but.

"That's good, since Mr. Whitehaven mentioned you to me. As in, we'll be working together." Nick's intent gaze said he was quite interested in my reaction to that information.

"Did he now?" I drawled out, past the tightness in my chest, a flash of anger sharpening my own smile.

Without waiting for either of them to respond, I turned and stalked toward the boss's office, just catching Kate's "Uh-oh" and the shifter's "What?" above the thump of my boot-heels.

Mr. Whitehaven's door was closed, but it usually was and I'd never let that stop me before. Giving a quick knock before twisting the knob and stepping into his office, I discovered he was on the phone.

Not even an eyebrow raised in surprise. "I'll be just a moment, Discordia. Please have a seat."

I chose to stand. The exact genetic mix that had resulted in Whitehaven was a mystery to me, but giant had to be part of it. My boss is eight feet tall and older than I like to think about. Standing didn't really give much of an advantage, but it felt like one. Having to wait was already leaching away my mad-on, so I needed all the help I could get.

If asked to sum up Dermot Whitehaven in one word, that word would be 'imposing'. I imagine he was terrifying when younger, before age had withered his appearance to something approaching cadaver status. Old or not, he didn't have a wrinkle, but the smoothest skin I'd ever seen on anyone.

"Yes, that will be quite acceptable," he told whomever he was talking to before ending the call. Reddish brown eyes focused on mine and his lips curved just a bit. "How can I help you, Discordia?"

Fists planted firmly on hips, I glared back. "Did you hire Maxwell to ride herd on me?"

"Your cases seem to be increasingly dangerous, and while I appreciate your ability to quicken the healing process for yourself, I thought it better to attempt prevention of injuries." His smile was fading.

"I can take care of myself, and don't need someone following me around. I'm taking self-defense classes."

Whitehaven pressed his lips together before speaking. "That's very commendable, Discordia. However, I think it better if Nicholas accompanies you on your excursions."

I had two choices: cave now or continue arguing, only to cave later. I always forget that I never win arguments with my boss. Before choosing which it would be this time, Nick appeared at the doorway. "I thought you said there wasn't a problem with my being a shifter."

"This isn't about that, Maxwell." I waved a hand, hoping he'd take the hint and truck his butt back out. "I don't need a babysitter."

Whitehaven focused on Nick, who shrugged. Neither wore an expression I could read, and I don't poke around in people's heads unless necessary, because it's rude.

"You are an invaluable asset, and I personally prefer that you remain as unharmed as possible. Nicholas will accompany you." My boss smiled again.

Caving was the only option when he used his fatherly tone. "Fine."

I spun around, only to halt because Nick blocked the doorway. He was taller by a good five inches. "Do you mind?"

"Babysitting you? No," he replied, a slow grin spreading.

"I meant move. As in *now*. I have work to do."

"Is it the dangerous kind?" The shifter turned sideways, giving me room to leave, but not without coming into contact with him.

"No." A nudge of TK pushed him out of the doorway, clearing my path back to my office. It was a childish reaction. Slamming the door shut before smacking down into my chair so hard it went through seven revolutions before stopping was too. I slowly spun myself round to face the desk and the tokens atop it.

Still not calm, I took a deep breath or ten before flipping the photo right-side-up. Zoe Blacke was a pretty blonde teen with a sullen pout enhanced by heavy magenta lipstick. The photo froze her in time at some family celebration, judging by the candles and tulip-shaped wineglasses winking around her as bubbles reflected the camera flash.

Probably a birthday. I tilted the photo to catch the light better. Sure looked like cherries in the middle of the slice of cake Zoe was mashing with her fork, so Black Forest gateau. Celebratory cake, family gathering, snapshots…and she'd been missing for days. There was lot more wrong with this picture than Zoe's lavish love for purple mascara.

Mr. Mitchell's attitude bothered me. He'd pushed the point that Zoe "hadn't adjusted" twice more before our meeting ended. I wondered if more than his being her stepfather had caused the girl to take off.

"Well, time to try to find out." Snagging the baggy and spilling the necklace it held onto my desk, I studied it. Nothing expensive, just a wire-wrapped, green kyanite strung on a leather thong. Both crystals and leather are great for absorbing living energy, so I began to clear my mind in preparation.

'Clear my mind' is a figure of speech. Maybe some people can manage to go blank, but I'm of the school that even when you're thinking 'nothing', that means you're still thinking about something.

Closing my eyes and counting backward from ten, I dropped my left hand onto the necklace while finishing. "One."

A few seconds passed before anything happened, and the images and emotions that swirled into my mind were too confused to make sense.

A boy's laughter. The sting of cigarette smoke. Heavy music and flashing lights. A faint, metallic taste that coated my tongue and faded. Zoe staring into a mirror, carefully anointing her pursed lips with lipstick.

It would eventually sort out into useful stuff. The truly important thing was the faint shimmer of golden "dust." It meant Zoe was alive–and still human. Plus it gave me a delicate connection to the girl that should alert me if I managed to get anywhere near her.

I'd set up the portion of my mind dedicated to work to look like my office. Creating a file folder, I tucked the golden shimmer inside of it before filing it inside the Active cabinet.

With any luck, my tracking ability would kick in at some point and lead me straight to Zoe.

Holding that hope close, I opened my eyes and put her necklace back into the baggy before tucking it inside a desk drawer. My next step was to take the photo down to Kate's office.

6

Two

Nick was there, but I ignored him. "Hey, Kate. Feel like trying for a location?"

"Sure." She pulled out a map of Santo Trueno before reaching a hand behind her neck to unhook the gold chain her locator crystal hung upon. Handing her the photo, I dropped into a chair to watch. Dangling the crystal over the map, Kate gazed at the photo, her green eyes going vague. Her lips barely moved as she formed a silent request to her chosen goddess for guidance.

I don't pretend to understand magic or to believe in any pantheon of gods, but it works for some people. Kate and the others of her coven are some for whom it works really well. They'd all chosen Aztec gods, so I couldn't pronounce half the names. Our city, Santo Trueno, is allegedly named after the Aztec god of thunder, so their choices seemed appropriate to me.

The crystal pendulum shivered twice before beginning to slowly circle. After a minute or so, it was swinging side to side. The witch moved it, letting the crystal guide the direction.

"Well, well," she murmured once the tip had stilled over a spot. "Looks like your favorite place to visit, Jones."

"The Barrows?" Leaning forward to have a look, I sighed. The Barrows were Vampire Central, located beneath the city.

"Stake?" Kate offered, opening her desk drawer to display several tucked among boxes of truffles, which were part of her emergency kit. "Damian delivered a few last night."

"She won't need one. I'm going with her," Nick said, and pulled a credible Yoda imitation. "Dangerous, the Barrows are."

Fighting the urge to laugh, I rose from my seat. Maybe he wasn't my idea, but the shifter was certainly big enough to choke a vampire long enough for an unhurried get-away on my part. "Fine. Let's go."

"You're bossy," he observed, but stood up to follow.

"It's one of my gifts." I smiled at Kate. "Thanks."

"My pleasure, Jones." She waved us out. "I'll let Mr. Whitehaven know where you're going. Have fun."

It was a rule that we kept the boss informed of our whereabouts. Safety precaution, he called it.

After a detour to my office for jacket and purse, I led the way out to the parking lot and to my twenty-eight-year-old sports car.

Nick balked, frowning at it, eyes hidden behind dark shades. "You've got to be kidding. You drive this tin can?"

Tin can? My baby? The glare and scowl made him back up a step. "There's more room than you think, but if you want to stay here, be my guest."

He eased the sunglasses down enough to look over the rims at me. "Is the trying-to-brush-me-off thing going to be a constant?"

"Probably." I grinned at him over the car's roof. "Coming?"

"Not yet, but I have hope." He winked while opening the door.

"Pervert." Settling in the driver's seat, I asked, "Is the innuendo thing going to be a constant?"

Nick threw my answer right back at me while pushing the shades back into place. "Probably."

"Great." I started the engine, which purred before the stereo kicked on. Stabbing a finger at the volume control to cut Pink's excitement at rattling her chains, I asked, "Ever hear of sexual harassment?"

"Do the seats recline all the way back?" His grin was friendly. Joking around, I could handle. If he really became a pest, I'd sic Mr. Whitehaven on him.

"Would you can the questions? What sort of dealings have you had with vampires? Any particular enemies I need to be aware of?" I hated taking someone I knew squat about into the Barrows.

"I'm the bodyguard," he replied, fastening the seatbelt. "Are we stopping for lunch first? I'm starving."

"Look, just because the boss thinks—"

"You really had both legs broken three weeks ago?" the shifter interrupted. I began sputtering in reaction and his near-permanent grin widened into a smirk. "What was it that happened? Oh, I remember: you were pushed off a roof."

My face grew hot. Throwing the car in gear, I muttered, "Shut up."

"I'm curious. Why didn't you use your telekinesis?"

I whipped the car out into traffic. "It's kind of hard to concentrate when you're falling, okay? Besides, that's the wrong ability."

"How many stories was it, and what is the right one?" Nick winced as I stomped on the brake then accelerated and yanked the wheel to pass another car. "Can I drive?"

"Fifteen stories. Transvection, which I don't have. No, you may not drive." I'd been lucky my legs were all that had been broken, panicked as I'd been. Unfortunately, my favorite jeans hadn't fared so well. E.R. nurses have an absolute fetish for cutting clothing off people.

"Watch it! Oh God." I glanced sideways, upper lip curling a bit at the sight of him cowering in my passenger seat.

Nick scowled. "Would you watch the damn road?"

"Wuss. I could drive blindfolded. Wanna see?" My grin broadened as panic bloomed over his face.

"No. There's...holy...! Can I please drive?"

"I already answered that question. It was 'no'. Your turn: any vampire enemies?"

"I'm a shifter, what do you think?" Nick grabbed the dash, still scowling.

"Names?" I persisted, making a sharp right that jerked him into the door. We were nearing an entry point for the Barrows, so I began searching for a parking spot on the car-lined street.

"No one you need to worry about. Are we stopping? Because I think I need to throw up. Has anyone ever told you that you suck at driving?"

"Yeah, and I'll tell you what I told them: kiss my ass." Spotting an open spot, I slowed down.

The shifter recovered quickly. "Ooh, can I?"

"No." Neatly parallel parking, I turned off the engine, catching his shrug from the corner of my eye as he took off his shades. Leaning toward him, I opened the glove box and began groping around inside. Nick sniffed at my hair. I angled my head to catch his gaze. "What are you doing?"

"You smell good. What perfume are you wearing?"

My fingers closed around the small, ruby-inlaid crucifix and I rolled my eyes while settling back into my seat. "Giorgio Red."

"It works on you." Nick watched me pull the chain over my head. "A cross? Seriously?"

"It's a ward. One of Kate's fellow coven members is muy kick ass in the warding department. This keeps me from looking tasty to younger vamps." Checking for traffic, I climbed out of my car. Locking the door and pocketing the keys, I glanced over at him and sighed.

The sunlight loved him, picking out cinnamon glints in his hair. His ready-to-rock stance gave wordless voice to the shifter's self-confidence. Nick met my eyes. "What?"

"Nothing. Let's go." Having him around was going to take some getting used to. Yet it was nice to know the boss cared.

This particular entry point into the Barrows was set between the brick walls of a club and a sex shop. It used to be just a narrow pathway to the alley behind them. Now an eight-feet-tall stone archway opened to a tunnel with steps leading down. If you came through the alley, you'd just walk through the arch and onto the street, because the entries are one-way deals.

The tourists love them, constantly snapping photos of friends appearing to float out of the tunnel's dimness. The Melding had returned magic to the world without much disruption as far as real estate went. The people and critters had been the real shockaroonies for humans.

Of course, I'd missed all the shock and awe. I'd dropped into a coma on the stroke of midnight as the Melding began, like a weird remix of the Cinderella and Sleeping Beauty fairy tales. Only my mom had been the one with the kiss of consciousness, instead of a prince, and delivered it to my forehead, not my lips because that would've been *eww*. By the time I'd rejoined the land of the awake, things had mostly moved past the *impossible* reaction.

Nick reached the archway a step ahead of me and led the way down. I followed, slightly amused by the appearance of his bodyguard attitude and his question: "Which area do we need?"

"How should I know?" My answer brought him up short, which wasn't a good thing in a stairway. I narrowly avoided bouncing my nose off his jacket.

He paused just long enough for a deep breath of his own. "Then what's the plan to find out?"

Grinning at his back, and noticing his shoulders were almost touching the tunnel's walls, I said, "Walk around until I feel a tug."

The shifter half-turned to look at me. "A tug?"

"It's a psychic thing."

"Uh-huh. The Barrows takes up a lot of space, uh...what am I allowed to call you?" Nick asked, head tilting just a touch left.

"Well, my friends call me Cordi, but you may call me Jones. You?" I was still grinning for some inane reason.

"I prefer Nick. How long before you decide someone's a friend?" His head tilted the other direction, as a curious dog's would.

"Depends on who it is. Daylight's a wastin', so get a move on, please." The sun affected vampiric powers even underground. I really didn't want to be in the Barrows after dark, having acquired a not-fan or two of the vampire persuasion.

With a shrug, Nick turned and began walking downward once more. A minute passed, then a couple of more. I noted my boots were the only ones scuffing the moss-encrusted stone.

"Stop." I frowned when he glanced back. "Can you see the landing?"

After peering down, he shook his head. "Not yet."

"This is weird, since we should be right at it now. It's ninety-seven steps down this entry point. I counted ninety-six, so you should be on ninety-seven." Leaning, I squinted into the darkness below, unable to spot the landing.

"You count steps."

"I like to be prepared if retreat becomes a necessity."

"I don't hear anything." The shifter sniffed the air a few times. "Vampire scents are faint."

"Okay. Time to go back up," I decided, but upon turning around, discovered that what should've been daylight from the opening had been replaced by the tunnel ceiling glowing. The entrance was gone, covered by something. "I don't like this."

"Don't panic," he soothed. "Go on up, we'll see if we can figure out what's going on."

Throwing a scowl over my shoulder, I said, "I'm not panicking. I just said I don't like this situation."

"Okay. Would you start climbing?" Nick poked me in the back.

"Hey! No touching."

"Is that a prejudice thing?"

"It's a psychic thing," I huffed, beginning the climb upwards. "I can pick up stuff when people touch me without warning."

"Oh. Sorry." The shifter was silent for a few seconds. "That must make sex difficult."

"Excuse me?" My voice was a squeak.

"Doesn't it? Sex does require a lot of touching."

"My sex life is none of your business." My face had gone hot and I was grateful he was behind me. It had been a while, and having a wet dream of a guy bring up the topic just made the lack all the more apparent to me.

"Oh, come on. You can't tell someone that and not expect them to wonder." Nick chuckled. The soft, husky sound hit me somewhere below the belt. "But I'm sorry I embarrassed you."

"You didn't," I lied.

"Right. That's why your body temperature just shot up about five degrees." Amusement laced his tone. "Your scent's grown hotter too."

"Thank you ever so much for sharing that and now, please shut up." I'd reached the top. "What the hell? There's not supposed to be a door."

"Switch with me," Nick demanded. "I'll open it."

"I think I can manage opening a door." He grabbed my arm when I began to reach for the door's ornate handle.

"But can you handle what might be on the other side?"

He had a point. I probably could, but why waste having perfectly good muscle around? Huffing out a breath, I shrugged. "Fine."

It took a bit of doing in the small space, but we traded places without tumbling down the stairs.

"Okay, I'm going to open it. Ready?" Nick glanced back at me.

"Yea- wait. What if it's something you can't handle?" The unknown was causing a chill of dread to ooze down my spine.

"Then you'll teleport us to your car."

"Who said I can teleport?"

"I need information to do my job, just like you do to do yours. Mr. Whitehaven gave me a rundown of your abilities." He paused. "He forgot to mention the no-touching thing, though."

"Whatever. Open the door," I demanded, making a note to find out later what all he'd been told. The shifter looked back at the door, reached for the handle, and paused.

"Maybe you'd better grab hold, just in case."

Shoving my fingers between his belt and jeans, I silently cursed my boss. He'd obviously mentioned my occasional tendency to panic. "Maybe you should knock first."

"It's a public door, it doesn't get knocked. Besides, element of surprise."

"Then open the damn door, I'm surprised enough."

"I'm opening the damn door." Nick pushed it open, but I couldn't see anything except his back. "It's a hallway. It smells like elves."

Huh. What did elves smell like to a shifter? I pushed the question away for later.

"We're probably okay then." Or should be, since I wasn't aware of having pissed off any. You have to be around the beings in question to manage that. "Go on."

"Shifters aren't welcome in faerie mounds, Jones."

Nick didn't move, so I released his belt to shove him into the hallway. "I'll protect you." The promise earned me a frown. "This is probably some kind of magical mix up."

"It's not a mistake, Miss Jones." An elf stepped out of another doorway about fifteen feet down the hallway. "If you'll join me, I will explain."

He no more resembled a spider than I did a fly but the elf had that gloating villain thing going big time. Typically gorgeous, taller than Nick by an inch or so, built like something out of a mail-order groom catalog for the stinking rich. Still, if he was playing the villain with Bond-esque panache, didn't that make me the hero? At least he'd called me Miss Jones without making it sound like a song reference.

"Both of us?" Leaving Nick alone was probably a bad idea. It would tick off Whitehaven if I lost him the first day.

The elf inclined his head, nearly royally. Nothing as ordinary as a nod of agreement, not from him.

"Okay then."

Nick was breathing down my neck by the time we entered what appeared to be an office slash library. The elf gestured toward a pair of spindly looking chairs placed before a massive desk.

A pair. As in *two* – for my unwelcome bodyguard and me.

"Please have a seat," the elf invited. "I apologize for the unorthodox method of meeting with you."

"You seem to know who I am. This is my associate, Nick Maxwell, and you are?"

"Thorandryll." He sat down behind the desk, not even nodding at Nick. "The information I was given said you work alone."

Yet there were two chairs waiting. I smiled. "Not anymore. Nick's my new partner. So what is this about, Mr. Thorandryll?"

Like most elves, he was gorgeous. Blue eyes the color of winter skies adorned a triangular, high-cheek-boned face Hollywood actors would pay a million bucks for. His hair was long, loose, and deep golden blonde. I hadn't been this close to an elf before, but could see why people became elf-struck.

Not that I would. It would be so unprofessional. As would be calling him the *Lord* he no doubt preferred.

"I wish to hire you to locate something."

My curiosity flared. Why would an elf need a psychic to track something down? "My employer pre-screens our cases at Arcane Solutions. You'll have to speak with him first."

"I prefer to keep this matter quiet." Thorandryll's icy blues focused on my face.

"Discretion isn't a problem, but you have to speak with Mr. Whitehaven first. I'm under contract—no free-lancing allowed." My urge to attempt to scan him was growing. What was it he wanted me to go after?

"I see." The elf studied me for a moment longer. He was probably judging his chances of success at bribing me, or whammying me with glamour.

Neither was a good idea. I like my job, and mystical crap aimed in my direction tends to piss me off.

Nick was fidgeting, his discomfort so intense that I felt sympathy welling up. "If that's all, Nick and I are sort of in the middle of something."

Thorandryll didn't take my attempt to dismiss him well. Brows drawing together, he gazed at me, and I'll be damned if goose bumps didn't bloom on my arms. After a long, silent moment, he rose. "I'll speak with your employer, Miss Jones. Allow me to escort you out."

"Sure." As the elf led the way out, I whispered, "Bit arrogant, isn't he?"

Nick grinned in response.

Three

"The spell will end when the door closes, returning you to the Barrows' entrance. It was a pleasure to meet you, Miss Jones." Thorandryll half-bowed after opening the door to the tunnel. Nick edged past, his expression blank and wariness exuding from him like a cloak.

"Likewise. I guess we'll talk later." Offering him what I hoped was a professional smile, I started down the stone steps after the shifter.

"Do you often visit the Barrows?"

Pausing, I turned to look back at the elf. "Just when necessary for a case. Why?"

"Merely curiosity, Miss Jones. It's dangerous." He frowned past me at the shifter's back.

"Danger comes with the job. Have a nice day." Two steps later, I heard the door click shut.

"I can see the landing now," Nick announced after a minute or so passed. "That was weird."

"Yeah. I wonder what Thorandryll's thing is? What do you think: stolen or lost?"

The shifter shrugged. "Who steals from an elf?"

"You mean apart from the suicidally inclined? I have no idea." We reached the landing and entered the false night of the Barrows.

Imagine every dark night movie scene featuring a decrepit old castle, and you'll have a decent idea of what the Barrows is like—minus the tourists, but you can't escape them. They're everywhere, even posing for photos in front of the fantastically designed iron gates blocking entry to the private residences of those with major standing in the vampiric hierarchy.

You enter the Barrows at your own risk. The cops will come to look for you if you go missing and it's reported, but vampires are usually experts at hiding the bodies.

They aren't supposed to kill anymore, and there's really no need for them to do so because there are always idiots willing to offer up blood. But everyone knows that killing does happen. People disappear, and have since the beginning of time.

Vampires are predators and seven years of civilized living hasn't made a dent in their conditioned hunting behaviors.

Nick appeared to be on full alert, his weight perfectly balanced and arms loose. Lower level vamps were taking care to avoid our path, but I wasn't convinced that was because of him.

Ronnie's anti-vampire ward was grounded in earth magic and seasoned with fire magic. The newer the vamp, the faster he or she would become a column of fire if they risked grabbing me for a snack. Overall, most vampires prefer to avoid being burned into true death.

I didn't see anyone I recognized as we worked our way up and down the main streets, but we did come across several groups of young humans. Emo kids, Goths, and punks for the most part.

Light scanning picked up their louder thoughts. I shook my head at the hope many had of becoming powerful creatures of the night. Stupid kids. But Zoe's so-called friends could be around, skipping school to play with the dead, so I kept scanning, and made a note to dig up some names. Maybe Zoe had a Facebook account.

"Anything?" Nick asked after we'd covered a rough square mile of streets.

"Not yet, or I would've said something."

"I'm starving. Let's stop for some lunch." He jerked his head toward a tavern across the street. "Good steaks there."

"You must hang out here a lot more than I do."

"I've been here enough to know where the good steaks can be found. Come on, I'll buy." He led the way across the street, and I reluctantly followed. My stomach was beginning to grumble a little about its empty state.

As was par for the course down here, the tavern's lighting was dim. Sighting Jo Morrison sitting at a corner table, head bent close to a vampire's as she listened to him speaking, surprised me.

What are you doing here? I 'pathed, startling her into looking up. I watched the vampire eye her neck while lounging back in his seat, despite the fact she wore another of Ronnie's warded crosses.

Book business floated from her in response. I smiled and waved for the vampire's benefit when he glanced our way. It couldn't hurt to let him know she wasn't down here completely alone.

Jo's a witch, and certainly not helpless, but I tend to be protective of those I call friends. There are few enough of them, and to be honest, they've pulled my fat out of the fire more often than I have theirs. I do my best to return the favor as much as possible.

"Who's that?" Nick was watching the byplay. Jo waved back.

"A friend of mine and a coven mate of Kate's. Her name's Jo." Slipping past him, I picked a table not too far from hers and sat where I could keep an eye on things.

The shifter followed, settling into a seat that let him watch the door and most of the dining area.

Who is he? Jo's question was a whisper, but I caught it because I was listening for her. She had a natural, thick mental shield and it had taken me a long time to tune in enough to be able to hear her.

New hire at the office. Kate would eventually inform them that Whitehaven had hired a babysitter for me.

Cute. She was grinning.

Yeah, I guess. Nick's good looks had paled during the meeting with Thorandryll, but the effect would wear off, at least until I met with the elf again. It was just a side effect of seeing what amounts to male perfection.

A menu was shoved into my face right then by a surly looking waitress. My guess was that being a vampire hadn't turned out the way she thought it would. From what I'd learned, it seldom did.

We ordered and there was nothing to do but stare around or make small talk. I chose small talk. "What made you take the job?"

"Babysitting you?" Nick grinned, his eyes sliding from me to the door and back. "It sounded interesting. I've never met a psychic before."

I scowled. "How about we say 'being my partner'?"

"A promotion already? Okay, sure." He laughed. It was a nice laugh.

"What were you doing before?"

"I've done some bouncing for a few clubs."

I rolled my eyes. "Great. Being a PI isn't all about throwing people around, you know."

"I do have a brain, Jones, and I'm a wolf. We're natural hunters." His grin said that I'd failed to offend him. The scowling vamp waitress returned with our food just then. After she'd dropped the plates in front of us, he asked, "How did you end up as a PI?"

"By accident. This smells good." The steak, medium rare and smoking hot with a side of marinated, grilled mushrooms, grabbed my full attention. "Let's eat and get back to work."

"Sure." With that, our mouths were busy with food rather than conversation. I kept an eye on Jo while we ate. The auburn-haired witch was having an intense-looking conversation with the vampire. He seemed to have lost interest in her neck, pointing out various things in the book they were studying.

Once lunch was disposed of, Nick excused himself for a trip to the Gents' Room. I decided to wait for him outside, and do a little scanning for any thoughts about Zoe.

Concentrating on that, I didn't notice the vampire approaching until he blocked my view. "Looking for someone?"

"Yeah." You couldn't trust them, but sometimes vamps could be informative.

He smiled. "Male or female?"

"A girl."

"Perhaps I can change your mind?" He moved, a quick blur, and semi-embraced me, pinning my arms while carefully avoiding the cross. He was obviously old and smart enough to know what it could do. Ugh, he wanted a donor. Then he tightened his hold, and it was easy to tell that he'd already fed. Sex was what he had in mind.

I shuddered in revulsion. "No thanks, bub. I'm not into necrophilia."

"I can give you pleasure you've never dreamed of," he murmured, voice silky smooth as he stared into my eyes. He was trying to cloud my mind, but wasn't powerful enough to.

"I said no thanks."

"I enjoy challenges."

"Yeah? Enjoy this." I head butted him, smashing his nose and knocking myself a little cross-eyed. The vampire stumbled backward, before disappearing as Nick grabbed him and threw him clean across the street.

"Are you all right?"

Blinking, I forced a scowl. "I totally had that under control."

"Uh-huh. How many fingers am I holding up?" The shifter raised his hand.

"Two?" It was a lucky guess.

"I guess your skull's in one piece." He shook his head. "That wasn't the best..."

"We need to get back to work," I interrupted, not needing a lecture that head butting a vamp was a bad idea. The burgeoning headache was enough information on that subject. "Come on."

Grinning, Nick turned me around before I completed my first step. "This way, Jones."

"Hmph."

The lack of luck in scanning an estate almost made me turn to look through the gates we were walking past. The two vampires standing guard kept me from acting on the impulse. I waited until we reached the end of the block before grabbing Nick's arm. "I couldn't get anything from this one."

"What do you want to do?" He didn't look around, gaining points in my book.

"I need to stay close, but not be obvious, to try again."

"How close?"

"Right here is good." The street wasn't one of the well-traveled ones, so there wasn't much in the way of a crowd to hide in. Just a few couples, pausing at intervals to snap photos. If I'd been alone, stepping around the corner out of sight would've been my first choice.

But I wasn't alone and that was too far to go.

Nick's intent gaze was making me nervous. "I have an idea, but it requires touching."

Suspicious, I asked, "What is it?"

He grinned and took a step toward me. I backed away and he followed, until the stone wall blocked further retreat. Placing his hands on it just beside my shoulders, the shifter began lowering his head.

"What the hell are you doing?" I hissed, hands moving to flatten over his soft blue polo and hard chest muscles.

"Providing cover for you to do your thing." His breath tickled my neck and he sniffed at my hair. "So get busy, Jones."

Keeping my hands where they were to preserve the few inches of space between our bodies, I closed my eyes and focused.

Mmm resonated from Nick. A vague image of a wolf rolling in grass flashed across my mind. The shifter apparently really liked my shampoo, pulling in a deeper breath while burying his nose in my hair.

Forcing myself to ignore him, I tried scanning again. If Zoe was inside, and held against her will, I could bring in reinforcements. Damian was a detective with the city police, not just a stake-carving warlock.

If she was there, I couldn't teleport to her without seeing where she was. Taking Nick in with me, then both of them out would be exhausting. I had to be in contact to teleport them, which wasn't a problem where the shifter was concerned.

His nose was traversing a downward path through my hair. I jumped when his lips brushed my ear, and goose bumps exploded on my arms.

"Sorry." It was a mumble.

Bored. I latched onto the thought. Tracing it back with as light a touch as possible, I gleaned enough information to know that the estate was that of a vampire lord named Derrick, and my contact was a volunteer blood donor.

A soft groan from Nick broke my concentration. I jumped again at the feel of his lips on the side of my neck. He leaned into my hands, trying to push closer, one of his rising to my jaw.

"Dude." The whisper didn't register on him, because his other hand slid between rough stone and my lower back. "Hey."

Want. His thought was guttural, barely coherent. I prepared to blast him with a firm *Back off!*, but a completely overwhelming wave of lust flooded my mind the second I created a crack in my shield.

My hands moved up and around his neck, my head turning as if drawn by a magnet. He growled, lips eagerly covering mine, tongue flickering over my bottom lip.

Mine parted, while my arms curled around his neck to pull him closer. A deep rumble vibrating his chest, Nick pressed against me. One of his legs ended up between mine, his thigh claiming a firm place against my groin.

He was hard, grinding an impressive feeling bulge against me while sliding his tongue in to tangle with mine. I suddenly remembered how much I liked kissing.

The connection to the blood donor forgotten, every bit of my attention locked solely on Nick.

Want he insisted, fingers trapping locks of my hair. Images flooded my mind, full of moonlight and trees. *Want.* It was a soft whine, pleading for permission.

A fraction of a second before granting it, I jerked as *Who's there?* roared through my mind. Nick froze as I gasped and tensed.

Who are you? came next, trailed by icy cold diving down the connection forged with the blood donor. The shifter pulled his mouth away enough to speak. "What is it?"

"We have to leave." I slammed my mental shield closed just in time. Stepping back, he caught my hand and dragged me around the corner.

I teleported us above, onto the street right next to my car. Shaking free of his grip and hurrying around to the driver's side, I unlocked the doors and practically dove inside.

Dusk was falling, painting the sky a hazy gray. I did not intend to be anywhere near the Barrows when the owner of that cold power came above ground, hunting for me.

Vampires are scary enough. Those with powers similar to mine are about a hundred times scarier. They've had centuries to perfect their control, while I have less than half a decade under my belt.

The engine purred to life at the turn of the key. A quick look around showed the way was clear to pull away from the curb. Seatbelt clicked into place, Nick leaned and groped for mine. His face was close enough that his breath warmed skin gone cool from fear. I let go of the steering wheel with one hand when he pulled the belt across. Another click and he straightened. "What happened?"

Fear has a tendency to make me bitchy. "We almost got caught, thanks to your idea of cover, that's what happened."

"Caught by whom?"

"I don't know. Maybe a vamp named Derrick. That's who owns the estate." I shot through a red light, but the shifter didn't notice. He was too busy watching me.

"You're shaking. Pull over."

"Hell no! We're too close to the Barrows." Shaking my head sent brown strands flying. I wanted safety, now. Safety was the office or home, both heavily warded. The office was closer, but the idea of leaving for home after full dark made me shudder. "Do you think those two guards got a good look at our faces?"

"No," Nick answered, just as his fingers made a surprise landing on the nape of my neck and began gently kneading the tenseness away. *Want.* It was barely audible and tinged with that pleading note. I wasn't sure he was aware of it, so didn't say anything. He glanced out the windshield. "Where are we headed?"

"Away from the Barrows."

"You're really spooked."

"Quick on the uptake, aren't you?" Terrified was a more apt description.

"It's one of my gifts." He grinned, not offended by my snarky response. "So this Derrick is scary?"

"I have never felt that kind of mental power from a vamp before." Shivering, I scowled at the truck ahead of us.

"Very scary," Nick amended.

"Friggin' terrifying," I corrected, relaxing a bit more. The gentle massage was rubbing the sharp edge of fear away. "I'll drop you off at the office, and then I'm going home."

His fingers went still. The need to say something about the kissy-face episode became important. "Um..."

Nick pulled his hand away, facing forward at the street ahead. It was probably my imagination that he looked disappointed.

On the other hand, maybe not, since a sneaky glance at his lap gave evidence to support the disappointed theory. Recalling the strength of his lust, I bit my lip and dragged my attention back to driving.

I don't like being alone after a bad scare. While I could call and arrange a stay-over with Kate, Ronnie, or Jo, they don't really fit the bill for clinging to. Neither did David or Damian, both having steady relationships.

Nick looked perfect for clinging to, yet he was a stranger.

But man, it had been a while.

Busy turning my choices over, I was startled when the shifter spoke. "I thought we were going to the office?"

I recognized the parking lot of my apartment complex. "Well, damn."

"This is where you live?" The disappointment was gone when I glanced at his face.

"Yeah. " Oh, what the hell. "Look, I..."

"Had a big scare and don't want to be alone?" Nick nailed it in one guess. I felt heat begin creeping up my neck.

"Yeah."

He smiled, not looking at me. "I'm open to hanging out for a while."

Four

Unacceptable to modern women everywhere as it might be, being tucked safely in my apartment behind wards with a big, strong man for company made me feel much better.

The shifter prowled around the living room, checking out my DVD collection while I pulled out dinner-making supplies after having checked the shimmer that represented Zoe. Still golden. I was elbow-deep in preparing a massive lasagna when Nick joined me in the kitchen. "Need any help?"

"No, I've got it. There's beer in the fridge if you want one."

"Thanks. One for you?"

"Yeah, please." He pulled two out, opened them both, and placed mine on the counter.

"Nice place. You watch a lot of movies."

"I stay home a lot when I'm not working." I scattered the last of the grated cheese over the top of the lasagna and sidestepped to wash my hands.

"Why?"

"Being around people all the time is kind of draining. I have to recharge." I'd learned to put the constant buzz of other minds into the background, but it still leeched my energy away.

Leaning a hip against the counter, Nick took a drink of his beer while I put the baking dish into the oven. "Is my being here interfering with your recharging?"

"No. One or even a few people aren't a problem." I was trying to figure out the rest of the evening. The shifter hadn't leaked anything for me to go by. It'd been a few months since my last relationship's end.

Realizing Nick was staring, and that I was doing the same to the oven's door, I snagged my beer and took a swig, which tickled my tongue and throat with cold-sharpened bubbles. "You want to pick out a movie? We can eat in the living room."

"Sounds good," he agreed, pushing away from the counter and sauntering toward the archway separating the two rooms. I watched him, or rather, his butt, before shaking my head and preparing a salad.

Meal over, dishes in the dishwasher, and movie halfway finished, I kept checking out Nick from the corner of my eye. He sprawled at the opposite end of the sofa, looking comfortable and totally absorbed in *The Matrix*. I was anything but absorbed and comfortable.

Send him home or ask him to stay? If he did stay, couch, or bed? Sex or no sex? If yes, then what? We'd be working together.

Damn it! I forced my attention back to the TV, admitting there were too many complications to think through. Besides, I had no idea how shifters handled such matters. Was sex with humans an entirely casual thing for them?

Nick moved, picking up his third beer of the evening. Without taking his eyes from the screen, he asked, "Am I staying the night?"

Caught by surprise, I responded without thinking. "Do you want to?"

"Yeah. But the question is do you want me to?" He took another drink of his beer.

Watching the line of his neck, the seal of his lips round the rim of the bottle, I swallowed a sudden mouthful of drool. "Um, yeah?"

The corner of his mouth quirked. "Then I'm staying. Next question: am I allowed to call you Cordi?"

"Um, yeah?" I sounded like a broken record.

"Last question. Can I touch you?"

"Please do." From the smile that blazed into existence, I had the distinct impression sex was in my immediate future. *Yay!*

"Good, because I certainly want to." He finally turned his head, meeting my eyes. His were more gold than brown and I forgot how to breathe for a few seconds, gazing into them. Smile fading, he confided in a low voice, "Your scent's been driving me crazy all damn day."

I had to clear my throat. "It has?"

"Yeah." The beer bottle clinked as he set it aside before moving to close the space between us. Our faces were only inches apart when he said, "Scent's very important."

"Oh." I was mesmerized as his eyes changed further, gold spilling from around the pupils, to flush away every trace of brown.

"So is taste," he breathed, mouth descending upon mine. All the cons I'd thought of went flying straight out of my head as *Want* growled out from his mind. Oh, hell yes.

Nick slid off the sofa without quite ending the kiss, to kneel on the floor. His hands ran up my thighs, then down, thumbs firm along the insides. When he stood, it was after wrapping an arm around me, and lifting me off the couch. The lack of effort required and my feet not touching the floor reminded me that he wasn't a regular guy.

"Wait," I mumbled, pulling away from his mouth.

"For what?" Nick tried for a second kiss, but I turned my head away.

"You're a shifter."

Releasing me, he took a step back, brows lowering and a frown beginning to grow. "I thought that wasn't a problem?"

"It's not, but I don't know much about shifters. I mean, I know you're a lot stronger and can change into an animal."

His expression smoothed out. "Yes, but I won't shift or hurt you."

"Okay, but that's not really what I was worried about. Um, you do know about safe sex, right?" I tried not to blush, but failed miserably. Doing was better than talking in my book. Yet talking meant less chance of confusion. Even though I was on the pill and religious about taking it every day, condoms were necessary. "I'm on the Pill, but I don't do bareback."

Nick slowly smiled. "Yes, I know about safe sex and I have a condom."

Moving into his arms, I buried my red-hot face into his t-shirt. "Okay, good. Sorry."

"No problem." He kissed the top of my head. "Where were we?"

"Uh...here?" Raising my head, I kissed him and he again picked me up, snugging my legs around his waist. When he turned toward the hallway, I broke the kiss. "Wait."

"Okay. Why?"

"Need to turn the TV off." Freeing a hand from around his neck, I pointed at the remote control. Nick sighed, but walked over and picked it up. Hitting the power button, he replaced it.

"There. Anything else, or can we go get naked now?"

I wiggled at the thought, and the feel of him pressed tight to my groin. "Is the door locked?"

"Let's check." Having 130 pounds hanging from him evidently wasn't a problem. Nick strode over to the door and tested the locks, one hand splayed across my lower back. "Yes."

"Okay." My security concerns settled, I focused my attention on diving my hands under his shirt. With a slight shake of his head, Nick turned again toward the hallway and my bedroom door.

An urgent, tongue-tangling kiss occupied us the second he carried me into the room. It wasn't enough. Dizzy from more than lack of air, I pulled away, slid down his body, and allowed my feet to discover the floor. We both took a step back to peel off our shirts. Footwear was next; I had to sit on the edge of the bed to take mine off.

Nick simply toed his running shoes off, unbuttoning his jeans at the same time. I watched while tugging my socks free.

"My turn," he growled while unzipping his jeans. "Wait."

"Okay." I paused, fingers on the button of mine. Since he was about to shuck his, waiting was fine by me. Warm golden eyes glued to my face, he worked the denim off his hips and down, neatly ridding himself of socks at the same time.

No underwear; he was a commando guy. I licked the corner of my mouth, gazing at him. "You're circumcised."

"What?" Nick looked down.

"Nevermind." For some reason, I hadn't thought he would be. Shifters healed fast - that was something else I knew about them. He was willing to move on, walking toward me and bending, fingers quickly unbuttoning my jeans

Unzipping them, Nick tucked his fingers over the edge of the waistband and grinned. "This is like unwrapping a present."

No one had ever compared me to a present before. Falling back on trembling elbows, I helped remove my jeans. He tossed them off to the side and crawled onto the bed, over me. "I'm not naked yet."

"Give me a minute." Another succulent kiss followed, his hand finding the catch of my bra, which fell loose. It slipped down, and Nick left my lips for my breasts.

"Condom," I reminded him, eyes closing as he nuzzled skin.

"I remember." He slipped backwards, off the bed and went for his jeans. While he dug for his wallet and the condom, I wiggled out of my panties, tossing them and bra to the floor.

"Mission accomplished." He came back, holding up the small package and paused. "Now that's something I haven't seen before."

"You don't like it? I think it's cute." I kept a small patch, currently trimmed into the shape of a heart.

"I didn't say that just that I haven't seen anything like that before." He ripped the package open, quickly rolling on the condom. Re-joining me on the bed, he asked, "Can we play now? Please?"

He took my laugh for a yes. We made out until we were both breathless and hot. Nick slid over me, settling between my legs to push tentatively, and slipped inside a bit. He wiggled like an excited puppy before pushing deeper, snuffling at my neck. In a thick, low voice, he said, "You smell so good, Cordi."

"Uh hmm." His first thrust was slow and careful. After a shivering pause, he moved into a firm, quick rhythm that had me panting for air in short order.

It felt fantastic, but when he slid both arms under me, changing the angle just so, it felt much better. Waves of pleasure radiated through me, continuing even when he groaned, thrusting deep and staying. I could feel the spasms as he came. Cheek pressed to my temple, he muttered, "Damn."

"What?" I was gasping for air.

"I only had the one. I want to do it again."

So did I, but without a condom, it wasn't happening. "You could go buy some."

He sighed. "I knew you were going to say that."

Another minute or two passed before he raised his head. "You're too warm and sweet smelling to leave right now. I'll bring more next time. If there's going to be a next time?"

On board with that idea, I nodded and found the energy to move my hand in a slow stroke down his spine. "Yeah, there is."

"Good." He kissed me, and then moved. "Need to borrow the bathroom for a few minutes."

I sat up. "We could take a shower together, but I'll want cuddling afterwards."

He chuckled. "Your wish is my command."

"Cordi."

"Hm?" I cracked open one eye to find Nick crouched beside my bed, fully dressed. "Is it morning already?"

The shifter grinned. "No, it's almost two. I have to go."

I needed a few seconds to process that. "Oh."

"I got a call; there's something I have to go help with," he clarified before my frown made an appearance. "Pack business."

"Oh, okay." Sitting up, I rubbed my eyes. "Where do I need to take you?"

"I've got a ride. I'm sorry I woke you, but I didn't want you to think that...uh, just leaving a note didn't..." he paused to start again. "I didn't want to go without saying bye or leaving your door unlocked."

That was sweet of him. "It's okay. Cool."

"I guess I'll see you in the morning." Nick leaned, but stopped shy of kissing me. "I had a really good time."

"Me too." His lips were on mine, and I almost had my hands round his neck to keep him longer, but he pulled free.

Chest heaving, he backed away and licked his lips. "Don't forget to lock the door."

"I won't." As he exited the room, I took a second before following to check again. Yes, the shimmer was still gold. If Zoe were turned, or dead, it would have disappeared.

Five

Everyone arrived more or less at the same time the next morning, so once we poured our coffees, Mr. Whitehaven called a meeting to issue our pay stubs. Our checks were direct deposited; I think he was just old-fashioned enough to like to hand out envelopes.

Slipping hers into a pocket of her ruby red, Fifties-style cap-sleeved dress, Kate asked, "What did you discover yesterday?"

"A vampire lord named Derrick who doesn't care for telepathic interlopers."

Nick jumped in. "He must be powerful. Cordi was scared enough to call it a day."

"Wary enough. It was dusk by then." They ignored my correction.

Mr. Whitehaven sat back, hands dropping from desktop to arm rests. "Did you locate the missing child?"

"She's a teenager. No. I couldn't scan this vampire's estate." Before he asked, I checked the shimmer for the third time since I'd woken up. "She's still alive. Oh, and there was another thing." I described the meeting with the elf, watching as the boss's face settled into blandness.

Since I didn't pry unless necessary in the line of work, I couldn't tell what he was thinking or feeling. The boss never leaked thoughts. As far as I knew, elves weren't clients the agency had taken on before.

"We'll see if he calls." Whitehaven left it at that.

"Kate, can you try and find out about Zoe's father? I'm curious as to why he wasn't here yesterday." Surely, someone had informed the man about her disappearance. My father would have been all over anything that involved my disappearance, driving people to drink until I was found.

"I'll do my best." She frowned. Searches weren't her forte, but Whitehaven hadn't found someone to hire as a specialist just yet. "I'll also see what I can uncover on this Derrick."

"Thanks. Will you be up to try locating her again?"

"Yes, this afternoon. I have a client coming in, and a lunch date. You need to call Mr. Fent, and set up another appointment to search for his aliens." She was also our acting receptionist to atone for her familiar's tendency to crap on select individuals, a habit that had driven the last one out the door.

"Right." The meeting was adjourned, and learning that Nick hadn't gotten a tour of the office, I took care of that before making the necessary call.

We took lunch early, Kate disappearing to meet her mysterious boyfriend, while Nick and I settled for burgers just down the block from the office.

Popping a fry in his mouth, he chewed while watching me douse mine in ketchup and pepper. "You're a fan of tomatoes in all their forms, aren't you?"

"You bet. I have tomato sauce running through my veins. Dad's family came over from Italy." The opening to tell each other about our families was there, but Nick didn't take it.

He changed the subject. "I'd like to take you out for dinner after work."

"That sounds like a plan," I agreed, picking at my fries and slightly regretting my leap of lust the night before.

We each ate a few bites before he spoke up again. "Sorry I had to take off like that last night."

"It's okay. Did everything work out all right?"

"Yeah." The shifter didn't offer any explanation, but whatever it had been probably wasn't my business anyway. We finished eating and walked back to the office to see a limo waiting in the parking lot.

I wasn't too surprised to find Thorandryll in the reception area. Just by lounging on the harvest gold two-seat sofa he turned our mellow reassure-the-clients-we're-sane atmosphere into a kindergarten art project. Damn gorgeous elves. Then again, arrogance like Thorandryll's kind of cut through the glamour. Nick's polite nod was ignored, and with a little helpful direction from my finger poking his ribs, he headed for Kate's office.

Left alone with the elf, I smiled. "Have you been waiting long?"

"Not at all. Your employer and I finished our conversation only a few minutes ago." He'd risen from his seat when we walked in, and began to offer his hand, but dropped it.

So, Whitehaven had given him the zoo speech. It was actually a 'don't touch the psychic unless she offers first' speech, but it reminded me of the signs on certain cages at the zoo. 'Don't feed the monkeys' or 'Don't touch the tiger's glass'. "Good. If you'll follow me, we can talk in my office."

"Certainly. It's a pleasure to see you again, Miss Jones." He followed, taking a seat when I gestured toward the chairs while shutting the door.

Once seated behind my desk, I asked, "What is it that you need me to find?"

"An item has gone missing from my library."

"So you want me to find a book?" Sitting back as he nodded, I thought he looked fantastic in the black slacks and a soft-looking green pullover he was wearing. Cashmere, I bet. Or thistle silk spun at midnight on a unicorn spindle and knitted by moths. He was having a terrible influence on me, if I was thinking things like that. "What kind of book?"

"It's an ancient tome, over two thousand years old."

"They had books back then? Wow."

"Yes, some did." His tone indicated sudden second thoughts about hiring me. I hid a grin, meeting those wintry blue eyes with what I hoped was an innocent expression.

"How long has it been missing?"

"Three days."

"Okay. Do you have a photo of it?"

"No."

Not helpful. "How about the title and author's name?"

"It's a journal, Miss Jones, so has neither stamped upon its cover nor written inside."

That was even less helpful. "Could you describe it, or better yet, visualize it and let me see it?"

"Your employer strictly forbade any attempts to mentally share information." He frowned, obviously not understanding Whitehaven's rule.

"Oh." I'd had some freaky episodes after mental contact with centuries-old vampires, hence that particular rule. The boss did the forbidding when a client was over a century old. The rule had come into play after I'd tried to bite him one evening. Even second-hand, the vampiric hunger for blood is a bitch. "Okay, do you have anything I can attempt to get some information from?"

"It's a large tome. The cover is lightly tanned leather. There aren't any symbols stamped upon it." The elf gestured with long-fingered hands. When he finished, a square of crimson silk formed in mid-air, then whispered down to pool on my desk's top. "The book was wrapped in that for the past three decades. Will it suffice?"

"Yeah, it should." I looked at the silk. It was older than I was by almost a decade. "No idea who stole it?"

"If I knew that, I wouldn't be here and the book would already have been returned to its place." He glared through me, jaw clenching and lips thinning. There was no trouble imagining him with a sword in hand, dressed in elaborate armor, and charging into battle.

"Aside from its age, what's important about it? Why would someone want to steal it? Is it worth a lot?"

"Only to a few, with myself being one of them." He smiled, not a confident curve of lips, but something cute and slightly crooked that called to mind little boys up to mischief. My brain stuttered to a halt. I didn't think he was using glamour to improve his looks, but that wasn't the only thing elves could do with that particular ability.

A quick knock on the door and Kate poked her head in. Her familiar, a parrot named Percival, stood on her left shoulder and Nick was behind her. The shifter focused on Thorandryll after a quick glance at me. Kate ignored the elf in favor of informing me, "I'm ready to try another location spell, Jones."

"Okay, just a minute." Their appearance broke the haze. I summoned up a professional smile, aiming it at the elf. "I'll let you know as soon as I come up with anything, and keep you updated on my progress as often as possible."

Both golden eyebrows rose. "You're not going to attempt psychometry now?"

I wondered if he'd been researching psychic abilities while answering, "I have a previous case to wrap up."

"I see." He nodded, gave another brief, devastatingly gorgeous smile and rose from his seat. I shadowed the move, stepping out from around my desk to offer a hand. Thorandryll didn't shake it. Too common, I suppose. He raised it with a quarter bow, breath and lips oh-so-briefly warming my knuckles. My skin tingled in reaction. "I look forward to hearing from you, Miss Jones."

"*Merde*," Percy remarked, turning his head and rustling a wing. "*Il la veut pour lui-même.*"

"Is that so?" Kate asked, eyebrows drawing down and green eyes locking on the elf's face as he turned toward the door.

"*Oui.* Asshole." The parrot chortled. Nick's lips twitched before he stepped out of sight.

Rolling my eyes, I pointed at Percy. "Manners, bird brain."

"Cordi, Cordi, Cordi," the parrot warbled in his Frank Sinatra imitation. "That's *amour!*"

"You have an interesting pet," Thorandryll remarked, walking toward the door. Kate stayed put, blocking it. Percy snickered as the elf was forced to halt.

"He's my familiar," she said, challenge gleaming in her eyes.

"My apologies." The elf inclined his head, and I sincerely wished I could see his face. Kate held position for a second longer before moving. Percy snickered again, one black eye watching the elf leave.

"What did he say? Was it rude?" I demanded, pointing at her familiar. "Aside from the obvious?"

"Only on the elf's part. Let's try the spell. I have a coven meeting this evening." She spun and headed for her office, Percy softly crooning in her ear.

Nick stepped up beside me. "Now that was funny."

"He's a client. Percy needs to show some manners."

"He is an asshole." Catching hold of my hand, the shifter tugged me into walking. His thumb slipped over my knuckles in quick sweeps as we followed the witch. "We're still on for dinner, right?"

"Absolutely." I was gearing up for another trip to the Barrows, hoping this time it would end with possession of Zoe, and complete avoidance of the telepathic vampire.

Unfortunately, Kate wasn't able to locate the girl, in spite of trying for a couple of hours amidst swearing and Percy's crooning impression of Sinatra to calm her down.

"Are you certain she's still alive?" Kate eventually demanded, putting the pendant down oh-so-carefully and rubbing the mark the chain had left across her palm.

A check of the filed shimmer gave confidence to my response. "Yes."

She sighed, flipping strands of hair from one cheek. "Well, I'm getting absolutely nothing here."

I had a reprieve, so it was guilt-flavored relief flowing through my veins as I stood up. "Try again tomorrow?"

"Definitely."

"Thanks, Kate." Nick followed me out of her office, brow creased in thought.

Six

"I'm starving." Constantly checking the Zoe shimmer was picking at my energy levels.

Ushering me out into the parking lot, Nick asked, "What do you want to eat?"

"Something heavy. Italian sound okay? I'll buy this time." Hunger was overriding tiredness. It demanded satisfaction loudly, my stomach issuing a ferocious growl.

Nick chuckled. "I invited you. Do you have a place in mind?"

"Yeah. Did you want to drive?"

Of course he did, given the opportunity. I kept a straight face at his quick "Sure."

Once we were in his truck, he started digging for information. "I get the impression you're not very fond of vampires."

"I'm not. One turned my best friend two years ago. She couldn't take it and asked me to stake her."

Nick quietly whistled. "Did you?"

"Yeah." I'd also paid for her funeral. Ginger hadn't been a vampire long enough to turn to ash. She'd just looked dead.

"That had to have been really hard."

"Let's talk about something else, please."

"Sure." He was silent for a minute. "So, what kind of music do you like?"

That and other general topics carried us through dinner, since he avoided any of my attempts to get him to open up on more personal subjects.

It was dark when we left the restaurant, and I looked around while we walked to his truck. The vampire whose mind had brushed mine still worried me.

Nick asked, "Would it be all right if I drove you home and stayed the night?"

"Hm," I pretended to think about it, and then grinned. "Yes."

"I'll drop you off at work, then run home and change," Nick said after swallowing the last bite of his omelet the next morning.

"No, that's okay. I can teleport to the office." I took a sip of my coffee. I'd slept well, snuggled close to him all night long.

"Well, I guess if you're sure?" Nick waited until I nodded. "Okay, I'll see you there in a little while. Thanks for breakfast, Cordi."

"You're welcome. See you there." He rose from his seat and bent, depositing a quick kiss on my cheek. We traded smiles and he left.

God, how domestic. Shaking off the bemusement, I followed to re-lock the door. It wasn't really safe even in the daylight, because vampires collect humans more than happy to do their dirty work.

Personally, I don't get the attraction of dying and returning to suck blood, never able to see the sun again. Don't get me wrong - the night can be beautiful. But watching the sun rise, chasing away black and gray with wide sweeps of pinks, purples, reds, and finally gold wasn't something I'd want to live centuries without ever seeing again.

I think they miss it, if vampires miss anything about being human. Most vampire-owned establishments have at least one, if not dozens, of sunrise landscapes hanging on their walls. Since I can't quite see them having such images around as a reminder of the limitation of their powers, it makes sense that they miss seeing sunrises.

Collecting our breakfast dishes, I frowned. This Derrick, what time was his deady-bye? Rinsing the dishes and loading them into the dishwasher, I made a note to do some research. If I've learned anything during the year I've been a private investigator, it's that no one is truly an expert about anything to do with the supernatural races.

They can surprise you, and those surprises are always nasty. My first nasty surprise had been learning vampires only needed six hours to recharge.

Retrieving my favorite pair of boots from under my bed, I slipped on the dark brown aviator-styled footwear and gave myself a once-over in the full-length, iron-framed mirror set in the corner of my bedroom.

Hip-hugging jeans, a wide belt in matching dark brown leather and a cropped, three-quarters length sleeved shirt in soft teal was the uniform of the day. I looked good, but after a quick application of black eyeliner, mascara, and pale rose lipstick, I looked even better.

Dropping phone, car keys, and slim card case into the inside pocket of my leather bomber's jacket, I slung it over a shoulder.

Satisfied I was as ready for the day as possible, I teleported to work.

I'd been studiously ignoring the red silk puddled on my desk while typing the initial case report for the elf's book. Hitting save and emailing a copy of the file to my boss, I sat back to stare at it.

Some might think being able to pick up impressions from objects, animals, and people is an awesome ability. Getting whammied by the memory of someone being messily killed proves how completely uncool psychometry really is.

I wore gloves for a long time after the first time it showed up in my arsenal of psychic abilities. That one was rather spectacular, involving a used sedan my mom was thinking of buying to replace her worn-out station wagon.

It was the first time I aided the police in an investigation, which led to meeting Damian and ultimately, Mr. Whitehaven. On bad nights, the memory of the victim and that gleaming, old-fashioned straight razor dripping with blood can bring me screaming awake.

Because that happens, my doctor diagnosed me with PTSD, and I have a couple of bottles of pills sitting in my medicine cabinet. After I lay trapped for hours, re-living one particularly brutal murder, I decided those pills weren't my friends and haven't touched them since.

I don't black out. It's not my memories that I flash back to in the dark of night. I wasn't there when any of those events took place.

The things I have witnessed firsthand don't haunt me the way those transferred memories do. Yeah, they bother me, but only during my waking hours and if I think about them.

So I don't as much as possible.

I reached for the silk, but a knock on my office door stopped my hand a scant inch from making contact. "Yeah?"

It opened to reveal Nick. "How's it going?"

"Good. Finished a report and I'm ready to rock on this." I pointed at the silk.

"Can I watch? I should probably learn as much as I can about how your abilities work, being your partner and all."

Nice of him to keep things professional at the office. "Sure. Come on in."

Stepping inside, Nick shut the door and chose one of the chairs in front of my desk. He sat down. "Thanks. So what is it that you're going to do?"

"It's called psychometry. The theory is that the energy of something is affected by the energy of whatever comes into contact with it." I paused to see if he was following along so far. Nick looked interested. "It can be a fluid change that isn't retained for long, or it can be a permanent change."

The shifter nodded. "Kind of like meeting people? Some barely register and you forget them immediately. Others make a lasting impression."

He was quick on the uptake – when he wanted to be. "Yeah, exactly."

"How do you keep it from happening all the time?"

"I block it. I had to learn how and practice, and still get taken by surprise sometimes." Hence the *no touchee the psychic* rule.

"Does it work instantly? I mean, do you not block, touch something and boom! See stuff?"

"Sometimes. Other times, I can handle whatever it is several times before getting anything. Or nothing at all, no matter how often I try." I shrugged.

"You can't really control it as much as ignore it when you need to. Except when it decides to surprise you." He was proving to be the Master of Summing Things Up. "Okay. Do I need to move back or anything?"

"No. Just be still and quiet, please."

"Wait," he said as I began to reach for the silk. "How does this help you find stuff? Won't you just see the elf's library?"

"Possibly, but I might also see the person who took the book. Plus, there's another ability that could kick in. It's like a tracking sense." I paused, but explained when he gestured for more. "Sometimes when I handle objects, it gives me a sort of sense of the owner, or people who've touched it. When I get close to the person, it can lock on and lead me straight to them." The tracking was still a mystery of sorts to me. It didn't always work.

"Okay. Sorry I interrupted." Nick settled back, arms crossing, and gaze focusing on my hands as I again reached for the silk.

Today was a good day, and it was eager to show what it found embedded in the silk's 'memory'.

A narrow, reddish view of a room. A clear view of Thorandryll's back and the legs of a woman circling his waist. Moans of pleasure from the woman he was making love to, her dark hair just visible above his shoulder. My face burned as I dropped the silk. The heat was so scalding that I knew it was probably as red as the silk. "Damn."

"What did you see?" Nick's question was a half whisper.

"Something I wasn't expecting to, not in a library." I had to fan my face, unable to banish the image of the elf's sleek backside steadily flexing. A sniff from Nick's direction drew my attention to him.

He was grinning. "It must've been something really good."

I silently agreed, realizing then that my panties were a little damp. "Um, I'll try again."

The shifter nodded. Taking a deep breath, I reclaimed the silk and images flashed through my mind.

Thorandryll and other elves, and all of them were doing normal library things. Browsing books, talking quietly, and reading.

As those faded, a feeling of heavy menace began to grow. The reddish haze faded to black. I sensed movement then the silk slipped to the floor, someone trampling it.

Wincing, I carefully folded it before placing it on my desk. "I couldn't see the thief. It was too dark."

"I've never seen that much red disappear so fast, Cordi. You've gone dead white." Uncrossing his arms, Nick leaned forward. "Are you okay?"

"Yeah. Whoever he is, he's a scary dude," I admitted, before attempting a careless grin. "Hey, bet you earn your paycheck on this one."

His return smile wasn't a happy one. Since psychic tracking didn't twinge, I checked the time. "I'm due out at Mr. Fent's in thirty minutes. Let's go."

"It's not really aliens, but Mr. Fent doesn't come into town very often. He hasn't had much contact with supernatural types, so he calls them aliens." Filling Nick in while zipping from lane to lane was fun. The shifter looked torn between listening and trying to figure out the best way to brace for the impact he seemed certain would occur.

I hadn't been joking about being able to drive blind-folded. It was another unnamed ability. I just knew what other drivers would do or how they'd react when behind the wheel of my car. Damian and his partner, Schumacher, had been the only two brave enough to ride with me during the blindfold test.

It was an extremely useful ability, one of my favorites once I'd grown accustomed to it. After all, it let me scare the pants off my passengers. And when the pants in question belonged to Nick, well... I pulled my mind out of the gutter before the car ended up crashed there, too.

"I don't know what they are because I haven't managed to spot one yet," I said. "Think I've tromped over all his land at least a thousand times, and gotten nothing except vague impressions that don't make any sense to me."

"What are they doing? Stealing stuff? Killing his chickens?" Nick's voice rose to a squeak when I accelerated to pass a big rig. "Do you always drive this fast?"

"Yup." I grinned. "Well, some things have come up missing, but not anything of value, from what I've gathered. Junk mostly. But one of the barn cats was attacked."

Nick pulled his wide-eyed gaze away from the windshield with an effort. "How badly? Was it killed?"

"Nope, a little scratched up. I'm not sure that it was really attacked, but Mr. Fent insists that it was. I think the cat just scratched its nose on a wire or something." Shrugging, I signaled right to exit.

Nick relaxed as we left the heavy traffic behind. "You're probably right, but it's possible some of the smaller races may have decided that city life isn't to their liking. Some are small enough for a cat to be a danger to."

"Like what?"

"Pixies, brownies, gnomes, and leprechauns."

"I've never seen any and don't know much about them."

"They're pretty shy and experts at staying hidden," Nick replied, and we pulled onto the dirt lane that led to Fent's farmhouse.

We spent the afternoon visiting with the elderly farmer and hiking all over his place, but didn't find anything. Calling it a day and beginning the walk back to my car, Nick suggested, "Maybe I should come back, stake out the place tonight?"

"Well," I hesitated, the idea of turning my case over to a complete newbie not palatable. Yet if something came up on the other two cases, he'd be busy, and I could handle it alone. That would be nice, even if it meant no playing before sleep.

"They might be afraid to show themselves to humans." He shrugged. "I don't want to step on your toes, but I might have some luck if I'm alone."

Scratching a mosquito bite, I decided to let him have at it. "Okay."

We spoke to Mr. Fent to arrange it before leaving. The drive back to town was quiet. I dropped Nick off at the office so he could pick up his truck, and then went home alone with one desire: a hot shower.

Seven

Showered and leftover lasagna devoured, I called Jo. The witch answered, her hello sounding distracted. "So what were you up to in the Barrows?"

"Trying to track down grimoires rumored to contain *muy* dangerous spells."

"Oh. How *muy* dangerous?"

Husky voice icing over, she said, "In the right hands, world destruction dangerous."

I smoothed the goose bumps that rose on the back of my neck and gulped. "How many right hands are there?"

"Couldn't tell you," Jo admitted. "Rumors we've heard over the past few years say that there are three grimoires with such spells."

"What exactly do the spells do?"

Her exasperated sigh numbed my eardrum. "That's part of the problem, Cordi. We don't know. One of them supposedly has the spell that divided the realms, but all we really have to go on is speculation."

"I don't think I want to hear speculation." Shivering, I asked, "What would happen if that spell was worked again?"

"In this day and age? Utter chaos. Maybe the Melding wasn't that long ago, but all the changes it brought to the world…"

"Wow."

"Yeah." We were both silent for a minute.

"Three books? You don't have the titles?"

"Grimoires," she corrected. "Books of dark magic. They don't really have titles, but are known by the name of whoever wrote them."

"Let me guess: finding the names is a big part of the problem?" I hoped she'd tell me I was wrong. It was a poor, misguided little hope.

"Exactly. The dark magical types were pretty secretive, so rumors are all we have to go on."

"So, what are you guys going to do with them when you do find them?"

She responded with no hesitation. "Destroy them."

"I'll sign on for that. If you come up with anything I can do to help, tell me," I offered.

"Thanks, girl." In a much lighter tone, she said, "Now tell me about Nick."

Sensing she needed a break from doom and gloom, I replied, "I totally schtupped him. Twice so far."

Jo squealed. "You did? I'm so proud! What was he like?"

"Kind of serious about it." An idiotic grin spread over my face.

"Serious about the sexing, or like 'let's relate' serious? Because you know you need to sow wild oats, Cordi." The statement was a repeat of what she'd been telling me since we'd met. Jo was of the opinion women should have just as much fun as men before settling down.

"The sexing. He's kind of careful about it."

She laughed. "Well, shifters are quite a bit stronger than humans."

"Yeah." We gossiped for a bit, until Jo convinced me to rate Nick on the old one to ten scale. "Um, I'd say eight."

"Not bad. Well, now that you've given me something to dream about, I'd better hit the hay. I've got a full day staring me down," she said.

"Okay. Talk to you later." Ending the call, I decided it was bedtime for me as well, but as I slid under the covers, another flash illuminated my mind, leaving behind a thick, silvery red thread.

Throwing the covers off, I hustled to my dresser for underclothes. Yanking panties on while heading for my closet almost introduced my nose to the floor. Grabbing jeans, running shoes, and a tee from there, I continued pulling on clothes while jogging for the living room.

It was a good thing none of my neighbors was out, because I didn't finish dressing until reaching my car. Tossing jacket and phone into the passenger seat, I pulled on the tee and climbed in.

Whatever my psychic tracking had latched onto was big, so I didn't think it was the Fent case. As my car shot out of the parking lot, I hoped it was Zoe. Solving that case as quickly as possible and returning her to her mother would be awesome.

The line led me to the outskirts of an area heavily populated by business buildings, where new construction was ongoing. It was flat out spooky in the dead of night, but my tracking sense was insisting that I check a certain site.

Buttoning my jacket against the surprise chill, I scanned the place with both eyes and mind before teleporting inside the chain link fence surrounding it. A sign declared it a future hotel.

Teleportation isn't one of my favorite abilities. It's disorienting and I haven't quite overcome the fear that I won't end up stuck wherever it is I pass through between Point A and Point B. But climbing chain link is noisy work, and while I wasn't sensing anyone, it felt like someone was watching.

Caution is always the smart move in my line of work, so teleportation it was.

Moving as quietly as possible, I picked my way through piles of building materials while focusing on that thin thread my tracking ability had presented. Stepping through a plastic-shrouded doorway, I paused when I heard a faint scuffling noise.

If life were like the movies, I'd be a dumb ass and ask "Who's there?"

I'm not that much of a dumb ass, thank you.

Waiting for my eyes to adjust, I stayed in place, listening and mentally scanning again. I heard a car start and drive off, the sounds distant. I didn't catch the slightest hint of another being physically present.

Probably just a cat hunting for its dinner. They were hard to sense. With a final blink, I was ready to trust my eyes enough to attempt navigating the mess.

Nick would be pissed if he knew I were out alone. Waiting for him might have meant losing the thread and that wasn't acceptable.

It led deep into the half-built hotel and straight to a pile of greasy looking ash. A stake made it clear what they were: vampire remains. Kneeling to one side of the pile, I stuck a finger into the ashes to check their temperature. They were still warm.

Not good. Halfway to my feet, I spotted a cord as it crossed my vision. Grabbing for it, I flung an elbow backward while twisting, striking my attacker in the stomach.

The garrote fell, but he punched me in the side of the head before I could get a look at him. Going down sideways, I could feel my ear already beginning to swell.

He landed on me, both hands going for my throat. I was too late to keep him from latching on, and digging my fingernails into his wrists didn't make him let go. The one bonus I got from grabbing his wrists was enough of a twist to my head that I could see his face. Only his face was gone.

Blackness swirled around his head, hiding him from me. A spell? Glamour?

Why the hell am I trying to figure that out now? I choked as the pressure increased. Letting go with one hand, I groped the floor, hoping for something to use as a weapon.

You can't concentrate enough to use psychic abilities when panicking. I don't give a damn who you are: no air equals panic.

Cold metal slipped past my fingertips. Grabbing, I picked up a can and swung it, hitting him through the black cloud. His grip eased enough for a gulp of air. I shoved the can toward the blackness and pressed the nozzle. A gagging noise followed the contents hissing out, and he released me to claw at his hidden face.

Then he fell over, bucking and flailing about. Coughing, one hand on my throat, I glanced at the can and wondered what in the hell I'd gotten him with. Not able to make out the label, I gave it up as his thrashing increased briefly and scrambled out of kicking range just before he went still.

Spell or glamour, the black faded, and I was left staring at a dead elf, yellow goo on his face and oozing out of his wide opened mouth. The goo leaked from his nostrils too.

Climbing to my feet, can still clutched in one hand, I studied his clothing and kicked his ankle to check for a reaction. His cheeks were puffing out, and his throat looked oddly fat. Bending down, I checked his pulse.

He was definitely dead. Elves were supposed to be immortal, yet I'd killed one. With what?

Unzipping my jacket pocket and pulling my cell phone out, I read the can's label by the light of its small screen: expanding foam insulation. "This is going to be interesting to explain."

A couple of button punches later, I had Damian on the phone, wondering which case the dead elf was connected to. Had to be Thorandryll's book, right?

We watched the coroner gesture the waiting EMTs to bag the body. "He was choking me. I didn't know what I grabbed until it was all over."

"So you just shoved the nozzle into his mouth?" Damian's lips twitched. He'd been having a hard time keeping a straight face since his arrival about an hour prior. In daylight, his eyes were summer sky blue, but night turned them indigo. Either way I was familiar with the gleam raised by the effort not to laugh.

I'd seen it often enough, and not just from him.

"Not on purpose. I was just trying to spray him in the face." I grimaced while swallowing. "Which was hidden by a spell or something. I hit him with the can first, and then sprayed."

"I'm thinking that this is luck of the legendary variety." He shook his head. "Damn, Cordi. Expanding foam?"

"I used what was available. Are you going to arrest me, or can I go home and see about my throat?"

He looked at it and winced. "No, not tonight and I doubt at all. Go on home. Do you want me to call one of the others to meet you there? I'll be here for a while, so can't help you with that."

"Thanks, but I can handle it." I stepped toward him, and landed an affectionate peck on his cheek. A flash of light startled me, and Damian groaned as we both turned to the source.

"Great, the press," he muttered. "Better get moving, Cordi."

"Going. I'll talk to you later." Deciding the situation called for it, I stepped through the plastic covering the future main entrance of the hotel before teleporting to my car. Mr. Whitehaven preferred we keep as low a profile as possible, to keep every kook in the city from showing up at the office.

€ight

I was kicked back at my desk and staring at the ceiling the next morning, trying to play connect the dots with what little I'd learned from the night before.

Thornadryll's book was old, hadn't been heavily guarded and had definitely been stolen. Zoe was a rebellious teen, presumed runaway with a vampire fetish. My psychic tracking had led me to a half-built hotel, a pile of fresh vampire ash, and an elf.

Something about the elf, aside from his being dead, nagged me. I needed to look at the body again.

Kate's locator spell for Zoe had led us to the Barrows, and the Mitchells seemed damned convinced she'd run off to be with a vampire. So were the vampire ashes related to her case? How good were the chances that the elf wasn't involved with Thorandryll's missing book?

Swinging my boots off the desk and sitting up, I spied my client walking into the reception area. For a moment, I wished I'd worn a dress, or at least a skirt. Something nicer than jeans, ropers, and the dark blue tee that said 'You think this is bitchy?' Today the elf was casually dressed in dark indigo jeans, a pale blue silk dress shirt left un-tucked with the sleeves rolled up. He wore running shoes, so new the white was practically blinding.

He paused at the door. "Am I interrupting?"

"I do have a phone call to make." I wondered if his long, golden hair were as soft as it looked.

"I can wait." He began to turn back toward the reception area.

"It may be related to your case, so you can wait in here." I concentrated on unplugging my phone from the charger while the elf strolled in, shut the door, and took a seat.

His icy blues focused on my throat when I looked up. "What happened?"

Having been too tired to stay awake long enough to heal all the damage to my throat, I had an ugly ring of green and yellow around it. "I ran into someone who wasn't friendly last night."

Thorandryll frowned. "Working on my case?"

"Working on a case. Which might be related to yours." I shrugged. "I need to make this call."

"Of course." A regal inclination granted permission before the elf returned to studying my throat.

Pushing buttons, I brought up my contact list and selected Damian's name. With another push, I was listening to it ring. He answered on the second one. "Hi, Cordi."

"Hey. So how much trouble am I in?" I pretended not to notice the elf's sharp glance and raised eyebrow.

Damian laughed. "You need to make an official statement. The DA isn't going to bring charges. He decided it was a clear case of self-defense."

A perk of aiding the police from time to time. "Cool. Next question: I need another look. Possible?"

"Entirely, after you make your statement. I'll take you down afterward," he promised.

"Okay. Be there soon." Glancing at Thorandryll, I had an idea that might help clear up which case last night's adventure belonged to. "I'm bringing my client with me. Maybe he can help with IDing."

"Good idea. See you soon."

"Bye." Ending the call, I smiled at the elf. "I hope you don't mind."

"Not at all. This would be the man who attacked you?"

Wasn't he quick to jump to sexist conclusions? It could've been a woman. "Yeah. We'll take my car." Rising, I collected my keys and phone, gleefully contemplating having the elf at my mercy. "I basically got a flash last night."

"A 'flash'?" Thorandryll gestured me out of the office ahead of him.

"One of my abilities is psychic tracking." I ended up spending the drive answering his questions about my abilities instead of explaining what had happened the night before.

To my disappointment, the elf didn't react to my driving. He emerged from my car completely unruffled, and played the gentleman all the way up to the detectives' division, opening doors and gesturing me through.

What can I say? It tickled my vanity that he seemed so interested in and impressed by my psychic talents.

A booming voice announced our entry into the big room. "There she is, our little menace to society." I blushed as Thorandryll's eyebrows rose. Detective Schumacher was grinning. "I have a gift card for a home improvement store if you need to reload, Jones."

"Ah, no. No thanks."

"That was really creative," he continued, grin widening as I squirmed in embarrassment. The detective absolutely loved teasing me whenever the opportunity arose.

"Dude, please," I begged, feeling the heat suffusing my face. Bright red isn't a good look on me.

Schumacher took pity, flapping a hand. "Aw, you're no fun."

"Cordi, back here." Damian's head popped out from behind a filing cabinet. Leading the way over, I introduced the elf to him. While I wrote my statement, he quizzed Thorandryll about elven culture. Once I'd finished, Damian escorted us downstairs.

"Why are we here?" Thorandryll was looking at the plastic sign beside the morgue's doors. "This is where the dead are kept."

"You didn't tell him?" Damian asked, pausing with one hand on the door.

"I didn't get the chance to."

"The man who attacked you is dead?" Thorandryll frowned.

"Yeah."

He switched his attention to my friend. "Who killed him?"

"Cordi did." With that, Damian pushed the door open and I followed, a little stung by the look of disbelief that appeared on Thorandryll's face.

All things considered, I think people should take me seriously. I'm not helpless. Occasionally clumsy and prone to panicking at times, okay, sure. But definitely not helpless.

At Damian's request, an attendant retrieved the body. The elf's face and throat were more horribly distended than I remembered.

"Um, so do you recognize him?" I asked while Thorandryll stared at the corpse.

"I highly doubt the woman who bore him would. What is that?" He pointed at the yellow gunk, in my opinion too calm to be viewing the dead body of one of his own kind.

"It's expanding foam insulation." Damian immediately rubbed a hand over his mouth and looked away.

"It's what?" Thorandryll looked my way, both eyebrows high, and caught me staring at his ears. His were elegantly pointed and extremely sexy looking.

"It's this stuff used to fill in spaces around water pipes or cracks in walls." I shrugged, bending to look at the corpse's ears. "It was a construction site. That's what was handy."

"You're a psychic."

"Yeah, well, he caught me by surprise and was choking the hell out of me. It's kind of hard to concentrate when you can't breathe, okay?" Looking up at the attendant, I asked, "He's had plastic surgery, hasn't he?"

He bent to check the corpse's ears, and looked up to compare them to Thorandryll's. They didn't look as elegant, being more bluntly pointed. "Yes, it looks like he has."

"Thanks. That's what I needed to know." Plastic surgery meant human. No wonder Thorandryll wasn't upset. I glanced at the elf. "Nothing?"

"I'm afraid not," the elf replied. Nodding, I turned and my arm brushed the corpse. The morgue disappeared, a rocky wall inches from the tip of my nose.

"Damian?" Stretching out a hand, I felt him catch hold of it. "A cave."

"What's happening?" Thorandryll's question earned instant shushing from the warlock.

"Need to turn around. All I can see is rock." Most visions were like watching a movie, but some were three-dimensional. This was one of the latter. I intended never to tell anyone about my fear of ending up locked forever in one.

Damian moved with me, a reassuring link to reality as my eyes scanned dimly lit rock. "It's a cavern. It's huge."

The space faded into darkness and my voice seemed to echo back. But there was nothing particularly remarkable about it. "I can't see...wait."

Flickering lights appeared in the distance, drawing steadily nearer my viewpoint. After a minute, I could make out torches carried by hooded figures, and whispered, "Something's happening."

They gathered around a flat-topped rock and one stepped forward, slipping the hooded cloak off. "A group of people. One's a woman and..."

She was nude under the cloak, long dark hair loose around her shoulders. Her back was to me. Stretching her arms out to either side, she didn't resist as two others took hold. They lifted her onto the rock, which I realized made a natural altar. Dread rose while watching them chain her wrists and ankles, leaving her face down and spread-eagled. Vulnerable. "I don't want to watch this."

"Watch what, Cordi?" Damian quietly asked.

"It's some kind of ritual." My stomach flip-flopped as chanting began. The figures formed a circle, beginning to march around the altar. I gasped when one raised a bone-handled whip, sending it slashing down onto the woman's back.

She jerked, but didn't scream. Drugged? More arms raised, fists clutching whip handles. My legs gave out when blood began flowing. Damian eased my descent to the floor, and kept hold of my hand while I begged, "Get me out."

We both knew from experience nothing could be done. I had no choice but to see it through. Closing my eyes made no difference.

The beating had reduced the woman's back to tatters of red. Her companions drew back, the chanting fading away. Into the newly fallen silence, another stepped forward, face hidden in the shadow of his hood. Lifting his hands overhead, he shouted out a harsh scrape of sound.

I scooted backward until my back hit something, staring in horror at the huge, winged beast that answered. Whimpering, I watched the demon wipe a hand over the sacrifice's ruined back and lift it to lick off blood.

"It's just a vision, Cordi. It can't hurt you," Damian murmured, having somehow managed to keep hold of my hand.

The cloaked ones knelt, heads bowing. Mine began to jerkily shake no, but that didn't do any good either.

Claws digging into her hips, the demon pulled the woman backwards as far as the chains allowed. Wings flicked, settling behind it, and I cringed at what the move revealed.

"No." My whisper had no effect. Lifting her hips higher, the demon took her. Now she screamed, the high keen ringing loudly. I let go of Damian's hand to clamp both of mine over my ears, sliding over and curling into a fetal position.

She screamed again, and it trailed off into a bubbling sob. Its third thrust didn't force a scream from her, but from me. I couldn't take it anymore, I needed to be free of the nightmare scene.

The demon's head snapped around, its baleful orange eyes boring into mine.

That did the trick. My mind shut down, allowing me to jump gratefully into its offer of darkness.

"It saw me," I insisted. I was sitting on a bench outside the morgue with my head between my knees. Unconsciousness hadn't lasted long; I'd come to as they were dragging me out into the blessed sunshine, away from the dark and horror. "It saw me, Damian."

"That's not possible. Your visions are of past events, Cordi. How could it see you?" He patted my back, but stopped when I flinched, the whipping still so raw in my mind that it spilled over to my flesh.

"I don't know." Moving with caution, I sat up and leaned back, hand shaking while pushing hair off my cheeks. "Just that it did. They raised a demon and it saw me."

Thorandryll offered the soda he'd collected from a machine in the foyer. I accepted it. "Thanks."

"You're welcome. I wasn't aware humans had mastered the art of calling demons forth from the nether realm."

Almost choking on the sip just taken, my response was a sputter. "Art? They beat a woman bloody and let it rape her to death."

"Forgive me. I misspoke," the elf apologized. "I wasn't aware humans could harness the power necessary to call them."

"Well, surprise," I muttered. "Some apparently can."

"So now we know he was a cultist." Damian sighed. "Captain's going to love this."

"I bet." Another cold sip of sugary goodness rolled down my throat, chasing away the last metallic dregs of fear coating my mouth. Funny how fear became a familiar flavor. "I'm never sleeping again."

The warlock nudged me. "I told you to adopt a dog."

"You could loan me Illy for the night." Damian's familiar, a goofy husky named Illusion, liked me almost as much as Kate's parrot did.

"I'll do that," he agreed. "I think nightmares are all you need to worry about, Cordi."

"Good thing."

Damian instantly defended the dog. "He can be quite ferocious when needed."

"Yeah, like when a stuffed animal goes on a rampage, or a trashcan plots world domination."

"Then why do you want to borrow him?" The warlock mock glared.

I shrugged. "He's cuddly."

Nine

"I'd planned to suggest that you visit my library," Thorandryll said as we neared my parked car. "In hopes that you might sense something useful."

"Yeah, I was going to ask about doing that." I hesitated, trying to decide if I was up for another vision hitting me. "No one's ever died in there, have they?"

He half-smiled. "No."

"Okay, I'm game to try."

"Perhaps tomorrow would be wiser," he suggested, giving me a critical look. "You don't look well, Miss Jones."

My tone was curt. "I'm fine."

"As you wish." The elf touched my arm and we were suddenly elsewhere. A wrenching sensation in my stomach followed the realization that it was his library.

"Could you warn me next time?" I demanded, shaking his hand off. Magic teleportation wasn't something I trusted at all.

"I'll endeavor to do so." His courteous expression raised the instant suspicion that he was laughing at me.

"Good." I began studying the ten-feet-tall bookcases surrounding the small nook we'd appeared in. There were empty places apparent in all of them. Aware of the elf's intent gaze, I selected one and turned in front of it, surveying the area. "This is where it was."

"Yes." His tone indicated I'd passed a test. Hiding a frown, I turned and slipped my hand into the empty spot. Nothing happened.

With a shrug, I knelt and laid my hand on the thick carpet. Roughly ten seconds later, I yanked it away, unable to stand the growing sensation of pressure. "Carpet's useless. Too many people have walked on it."

"You received nothing from the shelf?" Thorandryll moved a bit closer.

"No, but sometimes it's not immediate." Standing again, I tried touching the wood once more. "Where's the door?"

"This way." The elf gestured for me to follow. We walked a mini-maze before reaching the door, which proved to be nothing more than a wide opening with a carved wooden support outlining it.

Not very secure. I stepped out to look both ways, and spotted the door Nick and I had arrived through. "Hm."

Returning to the former resting place of the book, I studied it. "Is there another way in?"

"No."

"Okay. It was dark..."

The elf interrupted me. "It's never dark in here."

"It was in the vision I had. Completely black." I paused. "Wait a minute. I couldn't see the dead guy's face when he was choking me. There was this black stuff, like a piece of night, wrapped around his head."

"Rather clumsy method of concealment. I'd think it would be quite noticeable." Thorandryll crossed his arms, one eyebrow rising and lips twisting into a barely there smirk.

"Maybe, but it worked. At least until he was dead." Hands on hips, I shrugged. "With nothing more to go on at the moment, I'm going to say that Dead Fake Elf Guy was the thief."

No response from the elf. I began pacing. "That vision means he was there, and was part of the cult. Why would cultists want it?"

"I have no idea. It's merely a journal, written by one long dead. A tedious record of the times that led to the dividing of our realms, including quite a bit of boring political commentary." Thorandryll smiled when I glanced in his direction.

My pacing had taken me away from the shelves. Leaning against a table's edge, I frowned. "Then why would anyone want to steal it?"

The elf shrugged, coming to stand directly before me. "I don't know."

Scanning his face, I wasn't entirely certain he was telling the truth and became uncomfortably aware that he'd invaded my personal bubble. Deciding to move, I set a hand on the table to push away. Heat flashed through my body and a loud gasp escaped my lips. I'd forgotten about the first memory from the red silk. The table was the same one the woman had been on. Lucky me: it was my day for extremely vivid visions.

The elf was close, his head lowering and hands rising to cup my face. As his lips covered mine, something quietly nagged at me. Something about this...

Bright light flared in my head. Hands flat on the elf's chest, I shoved hard. He stumbled back, but the fact the vision had become real wasn't immediately important.

The thin, silvery line in my mind was. Taking off at a run, I hoped it wouldn't fade before I located whatever had triggered it.

Barely aware that Thorandryll was chasing after me, I slid out into the hallway, dodging into another room not but a few strides later. Crossing it, I threw open the balcony doors without slowing down much. The eight-foot drop was a little jarring, but nothing twisted or cracked. Still sensing the trail, I increased my pace while cursing the fact I'd worn boots instead of running shoes.

Slick underfoot, the grass blurred by, as did ornamental shrubs. I heard a shout, but didn't look back or slow down.

Not until an ancient-looking archway of vine-covered stone appeared. The pebbles marking the path to it rolled under my boots, so that I almost fell on my ass while sliding to a halt.

Catching my balance, I focused on the line's termination point. Panting, aware of sweat trickling down between my breasts, I scrambled to the patch of grass and dropped to rake my fingers through it in search.

All that effort and the prize was a thin braid of what looked like embroidery threads. Holding it up, I had no clue what it might mean. Thorandryll arrived, so I held it up for him to see. Sweeping his hair back over a broad shoulder, the elf focused on it. After a minute, he crouched down for a closer inspection. Finally, he murmured, "It's not our magic."

Twirling it briefly, I shrugged and tucked it into my back pocket. He'd wanted to keep the missing book quiet, and another elf was approaching.

"I haven't seen you chasing after a woman that quickly since we were young. Losing your touch?" He clapped Thorandryll on the shoulder while looking me over.

The newcomer had rich, mahogany hair and grass green eyes. Dressed in shades of brown, he made the archaic tunic, leggings, and boots look fashionable. Something about him seemed vaguely familiar.

"Is she your new lover?"

Rising, my client's eyes cut to mine before turning to face him. Before Thorandryll could answer, I stood up and planted a kiss on his cheek. "I'm going to be late to work."

"I'll return you to your vehicle." He reached for my arm. Skipping backwards, I plastered on a smile. Being alone with him seemed like a bad idea.

"That's all right. Call me." With that, I teleported away.

56

Ten

"You'd be better off having David look at it." Kate shook her head. Somehow she managed to make me feel like a cat who'd just spat a rat's tail at her feet. Not a bad prize, but a whole rat would be more useful. "String magic isn't my forte."

"Cool. I'll go over and," I saw Nick pulling into the parking lot. "Uh-oh."

Kate's gaze swept my throat, and she snickered. "This should be interesting."

The smile he greeted us with while entering the building became a scowl as the shifter saw my neck. "What happened?"

"Jones had a little adventure last night," Kate answered in her most helpful tone.

His "Damn it, Cordi" was a frustrated growl. "Why didn't you call me?"

"Didn't have time to. Where were you all morning anyway?"

"I spent the night out at Fent's farm, remember? Brownies. I introduced them this morning and the old man's thrilled to have some company. He's letting them move into the cellar." A grin reeking of smug appeared on his face. "Case closed."

"Then you can write up the report while I go—"

Nick shook his head. "Not without me. I want to know everything that's happened since last night."

"I'm gone. Still trying to track down Mr. Blacke," Kate said as we squared off with each other. "You can tell me who won later." Wiggling her fingers in an abbreviated wave, the witch escaped out to the parking lot.

"Reports are important," I began, determined to keep the matter on a professional level.

"Screw the damn report. Who did that? Who hurt you?" Nick jabbed a finger at my neck, his eyes narrowing and a scowl appearing.

So much for professional behavior. "He's dead."

The shifter blinked. Having regained the upper hand, I crossed my arms and raised an eyebrow, trying for amused boredom. "Regardless of what you and the boss think, I can take care of myself."

"Yeah? And just how did you take care of yourself while being strangled?" Nick mirrored my pose, arms flexing as he crossed them. It looked more impressive when he did it.

I wasn't about to admit it had been pure luck. "I've been taking self-defense lessons."

Nick shook his head. "I guess that's good if you get mugged. By a human."

"My instructor's an ex-Marine."

"Then he should be teaching you how to handle a gun. That would be a lot more useful against vampires, Cordi."

Actually, I had a concealed carry license and a gun. It stayed in a desk drawer, because I didn't like carrying it. "Did you not see me head butt that vamp the other day? It totally worked. Go, Marines!"

He laughed. "You got lucky."

"Uh-uh. I did what Jeff taught me to: I surprised him." The supernatural superiority complex was beginning to irritate the hell out of me.

Rolling his eyes, the shifter suddenly bent, grabbed my left ankle, and yanked. I ended up on my ass. "Ow!"

"Surprise works both ways," he said, grinning down at me.

"Jerk." I accepted the hand he offered, and he pulled me to my feet. Nick's grin disappeared the second we were face to face. Searching mine, he let go of my hand and stepped back.

"Why did you kiss him?"

"What?"

"I can smell the elf on you, Cordi."

From the way his jaw clenched, Nick didn't like it one bit. "Oh, it was nothing. One of his buddies showed while I was following a trail. Thorandryll did specify 'discreet', if you'll remember."

A slow nod was his response. "The guy was kind of nosy, and asked if I was his new girlfriend, so I kissed his cheek and left."

It wasn't the whole truth, but it wasn't as though Nick was eager to share much more than his body. I held up the string. "Found this, and I'm going to the Orb to ask David to take a look at it. Are you coming?"

"Yeah."

He was back to normal by the time we arrived, because I'd spent the drive bringing him up to speed while he hung onto the Jesus handle.

The Blue Orb sat tucked among other businesses in a cul-de-sac off Main Street. Its façade matched theirs, being adobe warmed to cream by the sunlight, and a dull red canvas canopy promised shade. Inside, a welter of scents from herbs and candles filled the air. I sniffed appreciatively, picking out hints of sage, rosemary, and frankincense.

The first thing I did was introduce Nick to David. Second up was handing over the string. After that, I excused myself and went upstairs, leaving Nick to check out the shop while the warlock studied the string.

David had been the hardest to win over of the witches, being shy and intellectual. Asking if he carried *Psychic Abilities for Dummies* hadn't started us off on the right foot.

We all kept emergency bags at the shop, in a spare closet. I got mine out and carried it to one of the guest bathrooms. Though not sure what was going on between us, making Nick jealous or hurting his feelings wasn't my style.

I brushed my teeth, washed my face, and reapplied makeup. My last step was a fresh squirt of perfume before returning my bag to the closet.

Once back downstairs, I hopped up on the counter. "Well?"

David was up to his usual high standards, ready with the answers. "Concealment charm."

"One strong enough to hide a human pretending to be an elf from real elves?" I gave his familiar's glossy black feathers a stroke. Copernicus rustled his wings, blinking sleepily.

"From the residual magic, I'd say yes."

"Cool. Dead Guy was the thief," I decided. "I need to remember to ask Thorandryll where that arch led to."

"I think the cultists are a bigger concern." Nick returned from wandering around the shop.

"Dude, I can handle humans just fine. Proved that last night." My defiance turned to a grudging admission. "It's their pet demon that has me worried."

"Meh." David shrugged, straightening his old-fashioned cardigan that always had stuff trailing from the pockets. "It takes quite a bit of power to call one up, Cordi. Even if that vision was of a relatively recent raising, it's quite likely the demon already completed whatever task it was set to, and has returned to the nether realm."

"If it takes so much to raise one, why wouldn't they keep it around? You know, like having a guard dog on a leash?"

David laughed. "A demon's not a dog. A dog, properly trained, will obey. Force is required to make a demon obey. It would take too much energy and blood to control one for any real length of time. If you can't control what you raise, it will take over. Few want to risk that happening."

Feeling much better, I smiled. "Thanks."

"My pleasure."

"Now what?" Nick was frowning, but I detected a hint of relief.

"Now we eat lunch. I'm starving." Sliding off the counter, I grinned. "And we learn how to hunt cultists."

"Jo's lunching at the cafe," David remarked.

"Cool. Want us to bring you something back?" He shook his head. "Okay, catch you later."

The café was across the cul-de-sac from the Orb. A tiny outdoor patio allowed the coven to have their familiars with them, specially created after David had taken possession of the building and opened the shop for business. In return, Ronnie had warded the place against theft, and natural disasters. Also against vermin of both the insect and small furry kind.

Or not so small. Santo Trueno's rats rivaled the tales told of New York's.

"The serious cultists love the poseurs and dabblers. They make good minions and fodder." Catching my grimace, Jo shrugged. "I don't make the news. I just report it."

"Fodder? Like, they feed them to demons?" My appetite for the scrumptious looking fried chicken on my plate disappeared.

"I suppose in a pinch, yeah. But minions are the fall guys, the living shields - the expendables." She petted her familiar, who was watching Nick strip fried chicken from bone with an unblinking gaze.

Though the shifter appeared to be ignoring us, I felt certain he wasn't missing a single word. "Okay, so where do we find where the serious types recruit their minions from?"

She grinned. "Think in clichés for this crap. Goth clubs."

"Don't vampires own most of them?" I picked at my chicken, uncertain it would stay down if I ate it. The cat transferred her attention to me.

"Yes, most of them. You want the ones owned by humans. Vampires don't look kindly on anyone poaching from their potential donor pool, so most of the cults steer clear."

"Which don't?" I asked, offering Trixie a bit of chicken. She sniffed before daintily accepting it.

"The stupid ones." Nick chuckled at her response, and Jo beamed at him. "Cordi didn't mention how old you are."

If the change of subject fazed him, the shifter gave no sign. "Twenty-three. Did she mention we're sleeping together?"

"God!" I shot a disgusted look at him as my face grew hot.

Jo laughed. "Yeah, she did mention that. Rated you an eight."

"I'll have to try harder and longer." He went back to eating, unperturbed by Jo's wicked cackling or Trixie's amused grumble.

Burying my flushed face into my hands, I wondered what would get me first: cultists, vampires - or my friends.

Lunch over, Nick and I returned to the office. There was a note waiting. Mr. Mitchell had called for a progress report, which struck me as weird.

"You write the Fent report," was my order, complete with handing over the case file.

Accepting it, he asked, "What are you going to be doing?"

"Detective stuff, after I return this phone call. Like researching the ownership of Goth clubs. We can start hitting them tomorrow night." I didn't even want to think about walking into a loud, crowded club.

"Okay. How about we go out for dinner after work?"

"Uh, no. Sorry." Seeing disappointment appear on his face, I added, "I'm exhausted, Nick. It was a rough morning."

"Right. Maybe dinner before club crawling tomorrow?" he suggested, disappointment gone.

"Sounds good," I agreed. "Now scoot."

"Scooting, Miss Bossy." With a grin, the shifter left my office. Going to my desk and sitting down, I received a faint impression of Kate's irritation at having to play receptionist when I picked up the call note.

Mr. Mitchell certainly hadn't given off any vibes to make me think he was worried about his step-daughter. Why would he call, instead of his wife?

Maybe to get back into her good graces? I bet he'd spent a night or two on the couch for his insistence she'd run away because she was a spoiled brat. If looks could kill, the ones Mrs. Mitchell had been shooting his way would've left my office a disaster area.

Picking up the phone, I checked the Zoe shimmer before punching in the number. The reassuring gold eased my mind.

"Mitchell and Associates. How may I direct your call?"

"I'm returning a call from," I checked the case folder. "Mr. Hugh Mitchell. This is Discord Jones."

"One moment, please, while I see if he's in his office." Elevator music filled my eardrum.

Two minutes passed before the music cut off, and Mitchell was on the line. "Miss Jones?"

"Yes. I don't have anything solid to pass on, except that I know for certain Zoe's alive and not a vampire." Before he could make any response, I plunged ahead. "However, I do have a few questions that you may be able to help me with."

"Of course."

I'd start with the easy and obvious question. "What can you tell me about Zoe's relationship with her father?"

"She idolizes him, so of course, I'm the interloper. He's been too busy to see much of her since the divorce. A weekend every other month or two."

"All right, so in your opinion, she would or wouldn't go to him?"

Mitchell snorted. "If she knew where he was, she would. He travels extensively. I believe he's currently in Japan."

"Do you know if Zoe has a Facebook account? I'd like to talk to some of her friends."

"No, I don't. She does have a computer in her room, but it's password protected."

And he knew that how? Before I could ask, Mitchell told me. "Lesley checked it when Zoe first disappeared, hoping to find she'd had plans with friends."

Logical. "Okay. I'll do a search and see if I can find what social media sites Zoe used."

"Didn't you find out anything useful from her necklace?"

"Not really, other than that she's still alive."

His voice carried a note of caution. "How did you determine that from it?"

I felt rather cautious myself, and didn't want to give him too much information. "She must have worn it a lot. Formed a kind of energy connection to it, which I received when I handled it."

"But you didn't learn anything about her current whereabouts?"

"No." I told the lie without a pause. "I'm sorry, I didn't."

"Well, you can only do what you can do." There was an unmistakable note of satisfaction in his voice. I wanted to reach through the phone and throttle him.

"What is your relationship with Zoe like?"

"Mine?" I'd surprised him, if the squeak in his voice was any indication. "Well, we basically ignore each other. She doesn't care for me at all. That interloper thing. I'm not her father, just the man her mother decided to marry."

63

He didn't sound bitter or upset about it. Shouldn't he be? "All right. Thanks for the help, Mr. Mitchell. I'll be in touch."

"You're quite welcome. I'll let Lesley know I spoke with you today."

"Thanks." I ended the call and sat back with a frown. After thinking about it, it didn't seem quite as odd that he wouldn't have any real kind of relationship with Zoe. After all, my dad's new wife would pretend I didn't exist, if she could get away with doing so.

I logged onto the computer to settle in for a few hours of tedium. Records research never fails to be brain numbing.

By six o'clock, I had a list of seven human-owned Goth clubs printed out, in order of closest to my apartment. Nick had stopped in briefly to let me know the Fent report was finished. We'd agreed to meet at my place the following evening.

Logging off, I was more than ready to end the day. Collecting my things and the list, I headed out to the parking lot. Damian's car pulled in with Illy's head hanging out of the passenger window. "Hey, guys!"

"Hi. Thought I'd drop him off so you didn't have to make a trip out," the warlock said. "He'll make his way home in the morning, Cordi."

"Cool. I appreciate it." Opening the passenger door, I shut it after the husky jumped out, and bent to wave. "See you later."

"Bye." With a wave and smile, Damian drove off. Illy trotted over to my car and waited patiently until I opened the door for him.

Once we were both in, I said, "I have to stop at the grocery store first. You stay in the car this time, okay?"

He grinned in answer, which didn't give me much confidence that he'd obey. When he poked his nose at the side window, I leaned and rolled it down. "I'm serious. Stay in the car, no begging treats from kids this time. There's a steak in it for you, bub."

Head tilting, he thought about it, and then licked his chops. Laughing, I started the car and put it in gear while the husky shoved his head out the window. He likes riding with me.

Eleven

Thanks to Illy's presence, my night wasn't nearly as horrible as I'd thought it would be - with the added bonus of steak-scented, dog-slobber facials waking me up each time the demon appeared in my dreams.

With no new insights or psychic sparks, and it being Saturday, I decided it was a good day to play hooky.

I hadn't seen or spoken to either of my parents in almost a week, so after watching the husky blink out for home, I left too. Mr. Mitchell's coldness had left an itch that could only be scratched by touching base with the people who'd created me.

My parents were an odd couple from the start, with my mom being twelve years older than my dad and a dyed-in-the-wool hippie chick. Dad was twenty-three when I was born, already beginning to climb the corporate ladder at the advertising agency. During my three-year nap, they'd gotten divorced.

It seemed that watching your comatose daughter slowly waste away to bones put a harsh strain on a marriage.

Mom was still single. Dad remarried a year after their divorce and presented me with two half-brothers by his new, younger wife, Betty. Because Dad does have his new family, I drove to the New Age center my mom works at first.

"Cordi!" She rose, leaving the circle of people where she was conducting a crystal loving session. The goal was to infuse various types of crystals with positive vibes, but it always looked like some make out session gone horribly wrong to me.

People sat around, stroking and hugging rocks. They're so serious about it that I can't laugh. One time, I'd brought Kate with me. The witch had taken a look, pivoted on one stiletto-heeled boot and told me she'd be waiting in the car.

Percy had stayed, until I threw him out for making too many X-rated suggestions on better ways to infuse crystals.

"Hi, Mom." She'd reached me, and we hugged. The smell of lavender and rose wafted into my nose, causing my eyes to water a little. It had been the first thing I'd smelled, as I woke from my coma while she kissed my forehead.

"You look tired." She smiled. "You haven't been balancing work and fun properly."

"It's been a little tough to lately." Though there was Nick, and sex with him was definitely fun, if not completely satisfying.

She patted my cheek. "I have an extra crystal."

"Uh…" I groped for an excuse and came up empty. "Okay."

The things I do for the woman who gave birth to me. Shrugging off my jacket, I smiled and said hello to those I knew while sitting down next to Mom. She handed me a large, decidedly phallic-shaped, pink kunzite.

After surveying it with more than a little disbelief, I reluctantly began fondling the damn thing. "So, what have you been up to?"

"Harvesting herbs and work. I was planning to call you this evening. Tina would like for you to come to her lying-in party."

And there you have the reason why I've developed an obsession about birth control.

Lying-in parties are home births. I challenge anyone to watch a woman sweat and groan while squatting to squirt out a bloody, furious baby, and see how scarred for life they end up being.

"Any idea when?" I was hoping work would interfere, because I couldn't say no without hurting both my Mom's and Tina's feelings. I've been to twenty-seven lying-in parties, and fourteen of them were prior to my coma. My parents had both been big on the idea of everything being an open book to me when it came to life.

Or maybe to scare me into waiting on sexual exploration for as long as possible. They needn't have bothered, what with my three-year time-out and then getting a handle on my abilities. I'd been twenty before I had dared risk getting naked with my boyfriend at the time.

He'd been a good sport the first couple of times about having to duck flying objects, but it got old fast, so he soon moved on to a girl who didn't have psychic abilities that went haywire in the middle of sex.

"Two weeks or so. Dates are allowed," she informed me.

The image of Nick's face if I asked him to go with me caused a mad case of the giggles to strike. Glancing down at the crystal penis I was holding caused a total loss of control. I laughed until tears poured down my face and I was in danger of dropping it.

Laughter like that is usually infectious, so I wasn't the only one disrupting the hushed atmosphere of the center. I tried to stop, but met the watering eyes of a sixty-something dressed in a truly horrendous chartreuse muumuu and lost it all over again.

It felt good, even though my sides were aching by the time I'd lapsed into sniffling hiccups. Say what you will about hippie and

New Age types, most are sweet people who love to share a laugh, even if they don't get the joke.

Eyes closed, hysterical bursts of giggles escaped while I listened to others trying to cool their hilarity jets. "God, I needed that."

"Looks like it," Mom gasped, patting my knee. I couldn't restrain myself. I had to ask.

"Dates? Really?"

"Yes."

Slapping a hand over my mouth, I muffled another explosion of laughter.

"Did you have someone in mind to ask?" Mom's question caused my eyes to pop open and all silliness to leak immediately away.

"Not really."

My mother is better than a vampire at sensing blood - metaphorically speaking. "But you're seeing someone?"

Uh oh, trapped. I will totally lie to her about my work, to keep her from worrying, but I can't do it about anything else. "Well, yeah. I mean, sort of."

"Tell me about him," she demanded, eyes lighting up. Since I had no choice, I complied.

"We work together. His name is Nick Maxwell and he's a shifter." Catching my breath, I held it to wait for her reaction to that bit of info.

She blinked, and then beamed. "I'm so proud of you for being open-minded!" Looking around at our erstwhile audience, she informed them, "I taught her that."

It was the truth, since Sunshine Breeze Jones was the most open-minded person I knew. That's Mom's name, which she had legally changed back in the mid-sixties. I have to admit that I do fall short of the whole open-minded bit when it comes to the 'vampires are people too' theory she has.

"What does he look like?"

I resigned myself to spending at least an hour satisfying her curiosity.

I wasn't far off the mark. Leaving the center forty-five minutes later, with the kunzite in hand because Mom had insisted, I was relieved she hadn't asked if I'd had sex with Nick yet. Talking to Jo about it was one thing. My mom? No way, even though she had the same sort of view as my friend.

Once in my car, I tossed the crystal into the back before pulling out my phone to call Dad. His first question was, "How's my girl?"

"Fine, dandy, and on my way over, if you guys aren't busy." I never just showed up, because of his new wife. The second time around, Benjamin Thomas Jones had picked out a woman who knew how to handle the corporate social scene.

"If you hurry, you'll be in time for lunch." Dad sounded pleased.

"I'll hurry. See you in a few." Putting my phone away and starting my car, I backed out of the parking space and waved at a couple of the crystal huggers on their way out. The drive wasn't long, with traffic proving no more traffic-y than usual at mid-day.

Their two-story home was in Elmhaven, a development only a couple of miles from my apartment. Jonah and Sean attacked the instant I stepped out of my car. "Cordi!"

Pretending to fall down, I rolled on the grass with them for a few minutes before we went to join Dad, who waited on the porch. "I think they've missed me."

"Looks like it. Give me a hug." Hugs exchanged, we went inside. Betty stepped out of the kitchen long enough to say hello and refuse my offer of help. We didn't hug.

Betty's afraid of me, but convinces herself that she doesn't like me because I'm a freak. She also has some deep security issues about Mom. After all, Dad was married to her for eighteen years.

Dipping into her mind wasn't required. Betty had no shield at all. Every thought slid right out, loud and clear. I strengthened my shield, to keep from hearing her.

There are times I wish my parents would get back together, but then I remember how devastating it had been to wake up and discover they'd divorced two years after the fact. My little brothers are five and three, and I adore them, so don't want them to have to deal with divorce.

I'd love to spend more time with them, but Betty's fear and paranoia are too difficult be around for more than a few hours at a time. She loves Dad enough to put on a convincing show of sincerely enjoying my visits. I have to respect her for that, and try to make it easy as possible for her to keep that façade in place.

Sometimes, people just can't help the way they feel. Of course, I could suggest that she not be afraid of me, and make things more comfortable for us both. But aside from being totally self-serving, it would cross the line I've drawn for myself in the sands of morality.

Gently nudging something already in place was one thing, in the interest of, say, saving someone's life. Making someone feel the opposite of their true feelings was entirely different.

Lunch was nice, with the boys telling their pre-school and kindergarten adventures, Dad a little about his work, and Betty chattering about how busy she was. She's a stay-at-home mother who doesn't stay home much. There are lunches with her friends, tennis lessons, and charity works. Betty's a real social maven.

After dessert, which was pineapple upside down cake, we went out to the backyard. The boys played fetch with the Cocker Spaniel Betty had decreed a proper pet. The poor dog's name was Amadeus. Neither of the boys could pronounce it correctly yet.

"How's work?" Dad asked once we were at the patio table, enjoying fresh lemonade.

I tell Dad everything. He's never been satisfied with just a highlights reel. Though he worries, he also has a hefty amount of confidence in my ability to take care of myself. "I have an elf as a client. That case seems to have a cult and demons involved."

"Demons?" Betty paused in the act of pouring lemonade, her eyes so wide, white showed all the way around. She's blonde and blue-eyed, like Mom.

"In a vision. I haven't seen one up close or anything. According to people who would know, that one is probably already back where he belongs."

"Oh. Well, good." With a weak attempt at a smile, she went into the house. I had to admire her control, having caught her impulse to scurry away screaming.

"I bet you could handle a demon, if you had to." Dad's smile was proud, but there was a hint of worry in his eyes.

Deciding it was time to change the subject, I brought up my visit with Mom. "She said Tina wants me to come to her lying-in party. Get this: dates are allowed."

Dad stared at me for exactly two seconds, and then we both cracked up.

He walked me out to my car about an hour later, arm around my shoulders. "You are being careful."

"Of course. In fact, I have a partner now. Whitehaven hired a shifter as backup muscle for me."

Dad's relief was barely perceptible. "Good. What kind of shifter?"

"Wolf. His name is Nick. Hates my driving." My dad is an intelligent man, but he completely lacks Mom's nose and never notices there's a man in my life unless told.

"I'd like to meet him. Maybe we can have lunch one day." I agreed, hugged him, and we said good-bye.

Halfway home, it occurred to me that we'd forgotten a key component for our evening's plan of club crawling. Digging out my phone, I called Nick. "Hey, about tonight. We need to dress the part."

"Go Goth?" He didn't sound enthusiastic about the idea.

"Yeah. We better meet earlier, so we have time to shop."

"Sure. I can be at your place in about twenty minutes."

"Sounds good. See you there."

A few hours later, shopping finished and dinner eaten, we were in my bedroom. Nick held up a hand when I headed for him. "No. I am not wearing lipstick."

"But it's black."

"Then you wear it. I've already let you paint my nails and put that gunk around my eyes." He wiggled. "These pants aren't comfortable."

Giving up the lipstick idea, I grinned. "But you look great in them."

"I feel like an idiot." Picking at the studded collar around his neck, he sighed. "This, I truly hate."

"It's hot on you, so deal with it." I collected a tiny black purse, dropping my phone and keys into it, and then struck a pose. "How do I look?"

"Sexy as hell." The shifter's leer was instant. "Can I peel you out of that later?"

"Yeah, if you'll stop bitching about dressing up." Lacing the purple and black corset had required his help. It wasn't coming back off without more assistance. "All right. Let's go."

The first club was a bust, but gave us a chance to practice the right attitude. Walking into the second one, Nick embraced me from behind every time we paused for a few seconds. "What are you doing?"

His head was lowered, lips and tongue playing over skin. I had to strain to hear him above the music and crowd. "Sex. There's a lot of people having sex in here."

"Seriously?" Looking around, I didn't see anything going on. People danced, drank, and stood around looking coolly bored. "Come on."

Moving through the crowd, we finally neared the back of the club. Nick's arms felt like steel bands around me when we paused, and I flinched as his teeth scraped my neck. "Stop that."

"Can't." It was a mumble, and he began to lean heavily on me, easing us towards a velvet covered fainting couch. Dropping my shield a little, I picked up his thoughts: he wanted us down, so that he could do something about the need that had begun building the second we entered the club.

My knees buckled at the heavy insistence of the lust he felt, but I managed to lock them by concentrating on and sending one loud thought. *I am not going to let you do me in front of an audience.*

The mental contact shocked him enough that his grip loosened and he straightened up. Dropping my shield more, a telepathic scan proved that he was correct. There were a lot of people having sex in rooms behind the back wall.

We'd walked into a Gothic sex club. The business records hadn't mentioned that. I had to fan my face. Great.

No one was thinking about demons, just their next sexual position. Closing my shield, I dragged the shifter back through the crowd and outside. It wasn't until we reached my car that I noticed his eyes were more gold than brown. "Nick? Are you all right?"

He took several deep breaths, expelling each in loud sighs. Shaking his head, the shifter offered a rueful smile. "I'm fine. Sorry."

"It's okay. I'm sorry about the brain smack." I had learned something new to add to my list of information about shifters. They became aroused at the smell of others having sex. "Let's call it a night."

As we were driving back to my apartment, the shifter glanced at me. "I'll go home."

"You did mention wanting higher than an eight." I was already anticipating his efforts to climb the scale.

Twelve

Sunday is the one day Arcane Solutions officially closes every week, so we slept in. It was almost noon before either of us stirred. We took turns showering, and I swallowed down my no pregnancy insurance while cooking brunch. Nick silently nursed a cup of coffee, until the food was ready.

"This looks good." He smiled.

"Cowboy omelets. Let me get the bacon." Grabbing that and the coffee pot, I returned to the table and sat down. "The next two clubs aren't open until Wednesday night, so we'll hit them then."

"Right. Mind doing a little more research to make sure they're not..." My giggles interrupted him, and he dropped his head over his plate. "It's not funny, Cordi."

I had to fight to sober up. His words to the contrary, he'd still been affected enough for three rambunctious episodes the night before. I could now mark 'done on the living room floor' off my bucket list. That was how far we'd made it before he'd unlaced the corset. "Sorry. Yeah, I guess it wouldn't be. Not anymore than when I couldn't control my cryo ability, and kept freezing every drink I picked up."

"If any of them are sex clubs, I'll get something to help block the smells." He took a bite, and I followed suit. "What are the plans for the rest of today?"

"I need to call Kate, and unless something pops up on either case, I guess we could watch some movies."

That's what we spent the afternoon doing, cuddled on the couch. Kate was able to confirm that Mr. Blacke was out of the country, as well as one of the inherited-type wealthy. She hadn't had much luck on the Derrick front yet. Another location attempt had come up empty. I was checking the Zoe shimmer hourly while conscious, so was able to assure her the girl was still alive.

At about six, Nick's cell phone rang. He went to the kitchen to talk after answering it, and came back out a few minutes later. "I have to go, Cordi. That was my Alpha."

Figured. "All right. I do have some washing and stuff to take care of."

His expression wavered between annoyance and apology. "I'm sorry. This was a lot of fun today."

Getting off the couch, I shrugged. "It's okay. I'll see you in the morning."

"All right." He went to the bedroom to grab his things, and then I walked him out. We kissed and said good-bye. Nick waved before backing his truck out of its parking spot, and I watched him drive away.

Re-entering my apartment, I wondered why I wasn't pushing hard to learn more about him. Normally, I knew quite a bit about a guy before jumping into bed with him, or letting him spend much time in my apartment.

Nick seemed to be a special case. There was a definite sexual attraction, and he was fun to hang out with, but he didn't share much personal information. It didn't matter what kind of opening I tried dangling in front of him, he didn't bite.

Maybe I'm not pushing because he's a shifter. That thought came out of nowhere, while I was sorting clothes, and was a sobering one. Vampires aside, I'd never considered myself particularly prejudiced before.

In my experience, most humans who knew that I was psychic tended to wander off after a while, uncomfortable with someone capable of reading their mind.

My friends and boss knew that I didn't actively pry into people's thoughts, and if the realization had occurred to Nick, he apparently wasn't worried about it.

Even when someone was trying to kill me, ripping his or her mind open wasn't my first defense. Or even my last - yet.

A time might come when I had to do something like that.

The flash signaling my psychic tracking had locked onto something was a relief. I threw the armful of clothing I had into the washer, started it, and went for some shoes.

The silver thread led me to a part of the city I'd never had any reason to visit: the Palisades.

I balked at the idea of parking my car on any of the trashed out, graffiti-marked streets. Half of the lights were out, the others casting weak pools of blinking yellow-pink. Pushing away the urgency, I drove back out and several blocks away after picking one of those lights, to leave my car somewhere safer. The parking lot of a mini-mall on the other side of the highway that divided San Trueno was my choice.

No one was around when I teleported to a spot beside the streetlight I'd chosen. I wasn't worried anyway, since humans don't really scare me unless they have guns. A small display of one of my abilities had always sent the average punk running.

Supernaturals, having their own abilities, don't scare easily and can usually move quickly enough to make my head spin.

Concentrating on the thread, I was relieved my side trip hadn't resulted in its fading any. Moving at a fast walk, I followed it. Ten minutes passed, putting me deep behind what the *Santo Trueno Daily* liked to call 'enemy lines'. It shouldn't have surprised me when I realized someone was following me. Two guys, both human and looking for some fun.

Their idea of fun wasn't the same as mine. Debating on whether to turn and handle them now, or wait until they were a little closer, a vision made me stumble to a halt.

A door, surrounded by blue and white graffiti. The vision faded away, leaving me aware of the fact my pursuers had gotten closer. I turned around to face them, goose bumps prickling my skin. "You really don't want to do this."

"Yeah we do," the one on the left said, an ugly leer appearing on his face.

"I don't want to hurt you. Just turn around and walk away." They laughed, nudging one another with their elbows. Well, I had warned them. It wasn't my fault if they hadn't run into anyone not quite human before. Spreading my feet apart a bit, I struck a defensive pose my instructor had taught me.

One of them laughed, genuinely amused. "Aw, she thinks she can take us."

"She's gonna take us, all right." Guffawing at his crude humor, they drew nearer. I waited until the first reached for me, and threw both hands out, palms outward. His buddy went crashing into a nearby wall.

"What the..." The first was hanging in mid-air, looking confused.

"I guess you don't need my help." A dark figure moved in the shadows about twenty feet away. How he'd managed to arrive without my noticing took secondary importance to the fact that the thread had disappeared. Damn it.

"No, but thank you for offering." I waved my hand to send the second crashing into the same wall. He slid down to sprawl next to his unconscious friend while I scanned the newcomer for aggressive intentions.

"Name's Logan Sayer." He took a few more steps forward, into a pool of light cast by one of the working streetlights. Helpful of him. "Are you a witch?"

"Psychic." I couldn't sense anything negative from him and relaxed a bit. "Discord."

He raised a dark eyebrow. "What?"

"Discord Jones, my name."

"Interesting name." He grinned, displaying even white teeth. Logan appeared to be about thirty, ruggedly good looking with dark eyes and hair, the latter brushing the collar of a blue work shirt. His name was embroidered on the front pocket in cursive script.

"I get that a lot." Curious, I asked, "What are you doing out here?"

"Being thwarted in my effort to rescue a damsel in distress." He grinned again, shoving his hands into the front pockets of his jeans, shoulders rising.

That grin was beyond cute, so I had to return it. "How about I scream and faint next time?"

"There's going to be a next time?" He glanced at the unconscious men. "Does this kind of thing happen a lot?"

"More than I'd like it to."

His grin faded while Logan studied my face. "Going for the cheesy line: what's a nice girl like you doing in a place like this?"

I laughed. "I'm a private investigator, and I'm looking for something."

"Oh. Could you use some help finding it?"

"Maybe. How well do you know this area?" Anything that might cut down on the time I had to spend in this part of town was welcome. Without the thread, I could wander for hours and never find anything but more trouble.

"I've lived here since the Melding. I'm a shifter." He watched for a reaction, but I just nodded. "Tiger."

"I work with a wolf. Haven't met a shifter of the tiger persuasion before." I grinned. See? No prejudice here.

"What are you looking for?" Logan eased a step closer, keeping his hands in his pockets. Nothing leaked from his mind, but I felt like he was trying to keep from spooking me.

"A door with blue and white markings on the walls around it. Any ideas?"

"This area is all gang territories. One marks theirs with blue and white. It starts about three streets over." He jerked his head to the west. "I can take you there, if you want some company?"

"Sure." I walked over, offering my hand for a shake. "Pleased to meet you, Logan."

"Likewise." He pulled his right hand free to shake, nostrils flaring a bit. If my scent affected him the way it did Nick, Logan gave no sign. When our hands met, his warmth slowed the adrenaline-induced beat of my heart back to normal. Calm seemed to flow naturally from him, much as it did from Whitehaven. "This door, is it glass, metal, or wood?"

"Metal."

He pursed his lips at my answer, turning slightly away to scan the street. "May be in an alley then. Do you have any more details?"

"Give me a minute." Closing my eyes and recalling the vision, I studied the door carefully. "It's kind of rusty, with a few dents close to the ground. It's padlocked, and the lock's new. There's a sign by it, but the graffiti covers it."

He was rubbing his chin when I opened my eyes. "It sounds like a delivery door, or maybe a basement entrance to an apartment building."

"Any ideas where to start?"

"That gang claims seven or so blocks of six streets. We'll start with the first alley."

"Okay." We set off, and I noticed his gaze constantly moving. "Are you watching for anything in particular?"

"It's been a little unsettled around here the past few days. Feels like some thing's brewing, but there haven't been any rumors the gangs are gearing up for a turf war."

"They really have those?" My astonishment earned a smile.

"Yeah. Guess that sort of thing's not commonplace in your part of town."

"Nope, no turf wars in Redwood. I get my share of violence during cases with vampires involved."

Logan chuckled, a rich murmur of sound. "Since you're still walking around human, I'm guessing no vamp's gotten the upper hand."

"Not for long."

He cast a quick, sideways glance. "But some do have psychic abilities."

"Yeah, but none of them have more than one. I do, not that I'm bragging." My reply received another chuckle. "Most of the time, it's a pain in the ass to have them."

"How's that?" We turned the corner, and he nodded towards the alley. "This is where their turf begins."

"Okay." I followed him to it, and we paused. "Well, for one thing, they take a lot of energy to use. For another, some of them aren't exactly cooperative. It's clear, except for small animals."

He grinned. "I know. Have a good sense of smell."

"Oh, right. Sorry." I could feel my face beginning to heat up.

"Caution's a good thing." Logan shrugged, the blue work shirt he wore over a white tee tightening at the shoulders with the movement. He didn't follow up with a remark about my body heat rising. Maybe tigers had better manners than wolves. Though it could be an age thing, since he was older than Nick.

The first alley proved to be a bust, and so were the second and third ones. We chatted, and I learned that he worked at an auto repair place. Halfway down the fourth, we hit pay dirt. "This is it."

"It's a delivery door for a smoke shop. The owner called it quits after the last robbery." He was watching me check the padlock. "Want me to break that for you?"

The lock clicked, and I held it up with a grin. "Psychic lock picking."

"Handy." He continued watching while I pulled the door open.

Hesitating, I smiled. "Thanks for your help."

Logan smiled back. "If you're going for a polite brush-off, forget it. I'm curious now."

"I'm kind of breaking and entering here."

His smile broadened. "You're just entering if the lock still works."

"It does, but I don't want you to get into any trouble."

"There's no alarm, so no cops. They stick to the outer edges around here, unless an alarm goes off. No trouble." With a shrug, he edged past to walk into the building.

"Okay, fine." I followed him inside. It was a storeroom, completely empty of anything but a healthy layer of dust. "Damn."

"I take it dirt isn't what you were hoping for." The shifter joined me in the middle of the room.

"No, it's a book." I huffed, turning in a circle to look around again. "Man, see what I mean about psychic abilities being a—"

The floor cracked underneath our feet, and we looked at each other with widened eyes. Before I could grab his arm, there was a roar as it gave way. I just managed to break my fall with a cushion of thicker air, but rolled down the pile of debris and hit what felt like concrete. Logan quietly called my name from somewhere above. "Discord? Are you all right?"

Sitting up, I waved at the glimmering dust swirling around my face and coughed before answering. "Yeah, I think so. Wasn't expecting that."

Sliding noises followed his low chuckle, and he appeared, crouching at my side. "It smells like vampires down here."

"Great." Did we land in the Barrows? The dust was settling enough to show the source of the weak light. Safety lights, recessed in rough stone walls.

"They're not my favorite people either. Are you sure you're all right?" Logan partially rose, settling on one knee.

"Nothing's broken, but I bet I have some terrific bruises on the way. Are you okay?" Having accepted his help, I hated the feeling of responsibility that crashed down on me for putting him in a dangerous situation.

Logan grinned, his teeth a faint gleam. "I landed on my feet."

"Cat thing, huh? Do you have nine lives too?" Taking the hand he stuck out in offer, I climbed to my feet while he smoothly rose to his.

"Some would say so." A faint purr seemed to underline his voice. Releasing my hand, he glanced up. "The way we came in is out of reach."

It was rather high overhead. "And the noise might bring unwanted guests." Turning to survey the tunnel ahead, I sighed. "Well, guess..."

A flare of light in my mind, tracking ability wide-awake and eagerly pointing the way. I took two steps before halting. "Um, look, this is the way I need to go. I'll teleport us up so that you can go home or whatever, and come back down."

Logan had followed me. Quietly sniffing the air, he shook his head. "I offered my help. I'll go with you."

"I really, seriously, appreciate it, but I'm getting paid to do this."

"That's fine. I'm curious." He shot a sideways grin at me. "It's the cat in me."

A giggle escaped before I could suppress it. "Well, okay."

We began walking, the dim light enough to keep me from smacking into any walls at turns. The air was damp and chilly, not helping the rising nervousness I was feeling.

Logan's presence did. The shifter moved silently, perfectly calm and at home in the semi-darkness. I was grateful for his continued companionship, because it was spooky as hell down here.

We weren't moving fast, but that was fine. Sneaky was the goal. The corridor was leading steadily downward, which I took to mean that we were near the Barrows, if not actually in them.

Everything was going great, until another corner appeared. Taking it brought me face-to-face with a vampire, and *You!* smacked my brain with the force of a speeding train.

Back peddling, I bumped into Logan. He snarled as the vamp blurred into motion, stepping forward. The vampire casually slung him aside. A white hand sped toward my face, and sent me flying.

I heard a loud crack, saw Logan leaping onto the vampire's back and then nothing.

Darkness and a soft vibration on one side of my body were the first things I became aware of upon regaining consciousness. Next were a pair of arms around me, and the discovery that I was in someone's lap. "Discord?"

I groaned in response, suddenly aware that my head was killing me. The events that had led to the pain surfaced. "I feel horrible."

Logan chuckled. "You remember saying you'd scream and faint?"

"Yeah."

"You forgot to scream."

I could smell the thick, coppery tang of blood all around, drawing in a breath to giggle. "Sorry. Am I bleeding?"

"No, that's me. He and two others kicked my ass," the shifter admitted, sounding rueful.

Remorse took over. "I am so sorry. How badly are you hurt?"

"I volunteered, remember? Besides, I've already healed." After a pause, he said, "He seemed to know you."

"He did?" The vampire hadn't looked familiar to me, being one of those broody looking Heathcliff types teenaged girls freaked out over. I vaguely recalled lace streaming from the wrist of the hand that had slapped the hell out of me. My jaw hurt.

"He knew your name."

"Did you happen to catch his?"

"Yeah. Lord Derrick." Logan re-adjusted his hold slightly. We were silent for a few minutes. "I guess I should've brought my cell phone."

"Oh. Mine's in my right jacket pocket. Let's try for the cavalry." A head full of jagged glass wasn't the easiest thing to concentrate through, so my attempt at fishing the phone out failed.

Logan took over the task. "No signal."

"Of course not. That would be too easy, right?" I sighed. "Okay, let me see if I can't fix my head enough to teleport us out of here."

"Sure." The soft vibration began again, and I realized the shifter was quietly purring. It was a soothing sound.

Speeding up the healing process is an ability I like, since I'm not a big fan of pain. It requires a lot of energy though, so my plan was to dull the pain to something bearable for now. I could finish it later, once we were safely away. Cradled against Logan's chest, my eyes closed and his soft, raspy purr rolling over me in a comforting blanket of sound, I monitored my energy level with care once the healing began.

An hour slowly passed. I was aware of Logan sniffing my hair from time to time, in between my gloomy thoughts.

Man, Nick was going to be pissed I'd taken off on my own again. I felt bad about that, but probably not as bad as I should've felt.

Eventually, the blinding agony ricocheting around my skull decreased to a dull ache. Sighing in relief, I lifted my head from his shoulder. "Okay, I'm going to try teleporting us now."

"Do we need to stand up?" Logan asked, shifting under me a bit.

"Let's not." I gathered a handful of his shirt. It was soft from repeated washing. "Here goes nothing."

Fresh air whispered of green things surviving despite the concrete city hemming them in. Yells over a thumping bass beat sounded in the distance. "Oh, my head." I lowered it back to Logan's shoulder with a groan. "Please tell me we're by my car."

"If your car is an '81 root beer brown metallic 280ZX in cherry condition, then we're by your car," he replied. "It's a nice car."

"Thanks. The keys are in my left jacket pocket. I need to call a friend to come get me." I was in no shape to drive, unwilling even to open my eyes.

"Okay." He slid an arm under my legs and began to rise.

"Ow, I..." was as far as I got before passing out.

Thirteen

I woke in Kate's guest bedroom, with Percy standing watch, perched on the headboard above me. Not the first time I'd woken there. The lacy bedspread was softer than it looked, and she'd once sworn on her favorite shoes that the heavy wooden bed frame with its tall spindle posts wasn't a relic from a convent. I still had my doubts. The walls were wine red, and a potted pineapple sage held court in the deep windowsill.

A low rumble of conversation leaked through the crack of the slightly open door, so I strained to listen.

"Calm down." It was Damian's voice, uncharacteristically sharp in tone. "He can't explain if you keep interrupting him, Nick."

"She'll be fine," David's soothing voice followed up. I wondered who he was trying to calm down, Damian or Nick? "In fact, by morning you'll never know that she was injured."

Nick's voice was a snarl. "I want to know how the hell her skull was cracked and what the..."

"This male posturing is becoming tedious." Kate cut off Nick's tirade better than a knife would. It sounded like I needed to get up and out there before a fight broke out.

Percy twisted his head to look at me upside down as I sat up. My head still ached, but the smell of David's favorite salve and greasy fingertips assured me one of them had magically tended to my injury. Holding my arm out, I told the parrot, "Come on, bird brain."

"Be nice. Percy loves Cordi," he loudly scolded, ruining any chance of making a surprise appearance. I scowled at him while he stepped onto my forearm. "Cordi, Cordi, Cor..."

Wincing, I pinched his beak shut. "Shh. Cordi's head still hurts."

Percy's answer was a muffled croon. I let go of his beak and shuffled to the door, then out into the short hallway, catching a glimpse of Kate's closed bedroom door. All eyes were pointed my direction, waiting for my emergence.

Logan sat in the plum-colored easy chair, dusty and with dried blood down one side of his face and neck. More spots dotted his shirt, jeans, and tee.

"You guys couldn't let him clean up a little?"

"We were a bit more concerned with your skull," Kate snapped. I shooed Percy off my arm and noticed that she was pouring coffee.

The woman had a complete coffee service in fragile china, plain white with silver edging. She even had snowy linen napkins at hand.

A check of the Black Forest chalet cuckoo clock showed the time at almost 2 AM. Talk about prepared for anything.

"It feels much better. Thanks, guys." I took in Nick's angry glare, as he stood at one side of Logan's seat. Damian stood at the other, and it appeared to me that he was ready to interpose himself between the two shifters.

Logan seemed perfectly at ease, offering a slight smile when I met his eyes. "I really appreciate all of your help. Are you all right?"

"Good to go." He shrugged. "You sure you're okay?"

"Much better."

"What the hell happened? What were you thinking, going out there alone?" Nick took three quick strides, coming to a halt directly in front of me and blocking my view of everyone else.

"Shh. Cordi's head still hurts," Percy announced from his perch on the back of the sofa. Nick threw a flat, disgusted look over his shoulder, but lowered his voice.

"What happened? Where'd you meet him?"

"Okay, he has a name. It's Logan Sayer." I poked a finger at his chest. "A couple of punks tried to jump me."

"Which she didn't need any help with," Logan remarked. "She had that under control, but I didn't know that at first."

"Right. He offered to help me find what I was looking for, and he did. Only the floor collapsed, dumping us into the Barrows, or somewhere close." I paused for air. "Can I sit down?"

"Oh, yeah. Sorry." Nick took my arm, the anger fading to just concern as he led me to the chaise. Once I was in place, he sat on the edge, shooting Logan a dark look while draping first a chenille throw, then his arm over my legs.

The other shifter took up the story. "We couldn't get out the same way, and Discord said she needed to go into the tunnel, so I went with her."

"We ended up running into a vampire. Derrick the vampire. He slapped me into a wall, and Logan jumped him, but that's where I went out."

"I got my ass kicked," Logan said, shrugging. "He had a couple of his guys drag us to a cell and lock us in."

"Which is where I came to." I rubbed my forehead with careful fingers before accepting the cup of coffee Kate finally parted with. Ah, coffee. A mild analgesic, plus the warmth and caffeine helped ward off the testosterone poisoning the air.

"She teleported us out, but I guess with her being injured, that was too much. She told me where her keys were and that she needed to call one of you before passing out." He smiled at me. "It was easy to figure out who to call."

David's number was listed under 'Witch ER'.

"See?" Damian frowned at Nick, who grimaced.

"Sorry." It wasn't heartfelt, but Logan accepted it with a grave nod.

"No problem."

Damian volunteered to give Logan a lift home. David muttered another spell over me while smearing more of his magical salve onto the lump at the back of my skull.

Kate offered cupcakes, but everyone declined, and then Nick announced that he was taking me home. It was a silent drive, the shifter's emotions tamped down tight. I gave up worrying about it and dozed off before we even left her street.

"Cordi, we're here." His voice roused me. "Come on, I want to get you in bed."

"Are you still mad?" I let him help me out of the truck and hitched up Kate's throw so it wouldn't trail on the ground.

"Yes."

"If you're going to yell, you can just go home. I don't feel like dealing with it tonight, bub."

"I'm not going to yell," Nick promised. "We can talk about it in the morning."

"Maybe I don't want to talk about it," I grumbled, leaning on his arm as we began walking. He didn't respond, not until we were in my apartment with the door locked behind us.

"First, I was hired to keep you in one piece. I can't do my job if you keep taking off without me. Second, I really like you, Cordi. I don't want you to be hurt." Nick wrapped his arms around me, gazing into my eyes. "I want you to be safe."

"I'm a private investigator who deals with the supernatural. Safe isn't a given in this line of work."

He sighed. "I know, and it's driving me crazy. You drive me crazy too."

"My scent drives you crazy. That's what you said the other night." I wanted to lie down. "My head hurts."

Nick released me, following closely as I headed for my bedroom. I collapsed on the bed, unwilling to bend to remove my boots or deal with getting undressed. Working quietly, he pulled them off and helped me out of my jacket. "Do you want a night gown or something?"

"I don't have one." I slept nude, or sometimes in just my panties. During the winter, I usually added a tee.

"Okay." He unbuttoned my jeans.

"What are you doing?"

"Helping you get comfortable so that you can sleep." Peeling my jeans off, he moved to my shirt. "Sit up, Cordi. Do you want anything to drink or eat?"

"No, just sleep."

"Okay." Once I was free of everything but panties, he tucked me under the covers and moved to the other side of the bed. Stealthy rustling sounded.

"What are you doing now?"

"Undressing. I'm staying here, in case you need something. David said I have to wake you up a few times too." A second later, his warm body was next to mine under the covers. Cuddling close, Nick softly sighed. "Go to sleep, Cordi. You'll feel better in the morning."

I did after a long while. For some reason, I kept expecting him to start purring.

Fourteen

The next morning, he dropped me at the office and went home to change clothes. I discovered Thorandryll waiting in the reception area, watching Kate growl into the phone while taking a message. "Hi. I don't really have any progress to report at this time."

"I've purchased a cell phone." The elf fished an expensive model out of a jacket pocket. He was wearing a charcoal gray suit today, teamed with a faintly silver shirt made of what I suspected was spinner silk. Spinners were a rare species of arachnid carefully shepherded by elves. "I came to leave the number with you."

He could have called. It would've been easier. "Cool." At my gesture, he followed me into my office. "I did get a lead last night, but no results to show for it. Cell phones work in faerie mounds?"

"Yes." Crossing to my desk, he selected a pen and wrote the number down on a notepad. Deciding something needed saying about the episode in his library, I shut the door.

"My empathic ability must have gone a little haywire the other day."

Turning, his eyes captured mine. "Is that what is known as the 'logical explanation'?"

Caution seemed like a good idea, especially when I realized looking away was impossible. "How would you explain it?"

"You're a beautiful young woman, Miss Jones. We enjoy beauty." A smile played over his lips.

"So what, you go around groping strangers a lot?"

"Of course not, and I'd hardly describe what passed between us as 'groping'." Smile gone, he took a step toward me. "Did you not enjoy the experience? You were quick to accept the part Alleryn designated for you."

The question caused a few seconds of replay. Remembering his taste, which was warm sunlight and spring breezes, heat uncurled down low. "That's beside the point."

"Is it?" How the hell had he gotten so close? There was barely a foot of space between us, and a definite dampening sensation happening in my jeans. Damn it, was he using glamour on me?

"Yeah, it is. You wanted discretion, and that seemed the best way to be discreet." Contrary to my intentions, the response lacked even a tiny bit of the *I wasn't impressed* I had tried to infuse it with.

Bringing up the matter had been a mistake. Somehow, I managed to find the doorknob. "I'll call you if I have anything to report."

"Miss Jones..." I sidestepped as he moved even closer, yanking the door open, and was surprised to discover Logan standing outside. Thorandryll frowned and moved slightly back.

"Hey. What are you doing here?"

"I wanted to see you, after last night." Ignoring the elf, he smiled and held up my car keys. "And I kind of forgot to leave these."

Bad me, I let that 'last night' hang there and develop implications while I returned his smile with interest. The elf deserved it. But Logan...I was pleased to see him, and he deserved truth more than Thorandryll needed his arrogance aerated. I accepted the keys. "Lump's gone, and my skull's in one piece again."

"You were injured?" Thorandryll asked, a hand rising as though he intended to touch me.

Logan answered. "She was slammed into a wall by an unhappy vampire."

"Vampires are involved?" The elf's brows drew together. "You failed to mention that."

"Because I'm not certain they're involved in your case. Yet." My explanation seemed to satisfy him.

Thorandryll dropped his hand and nodded. "Very well. I look forward to our next meeting, Miss Jones."

"I hope I'll have better progress to report then." My smile froze in place upon meeting his gaze, and I sort of lost track of time until Logan shifted his weight while clearing his throat and the elf blinked.

"Until then." With a faint smile, Thorandryll left my office. Logan, having silently moved out of the way, turned to gaze after him.

"Have a seat. Would you like some coffee?"

"Sure." He chose a chair while I went to the sideboard to start some.

"It'll take a few minutes." Keeping my hands busy with setting out cups, and silently blessing the shifter's arrival, I started when he spoke.

"Is he the one whose book you're looking for? Or should I not ask?"

"Yeah, Mr. Arrogant's my client." Turning around, I noticed that close proximity to the elf did not do a damn thing by way of dulling Logan's good looks. He wore jeans, mechanic's boots, and a warm, yellow-gold tee under a jean jacket. Casual and oh-so-sexy on him. The tee's color brought out the gold flecks dancing in his pine green eyes. We traded smiles.

His faded first. "You might want to be careful around him, Discord. Elves have a history of kidnapping humans."

"They do? Why would they do that?"

He glanced at the coffee maker, fingertips tapping the arms of the chair. "They weren't above rape."

My jaw dropped. "No way."

"Yes way. They kept the women until they were completely elf-struck." Scowling, he said, "They tell people how cruel the rest of us are, but elves are the masters of cruelty."

Reminded that I wasn't dealing with humans daily, I turned around to check the coffee and managed a careless shrug. "He'd better mind his manners around me, or I'll teleport him inside a wall and leave him there."

Logan's laugh rolled out, a deep, joyous sound that made my lips quirk into a smile. "You can do that?"

"Yeah, I can do that." The coffee was ready. I poured two cups. "Cream, sugar, or both?"

"Black is fine," he said. "If you decide to do that, can I watch?"

It was my turn to laugh, while handing him a cup. "Sure thing."

We chatted for a while, and exchanged numbers after I offered to buy him lunch sometime, in return for his help. It's unusual for me to be comfortable with someone I've just met, but something drew me to him. It wasn't physical attraction, or not just that, but something else.

It almost felt as though we'd been best friends for years.

Cup empty, he rose from his seat. "You probably have work to do, and I shouldn't keep you from it. Thanks for the coffee."

Jumping up to walk him to the door, I touched his arm as we paused before it. "You're welcome. I'll call you. I mean, for lunch."

"Looking forward to it. Bye, Discord."

"Bye." I wanted to say something else, but didn't know what, so opened the door and smiled. The corners of his eyes crinkled a bit when he returned it.

Logan wasn't gone fifteen seconds before Nick came into my office. "What did he want?"

"Well, good morning to you, too. He came to see how I was. Is that all right with you?" Feeling crowded, I moved behind my desk and sat down. "I would've been in big trouble without his help last night, and he got his ass kicked because of it."

"You should've called me." Nick planted both hands on the desk, leaning across. His brows lowered, teeth showing even when he paused for air. "I'm supposed to back you up. To protect you."

That close, his anger and hurt were all too apparent, flooding me with guilt. "I'm sorry. When my tracking sense kicks in, I have to act on it. I can't wait, or it might fade."

My explanation did nothing to ease his upset, but Nick relaxed slightly. "I think he likes you."

"Whoa." Holding up a hand, I shook my head. "Whether he does or not, it's none of your business."

Straightening, he blinked. "But..."

"This is a rule: no talking about personal business at work, okay?"

His lips tightened into a thin line, jaw clenching. He ground out "Fine. Can we talk about it after work?"

"Not tonight." Just call me chicken. "I need some alone time. It's been a hard week. Fun too." I threw that last bit in because his eyes narrowed.

Taking a deep breath, he gave a jerky nod. "Okay."

"Are you up for driving me around the Palisades? I want to see if that triggers anything."

He agreed, so we went to let the boss know. Mr. Whitehaven, fingers steepled, lectured me about not informing anyone before haring off the night before, ending with, "Especially to such a troublesome area."

Nick smirked, arms crossed. I smacked his leg. "Stop that. You had to go home, remember?"

"I would've come back if you'd called me."

"It was getting late, and I told you that I can't wait when it comes to that kind of thing."

Whitehaven interrupted before our bickering increased. "Which case do you think the event was related to?"

"I don't know. Vampires would seem to indicate Zoe, but then again, Derrick may be one of the highly territorial types who didn't appreciate my attempt to spy." Feeling a little put upon, I pointed out, "I did have some backup."

"Yeah, a total stranger." Nick's scowl could've blistered paint.

"Yeah, well, you were a total stranger five days ago, bub." It wasn't until the words left my mouth that it occurred to me that wasn't the best thing I could have said, especially since he was worried that Logan was attracted to me. Nick flinched, and opened his mouth, but I beat him to the punch. "So not every stranger is a bad guy, okay?"

He didn't buy it, but said, "Sure."

"Anyway, we're heading out to the Palisades to drive around and see if anything else pops up." Standing up, I headed for the door. "Come on, Nick."

To my relief, Mr. Whitehaven didn't call us back and make me promise not to run around on my own again.

We tiptoed past Kate's door and headed for Nick's truck. The drive across town was silent, but Nick spoke up as soon as we crossed Hwy 83, which was one of the Palisades' borderlines. "This area sucks."

"Not everyone can afford better." I stared out the window. It looked worse by day, with the sunlight baring the dinginess of the buildings, and the crowds of people. Teenagers hung out in groups, the boys wearing jeans that hung low on their asses, while the girls were dressed like aspiring skanks. Harried young mothers, some not out of their teens themselves, shepherded anywhere from two to four kids.

Graffiti was everywhere, as were boarded-up shops. Homeless people shuffled along, pushing crazy-wheeled shopping carts, or sat in squalid splendor against walls, just staring into space. "God, this is depressing."

"And dangerous. Half of them will gut you for looking at them wrong." When I looked at him, a sneer twisted his lips.

"Where do you live?"

"With my pack."

Rolling my eyes, I returned to scanning the sidewalks. "I mean, what part of the city do you live in?"

"We don't live in the city, but a few miles outside, to the north."

Staying quiet didn't elicit any further information. It was irritating. "Is it a secret or something?"

"Not exactly, but our Alpha doesn't like uninvited guests. We're not supposed to make it easy for anyone we meet to just drop in."

"Oh." My irritation began to fade.

Nick braked for a light and looked at me. "Humans aren't really welcome to visit, because they get bent out of shape over us being ourselves. Our land is the only place we have where we can do that, Cordi."

Pleased by his opening up a bit, I went for a joke. "What, do you guys lie around all day licking yourselves or something?"

He laughed. "You have the weirdest mind, Cordi. Some of the pack doesn't bother wearing clothing most of the time. Others like to stay in wolf shape a lot."

The light changed, and he faced forward again. "I spent most of my childhood in wolf shape, before the Melding. Some haven't adjusted to the changes. Mostly the older members."

"I can understand how that would be hard." Recognizing the street we were on, I pointed ahead. "Take a left there. That's the start of the section we were in last night."

"Right." We covered the whole section tagged in blue and white without any results. Nick found a place to pick up some lunch, which we ate in his truck.

After driving around for another few hours, he called it a day. "We don't need to hang around here after dark, unless it's necessary."

"Okay." I was ready to go home. "You can drop me off at Kate's, so I can get my car. "

"Sure. Just remember to call me if anything pops up tonight."

"I will." That eased the last bit of tension from him, to my relief. When we stopped for a red light, I unbelted and scooted to the middle of the seat to sit beside him. After I'd hooked the lap belt, Nick put his arm around me and smiled.

He brought up his home just before turning down the witch's street. "Since you're my girlfriend, I could probably get permission for you to visit. If you wanted to." His tone was casual, but he was watching me from the corner of his eye.

My mind went blank for a few seconds. Girlfriend? I was his girlfriend? "Well, I wouldn't want to like, harsh anyone's mellow or anything."

With a shake of his head, he laughed. "What the hell does that mean?"

"That I wouldn't want to make anyone uncomfortable, invading their space." Or be uncomfortable, if they didn't bother to dress when company came over. "Besides, I've never even been to a nude beach. My eyes would pop out of their sockets."

Pulling over, he stopped the truck behind my car while chuckling. "Well, maybe later on."

"Yeah, maybe later. I'll see you in the morning." I kissed him, and then scooted down the seat to climb out of the truck. "Bye."

"Bye." He waited until I was in my car and had started the engine before leaving.

Girlfriend. He'd said it, but I didn't feel that warm thrill I'd gotten other times I'd heard the word. I didn't feel like a girlfriend.

Was it really because he was a shifter?

Fifteen

I made one stop, to pick up some take-out, which I ate in front of the TV. That's also where I dozed off. An itching sensation woke me a few hours later.

Glancing at the clock told me it was 11:37 pm. Scratching at my hair, a huge yawn escaped while I got up and shuffled toward the hall. My immediate goals were the toilet, a shower, and bed.

My abilities had a different idea. Halfway to the bedroom, a vision took over. I stood on a dark street, under a buzzing, damaged light post. There was an anemic-looking tree a few feet away, its pitiful circle of dirt marked out by cracked, red bricks. Trash scattered and rustled, pushed about by a breeze.

"Aw, man." My complaint broke the quiet of my apartment, and the vision faded away. "Damn it."

It looked like I was heading back to the Palisades. Turning around, I went for my jacket to dig out my cell phone, only to curse again. I'd forgotten to put it on the charger.

For once, I wished that I'd gotten a land line, but the lack of one wasn't going to put a stop to anything. There was a charger in my car.

With a quick detour to the bathroom before grabbing purse and jacket, I left my apartment. Once in the car, and plugging the phone in, I called Nick. He didn't answer, so I left a message.

Whether or not he showed, I had to go.

Parking my car, I teleported to the dark street in my vision, and studied the blue and white graffiti. I'd returned to the area Logan had led me through the night before.

Another flare of brightness in my mind pushed me forward, excitement beginning to build. The silver thread was so thick this time that I thought that maybe one case would be finished tonight.

So it was a little disappointing when it ended at a small clutter of trash at the opposite end of the alley. The same alley where my previous vision had shown me the door. Going to one knee with a sigh, I gingerly shuffled through the pile until my fingers closed on something that caused tingles. Pulling it free, I rose and walked to a working streetlight to examine my find.

The paper was parchment, covered with spidery writing in rusty brown ink. Unable to read the language used, I unzipped my left jacket pocket and tucked it away for safekeeping. Securing it and turning to head back to my car, I froze as four vampires melted from the shadows to block my way. One moved a few steps closer. "Discord Jones. My master wishes to speak with you."

"Sorry, I'm a little busy right now. Have him call the office and make an appointment." I was frantically making a plan. Vampires move much faster than humans.

"He's an impatient man."

"Really? You'd think a master vampire would know that patience is a virtue."

He scowled. "You will come with us. There's the easy way, human, or..."

"The hard way?" I sent him flying into a wall with a shove of TK. Another vampire sped toward me in a blur of movement and I screamed as he tackled me.

We rolled for several feet, but I managed to break free and shoved, slamming him into the other two. While scrambling to my feet, the first blurred toward me, hands outstretched and fangs bared.

Something big and black with white streaks dropped onto the vampire, taking it to the ground. Logan's mental voice was deep and velvety sounding: *Discord*.

I scrambled backwards, spotting another of the vampires rushing toward us. Flinging a hand out, I called fire from the air around him and he burst into flames. A shove sent him flying backwards and directly into one of the others.

The tiger, bigger than a pony, was in front of me then, baring gore-stained fangs in an echoing roar. His eyes were pale green. Grabbing handfuls of thick fur, I locked both arms around his neck and used my TK to loft us into the air and onto the roof above. The second his paws touched down, Logan said *This way*.

Sounds of bodies landing behind us sent me racing after him, and he led me over the rooftops without looking back. All too soon, we reached the end of the block, but Logan turned and rose, wrapping thick forelegs and heavy paws around me before throwing us off the roof's edge.

I squeaked, feeling his muscles writhing as he shifted, certain I was in for another fun time of healing broken legs. Logan landed on his feet, taking the force of our landing, one arm having secured my legs at some point.

Arms around his neck, I looked up because he did. The two vampires left peered down at us, but faded from sight as a deep, low growl erupted from his throat.

"You do tend to attract trouble, Discord." Logan was fully human and grinning when I turned my head to look at him. "Must be that name."

"My middle name's Angel," I said, breathy as a rescued damsel, but hey, I had the excuse of that stunning drop.

He laughed. "Maybe you should start using it."

Logan released my legs, setting me neatly on my feet without letting completely go. A slight glance downward pointed out that he was nude. Blushing, I half-turned away before curiosity took complete control and my gaze wandered any lower. Letting his arm drop from my back, he moved a few steps away. "Give me a minute to dress."

"Sure." I studied graffiti and brick, listening to his movements and fighting the urge to peek.

"I'm decent. Where's your car?"

"Uh, back that way, I think. The strip mall parking lot on Ironton Ave?" He nodded and set off, so I hurriedly fell into step with him.

"Still searching for that book?" he asked.

"I found a piece of it." I patted my jacket pocket, checking to make certain it was zipped closed. "I can't read the writing on it, so I'll have my friends take a look tomorrow."

"You're a very determined PI." Logan glanced at me. "Vampires scare you."

"Well, yeah. I do prefer breathing to not," I admitted.

"Yet you came out here without Nick. Again." He sounded vaguely disapproving.

"I did call him." Eyes falling to the sidewalk, I debated before adding, "My boss hired him to babysit me."

"He wasn't acting like a bodyguard. More like an upset boyfriend," Logan quietly observed, hands diving into his jacket pockets.

"He's not my boyfriend. He's...I don't know what he is."

"Okay," he agreed in a mild-sounding voice. The last few blocks passed in complete silence. "I think that's your oh, damn."

"What?" I looked up and stopped. It was totaled. Pounded into a pile of scrap. "They trashed my car? Are you freaking kidding me?"

Logan began circling what was left of my baby. "They really don't like you."

"I'm going to kill them." My shout rang off bricks and concrete, echoing hollowly into the night. "It's on, you bastards!"

Logan touched my arm. "I'll take you home, Discord. And I'll take your car to our garage."

"They trashed my car." I couldn't believe it.

"I'm sorry." He put an arm around me. "You're shaking."

"I'm so unbelievably pissed!" The car hadn't been just my pride and joy, but the first symbol of my independence. Waking up three years older and chock full of psychic talents demanding to be used hadn't been easy to deal with. It had taken a massive amount of hard work to be able to move around in public without turning into a whimpering mess or inadvertently setting something on fire. Or doing something else equally disastrous. "My poor baby."

He guided me back into the Palisades, and down a street whose name I didn't bother catching. By then, my anger had faded and I was seriously mourning my car. We ended up in front of a garage bay door. It rolled up in response to his knock, another dark-haired man just inside.

"Need my truck," Logan said. "I'll be back in a little while."

The other just nodded, giving me the briefest of once-overs. Logan's truck was an older model, dark blue single cab. He handed me in and asked for my address after taking his place behind the wheel.

My sniffles as I fought tears were the only sound during the drive. Logan broke the silence as we arrived. "Which entrance?"

"The second one." Pulled out of my unhappy trance, I pointed out my building and then my parking space. "You can park there."

"This looks like a nice area," he remarked, pulling into the space.

"It's quiet. You wanna come in for a beer?" To my surprise, I really hoped that his answer would be yes. He was so calm. I needed calm.

"Sure." Cutting off the engine, he met me at the front of the truck and followed me to my apartment door. Digging my keys out of my pocket, I fumbled and dropped them. We both squatted down to retrieve them, putting us face to face.

Meeting his eyes, after almost seeing him completely nude earlier, I realized he was damn hot and regretted not looking my fill. Logan offered my keys, and a tingling flashed from my fingertips to my elbow as our fingers brushed during the exchange.

It was stronger, when he held out a hand and pulled me to my feet as he rose. Busying myself unlocking the door, I remembered feeling the same kind of sensation when Thorandryll had kissed my hand.

But not from Nick, and he'd done a lot more than hold my hand or kiss it. I wondered what it meant. "Come on in."

Logan followed me to the kitchen, and took a seat after accepting the beer I offered. I cast about for something to say while joining him. "So, how old are you?"

"Twenty-nine. You?" Spotting the trash can, he tossed the beer cap toward it, and it dropped right in.

"Nice shot. Twenty-two."

Logan settled back, focusing on my face. "What was being a psychic like before the Melding?"

"I don't know. I wasn't psychic before then." I grinned when he raised an eyebrow while taking a drink. "Dropped like a rock when the Melding began, and was in a coma for three years."

"A coma? So you came out of it with your abilities?"

"Yeah. From what I've heard, everyone who's psychic or a witch now had the same thing happen. Most were only down for a few days to a couple of months. I hold the coma record, as far as I know."

He frowned. "I wonder why?"

"Don't know. Hey, are you hungry? I am. I can make some sandwiches or something."

"I don't want to put you out."

"You're not." I got up and moved to the fridge. Within a few minutes, and with his stated preferences, I had the makings spread out on the countertop. "So, what kind of tiger are you, aside from really big?"

"Siberian."

"I don't know jack about tigers, other than the ones at the zoo are orange, black, and white. Are all Siberians black?" I spread mustard over bread slices.

Logan chuckled. "No, it's a rare color, like white. Rarer than white."

"Cool." Picking up a tomato, I began slicing it. "That guy at your garage, is he a tiger too?"

"No, he's a lion."

Since he seemed so willing to answer, I wasn't going to waste the chance to learn, and there certainly wasn't a *Shifters for Dummies* out. "How many different kinds of feline shifters are there?"

"Six that I know of. Tigers, lions, cougars, jaguars, leopards, and cheetahs."

Having finished my sandwich building, I put everything away before carrying our plates to the table. "Here you go."

"Thanks."

I sat down. "Do you know all the different species of shifters?"

"Probably not. I know some are extinct, and there could be others that don't have enough of a population to be much known."

We ate without talking much, and then kicked back with the remainder of our beers. After a good swallow, I asked, "So what were you out doing tonight?"

"Just walking. It's quieter at night." Logan grimaced. "The noise has been one of the hardest things to get used to."

I had to laugh. "It was a lot noisier to me when I woke up too."

"Telepathy?" At my nod, he grinned. "I wondered if that was one of them. Hoped you'd hear me, instead of slamming me against a wall."

"Yes, I heard you. And man, you should've seen the look on that vamp's face." I started laughing. "He totally wasn't expecting squashing by tiger."

Logan's grin broadened. "Most people aren't." He polished off his beer and rose. "I should head home."

"Okay." We walked to the door, and he stepped outside, half-turning while digging his keys out of a pocket.

There was a grin on his face again. "Just remembered something."

"What?"

"This time, you forgot to faint."

Another laugh bubbled out. "I'll get it right someday. Promise."

"I'll hold you to it. Thanks for the meal, Discord."

"You're welcome. Thanks for the backup."

"No problem." With a wave, he walked away. I shut and locked the door then remembered my car.

"Damn it!"

Sixteen

Since I was without wheels, teleportation was my only option for getting around, unless I called Nick for a ride. His fit the previous day, followed by his failure to return my call, and my still glowing hot anger over my car said that would be a disaster in the making.

Teleportation it was.

David startled when I appeared, hand flattening over his heart, the glasses he'd added to his ensemble almost popping off his nose. "Good lord, Cordi."

"Sorry. Do you have a few minutes?" Trixie butted her head against my shin, demanding I rub behind her ears. David's familiar, Copernicus, demanded love too. His feathers slipped coolly under my fingers. "I've found something I need your help with."

Jo came out from the back, slipping rings onto her fingers. "Hey, Cordi."

"Hi."

David was frowning past me, looking through the plate glass at the parking lot. "Why aren't you driving?"

"Because some vamps trashed my car last night." Scowling, I pulled the scrap out of my pocket. Behind me, the bell over the shop door jingled. It was Damian and Illy, the former carrying a cardboard tray of Styrofoam cups.

"Good morning. Where's your car, Cordi?"

A wide-eyed Jo answered before I could. "Vampires destroyed it."

The warlock halted, jaw dropping. Even the familiars were quiet and staring at me. Clearing his throat, Damian asked, "Case-related?"

"I don't know yet. Possibly. The mouthpiece said his Master wanted to speak to me before I introduced him to a brick wall."

"How many vamps have you pissed off lately?"

His calm tone cooled me down. "I can't breathe without pissing off a vampire, but I can only think of one in the recent category. When I find the two who trashed my car, I'm going to do more than piss them off."

"La-la-la," Damian half-sang. "I didn't hear that."

"I'm pretty sure self-defense will be a valid excuse." Legally, vamps were citizens, so taking one out was murder. Even so, the law tended to look the other way much of the time. Murder reminded me of Dead Guy. "Any clues about the vamp the fake elf staked?"

Shaking his head, the warlock crossed to the counter and set the tray down. Four cups, so Illy had a dog-acinno. I remembered the scrap in my hand, and raised it so that they could all see it. "I found this. Think it might be part of Thorandryll's missing journal. Can you tell me what it says?"

I set it on the counter in front of them, and they bent their heads forward to have a look. Then Jo touched it with the tip of her finger. Flames poured over her and David.

Horrified, I began pulling the oxygen away from their immediate area to kill the flames as Damian chanted a spell. There no way to tell which of us caused it, but the flames suddenly winked out a breath before a second spell resulted in a downpour of water. Sodden, the two and their familiars glared at us.

"Oops?" I offered, hoping to break the tension of the moment.

David pushed wet strands of hair off his forehead. "Yes, 'oops' is just the word."

"Some of us need to work on our illusion recognition," Jo said in a flat tone, staring at Damian. Hearing his name, Illy began wagging his tail and gave her a tongue-lolling grin.

"She wasn't speaking to you," Damian muttered, nudging the husky with his knee. Unperturbed, Illy kept grinning and wagging.

"I think we'll change before continuing." David blinked, his ferocious scowl disappearing. Jo leveled a final withering glare before she and David went upstairs, their familiars close behind.

"Yes, well, I guess we'd better clean this mess up before the water spreads," Damian suggested, eyes bright with repressed laughter.

We took care of the water with a combination of towels and my *encouragement* for the wet to dry out. Everything was shipshape by the time the other two came back down.

The scrap had somehow escaped the soaking.

I wandered around the shop while they conferred over the parchment. Herbs sat waiting in glass jars. Candles in every color brightened one aisle, while the crystals lay in state on display tables that led from the entrance to the counter. I always found some new curiosity to wonder over. Sometimes, I even asked what my discovery was.

Jo's soft "Dear god" pulled me back to the counter. "What? Is it some kind of kinky elf sex diary?"

David shook his head, fine blonde hair waving and rising in reaction. "No, this is from a grimoire. It's written in blood ink."

"Possibly one of those we're looking for," Jo added, studying the scrap with fingertips poised just above it.

"Not to argue here, but I'm pretty certain it's a scrap of the book the elf wants me to recover. Elves don't keep grimoires. Do they?"

"Not that I know of," she replied. "Their magic is innate. A part of them and what they are. They don't have to memorize spells or write them down. They just produce whatever effect they're aiming for, with simple words of power."

"Color me confused." I scowled at the scrap.

"They do keep written records of medicinal potions," David mentioned. "But a page from such a journal wouldn't be tainted like this is, and certainly wouldn't be written in blood ink."

"Great." I felt like beating a certain elf into a bloody pile of spare parts. "Looks like someone flat-out lied."

"Does look that way, yes," he agreed.

"Damn him." After fuming for a few minutes, I yanked out my cell phone and hunted for the right contact listing. Two rings before the elf's deep voice filled my ear.

"Thorandryll here."

"I think I prefer 'lying jerk' right this minute." He hung up on me. "You son of...ooh!"

I hit redial, and when he answered, blasted him with "Listen up, you pointy-eared jackass, I—"

"Will refrain from cursing at me or I won't speak with you," he cut in.

"You arrogant—"

"Did you find something?"

"A scrap from your missing book which turns out to be a grimoire. You have some explaining to do, bub." I snapped out the words with enough venom that Jo and David both looked up from the piece of parchment.

The latter winced. "Cordi? Would you please put the crystals down?"

"What?" I turned when he pointed behind me. A whole display of crystals hung in the air, shivering as though cold. "Oops."

"Temper, temper," Jo murmured while I groped for my TK ability, intending to lower them back onto their display table.

"What does it matter what the book is?" Thorandryll sounded impatient. "I'm paying you to find it."

"Hello, dark magic? Danger you should've warned me about!" The crystals climbed another three inches and David made a panicked sound behind me. "I'm working on it!"

Copernicus squawked, fluttering by to land and gaze at the crystals with his beady black eyes.

"Shut up," I told the raven, hissing in exasperation.

"Excuse me?" The elf's tone climbed to cold haughtiness.

"You too. Everybody just shut up for a minute!" Narrowing my eyes, I managed to take control of my errant TK. David sighed in relief when the crystals began a slow descent to the table.

"Thank you."

"I'm sorry." Raking a hand through my hair, I crammed all things psychic into a dark corner and slammed a mental blast door shut before saying anything else. "Look, Thorandryll, I want everything you know before I take another step on this case, or I'm done with it."

"I've told you..."

It was satisfying, in a totally petty way, to cut him off with "Fine. Your refund check will be waiting at the office. Minus my hours and expenses already occurred."

"You gave your word..."

I grinned at my listening friends. "I agreed to take your case based on the information you gave me. It wasn't truthful, so the deal's off." Before he could respond, I hit the button to end the call.

Damian took a sip of his coffee before asking, "You're not serious, are you?"

"Nope. You know I have to find it." A smile was still plastered across my face. "But it sure felt good to hit him over the head with that."

Jo laughed. "Are you starting a new list? 'Elves I've pissed off'?"

"You bet." My phone rang. It was the elf, and I enjoyed turning it off.

"Cordi, do you have time to take trip out to the crime scene with me? Perhaps you'll pick up something we can both use." Damian grimaced. "Anything."

"Sure."

"We'll work on deciphering this," David muttered, head once more bent over the scrap.

"Thanks. I'll buy lunch today," I offered, and everyone accepted.

Illusion was sent home after he finished slurping up his dog-acinno. Once in Damian's car, we tossed around ideas.

"Dead Guy stole the book, with magical assistance to help him sneak into Thorandryll's faerie mound." I paused, rethinking the last part, and snickered. "Is it just me, or did that sound dirty?"

He laughed. "It does now."

"Okay, so Dead Guy staked a vampire at the construction site. But why were they there?"

Slowing the car for a red light, he shrugged. "Maybe that's where the book was passed off? By the way, Dead Guy's name is Thomas Merricott. He had the plastic surgery roughly ten months ago."

"Huh. Do you think he was planning to steal the book that long ago?"

"Since we now know that it's a grimoire, I'm leaning toward 'yes'. Faerie mounds aren't easy to get into without an invitation." The light changed, and he eased the car forward.

"True. But if he was using that concealment spell, I don't get why he had the implants." Puzzling over that for a minute, I shrugged it off. "Grimoires, how often do they have spells or wards in place to protect them?"

"It's a standard practice. Dark magic users are secretive, and jealously protective of what they learn or create."

I made a note to ask Thorandryll what sort of protection the book had other than a flame illusion. "Jo said that vampires and cultists don't mix well, so what was a vampire doing there?"

"She's right, and the vampire did end up ash." Damian frowned while signaling a turn. "A cult trying to acquire a grimoire by any means necessary makes sense. But vampires can't do magic."

"As far as we know." We'd reached the construction site, and traded a look once he'd parked his car. "Maybe the vampire was a case of wrong place, wrong time. The book is probably in Dead Guy's cult leader's hands."

The site was a lot less spooky in the daylight. A soft breeze rustled the plastic covering piles of building material. I continued with a glance up at the cloudless blue sky. "Nick and I are checking out human-owned Goth clubs. I'll let you know if we find anything."

"All right." Damian produced a key and unlocked the gate. "Maybe we'll find out something today."

We didn't. I went over every inch of the unfinished room, but nothing happened. Two hours of trying with nothing to show for it was exasperating. "Sorry."

"Something could pop up later." He shrugged, patting my shoulder. "Let's go back to the Orb and see what they've managed."

We'd just cleared the building when I had a flash, and a red thread stretched out, ending just ten feet before us. "What the hell?"

Damian glanced around. "What…"

Something swirled into existence before us in a cloud of black and red. I felt an internal click, and a faintly green bubble enclosed us. Damian huffed out a breath. "Very quick."

"Thanks. Uh, is that...?" I pointed at the being taking shape. Later was time enough to figure out how the hell I'd just created an external shield.

"A demon, yes." He straightened his jacket and spoke into the air while tidying sun-streaked hair. "Illy, I need you."

A soft whisper of sound. The husky faded into view with a guilty expression and an empty meat package in his mouth. Damian sighed. "What is it with you and the damn trash?"

The dog dropped his prize and sat on it, offering up a big tongue-lolling grin.

"Uh, demon?" I prompted, and then gaped as Illy leaped to his paws, spinning around. The husky went from goofy and cuddly to a teeth-baring, hackles-raised danger on four paws. It was an impressive sight.

"We're ready." Damian's tone was calm and mild.

"I see that. Wow, Illy, I didn't know you had it in you." I looked from him to the warlock. "Uh, what are we doing?"

"Sending it back. You'll need to drop the shield, Cordi."

The demon was now surveying us, one red-skinned, clawed hand palm up. Fire sparked and grew above it. Panic began creeping in. "What about that?"

"Just jump out of the way." Damian was way too calm about the situation for my taste.

"Okay." Maybe frying me would distract the ugly beast long enough for the warlock to cast whatever spell he was planning.

Cordi. It was a sharp mental poke. Dropping the shield, I dove to the left and rolled, pushing hastily to my hands and knees. The demon hesitated. Damian's voice rose as Illusion began growling.

The fireball went streaking toward his head. I threw a hand up, forcing the oxygen away directly in front of him and Illy. Out the fire went. Blue and green lightning crackled from Damian's hands, lancing out to weave a net around the demon. It roared and Illy began barking.

The net slowly shrank with each bark, the trapped demon becoming insubstantial and finally, it exploded into gritty black ash. Damian sank to his knees, the lightning fizzling and fading. "Whew. Tough one."

"You're incredibly awesome. Have I told you that lately?" Checking to make sure my heart was still inside my chest, I made it to my feet and had to wait for my legs to stop shaking.

Uttering a weak laugh, the warlock leaned on his familiar and rose. "Thanks."

Familiar. I'd like one of that persuasion. Granted, even Illy probably couldn't stop Damian from feeling fear, but he could do something to diminish the aftermath. Me, I had to settle for those increasingly ineffective deep breaths to dilute the metallic flavor of it in my mouth.

But this particular flavor of fear was familiar. I'd tasted it before, just a hint of it.

I'd tasted it in the impressions I'd gained from handling Zoe's necklace.

Seventeen

Nothing. Dropping the necklace with a sigh, I leaned back and propped my boots on the desk. After feeding everyone lunch, returning to the office was my obvious course of action since Jo and David weren't finished with the scrap.

Didn't want to miss the elf's arrival.

Both Kate and Mr. Whitehaven were still out to lunch. I took a few minutes to enjoy imagining Thorandryll's fuming over my quitting the case. Maybe he was fuming about the lack of success in kissing me again too.

We enjoy beauty was shaky ground as an excuse for macking on me. Oddly enough, I trusted Logan's warning to be careful, even though the elf fascinated me.

Elves are a beautiful, charismatic people. Since I'd never been in close proximity to any before, I decided my first brushes were the cause of the hazy-mindedness that struck whenever I looked Thorandryll in the eye.

Or he could be using glamour. Sensing subtle magic wasn't in my repertoire. Dismissing that idea, I scowled at the ceiling while moving on to Nick and his attitude. I had no clue where he was. Probably lunch as well. "Whoops."

Or maybe out hunting for me. I'd forgotten to turn my cell phone back on. Digging it out of my purse and hitting the button, the voice mail app informed me of a dozen messages the second it finished booting up.

They were all from Nick. It was probably logical that he'd assume I was okay with being designated his girlfriend. He was sexy, protective, and funny. Normally, I'd jump all over the opportunity to be the girlfriend of such a hot guy. Was my lack of jumping really because he was a shifter?

The thought was just as sobering the second time around. Also unproductive. Right. Time to concentrate on work.

Why had the vampire been at the construction site? They did have some powers, but more in line with my own abilities, and not magic. If he couldn't use the grimoire, why would he want it?

But that taste of fear…that was Zoe-related. The first location spell had indicated the Barrows, while the second hadn't pinpointed her anywhere. I checked the shimmer in my mental folder. She was still alive, still human.

Recalling Mr. Mitchell's coldness during the client meeting, and his follow-up call, I wondered how convenient it would be for him if the girl disappeared.

Okay, that might be taking things a bit far. Surely he wouldn't have Zoe kidnapped just to rid himself of an annoyance. Disliking his stepdaughter didn't necessarily put him in the villain category.

Plenty of people didn't care for teenagers.

It was a dead-end line of thought, so I called voice mail to listen to the messages. The first one was "Good morning, see you at the office." Nick sounded a little concerned in the second one, wondering why I wasn't at work yet. He said nothing about returning my call.

Just as the third one began (*Where the hell are you?*), a noise out in the reception area caught my attention. Setting the phone down, I left my seat to check out the sound. Maybe Thorandryll had finally shown up. *Yippee.*

The man standing in front of the doors was short, muscular, and had strange-looking eyes. "You are Discordia Jones?"

"Yeah. How may I help you?" What was it about his eyes? Taking two steps, I had a better look, and mine must have gone wide, because he chuckled. It was an evil sound, like the scrape of blood-rusted metal over rock.

His eyes were solid black. Watching a smile crawl into place, I shivered when he said, "Yum."

"My boss will be back in—"

"I'll be finished before then." He moved incredibly fast, and I barely managed to dodge his grasp by dropping to the floor. There wasn't time to get up before he bent down and slapped me. The heavy blow rocked my head to one side.

He blocked my attempt to kick him between the legs, and took a second to laugh at the effort. I called on my TK. Three chairs broke as he landed across them.

He was up instantly, smile gone. The snarling expression that replaced it wasn't comforting. I tried to recreate the shield that had popped up earlier as he charged toward me, but found myself choking.

One hand wrapped around my neck, he hefted me into the air, taking two swift strides and slamming me against the wall. Everything but my legs went briefly numb, feet kicking uselessly in reaction. Both of my hands found his wrist, nails digging in to rip at skin.

"Pitiful. I expected more of a fight."

If I could just get some air, I was more than willing to try harder at giving him one. But the pain around my throat was escalating, and my vision was going dark.

"Cordi!" Nick's shout brought a wave of relief. Abruptly free, I sprawled to the floor as the man turned to face the shifter, and then he and Nick were trading fast, powerful blows. They knocked each other around the reception area, doing a thorough demolition job on the rest of the furniture.

The boss was going to be pissed. He'd spent a mint, hiring an expensive interior designer from San Antonio to make everything soothing for clients.

Each drag of air felt like fire burning down into my lungs. My eyes squeezed shut, but tears poured free anyway. A yelp from Nick made them shoot open, in time to see the man throw him face first through the two-inch thick glass of the doors.

The shifter landed in the parking lot on his back, an avalanche of glass falling with him. Blood was suddenly everywhere, and I crawled forward, wheezing out his name.

It drew the other's attention back to me. When his black eyes focused on mine, pure survival instinct set in. I flung both hands out, and he flew backwards, through the broken doors, landing almost in the street.

Nick was rolling over. Sparing a glance for me, he went after the man, who was already on his feet.

Before they collided, Percy popped out of thin air. The parrot dived and dropped something. It hit the man in the face, breaking and splashing a faintly glowing liquid over him. He exploded into a cloud of black smoke and ash.

The parrot screeched, circling the cloud. "Bad demon! No attacking Cordi!"

Damn if I didn't love that bird.

Nick was standing still, watching the dissipating cloud. Somehow managing to get my feet under me, I limped out into the parking lot. My voice was a croak. "You okay?"

He turned, showing a blood-streaked face embedded with bits of glass. Some slid free while we stared at each other, to make tiny sounds hitting the asphalt. His eyes were dark gold. "Nick?"

"What the hell was that? Did Percy say it was a demon?" He grabbed hold of my left arm. "Are you all right?"

"Battered but breathing." It really hurt to talk. Kate's low-slung, silver Italian sports car roared into the parking lot, brakes squealing as she spotted us. Her familiar landed on my shoulder. Rubbing his head against my cheek, he said, "Percy loves Cordi."

I ruffled his feathers with my free hand. "Love you too, bird brain."

Sirens wailed. People were staring from the entrances of other businesses on the street. Kate was on her cell phone as she left her car, hurrying toward us. More glass slipped from his skin, apparently escaping Nick's notice. "I thought this place was warded."

"It is. Was." Percy crooned something about '*petite déesse*' in my ear.

"Don't just stand there, Maxwell. Get her inside," Kate ordered as she reached us. "Now."

I was happy to have her take charge, wanting nothing more than to lie down and get busy healing. My face and throat were on fire, while my back felt like it had had an up close and personal encounter with a truck. One with a big brush guard installed, or maybe a semi.

"Percy, get off of her. She's injured." The parrot hopped from my shoulder to hers without protest. Nick quickly obeyed, hustling me inside the destroyed reception area. He cleared debris off the couch with a sweep of his arm.

"Here, Cordi. I'll get some ice or something."

"Okay." God, it hurt to talk. He scowled around the room, and disappeared from view. I closed my eyes, listening to Kate make another call, whispering in an agitated tone, and then she began dealing with the cops.

The shifter was back, his fingertips skating over my abused flesh. His touch was so light I barely felt it. "You're burned."

Opening my eyes, I watched him wrap a baggie of ice in a dishtowel. He arranged it on my throat, and bent to kiss my forehead. His face was covered in drying blood, but all of the glass damage looked to have healed. Cold leaked through, feeling wonderful. "I'll go get another one for your cheek."

He was back with another makeshift cold pack in less than a minute, and gently pressed it to my cheek. A cop came over. "I need to ask some questions."

Nick didn't even look at him. "Ask."

"What happened here?"

The shifter described what he knew, but protested my answering any questions. I tried anyway, but my throat didn't cooperate, and the cop waved away my croaked attempts. Mentioning demon ended the questioning. He offered to call for an ambulance, but Kate intervened. I decided beginning to heal my throat was a good idea.

Nick dug out some of the decorative pillows to prop me up, so I had a great view of Whitehaven's luxury SUV rolling over the curb and sidewalk to avoid the cop cars. The man himself appeared, smooth strides not hinting at any urgency as he walked toward the building.

He paused outside the broken doors, glass crunching under his shoes. He glanced briefly at us before he scanned the reception area. His gaze settled on my face.

"Wasn't my fault," I managed to rasp out, and Whitehaven smiled. Stepping inside, he picked a path through the mess, and stopped beside the couch.

"They were merely possessions, easily replaced. Unlike people. How do you feel, Discordia?"

"Awful." A touch of my hand made Nick lift the cold pack away. Whitehaven's smile disappeared. He bent low, studying my face. When he glanced at the shifter, Nick moved the other from my neck.

"He had her up against the wall, choking her, when I got here."

"You did well, Nicholas." The boss patted his shoulder. "Let me assist Kate, and then we'll do more for Discordia."

Both cold packs were replaced, the shifter's eyes once again dark brown. He smoothed my hair back, and moved to sit on the edge of the couch. "You have a hand print burned on your cheek. Am I putting too much pressure on it?"

"No." Lying there, watching him watch me, I realized that he'd saved my life. Of course, that's why he'd been hired: to pull my fat out of the fire when I got in over my head. Knowing that didn't keep a warm, tender feeling from spreading, along with confusion about why he hadn't returned my call the night before.

He took my hand when I lifted it, and pressed a kiss to the back. "If this ever happens again, your job is to haul ass while I keep them busy. Got that?"

"Yeah."

Nick grinned. "You have no intention of following orders, do you?"

"No." I only ran if everyone was running, or if I was on my own.

He shook his head, and looked over his shoulder. "I think they're finishing up."

Kate smeared salve over my back. "The bruises are forming Rorschach blots. I see a bird."

"Ha. Ha." I dabbed some of the salve on my cheek. "It didn't burn when he hit me. Just hurt."

"Demons are strange creatures." The witch let my shirt down. "There. Put some on your neck, Jones. Ronnie's here, and I want to see what she has to say about the ward failure."

Being unable to talk without pain hadn't been much fun, so my throat was almost healed. Scooping more salve from the jar, I covered the faint yellow brown band still visible. "How'd you know what was happening?"

She smiled, opening the restroom door. "A little bird told me."

"Percy?"

"He demanded a banishing potion and said he was going to save Cordi." Kate shrugged. "I had one in my bag, and followed as quickly as possible."

"But how did he know?" Wiping the excess off my fingers, I followed her into the hallway.

"He has his ways of keeping track of those he's fond of." She went toward the reception area. Deciding that I owed the parrot some major treats for a while, I headed for my office.

My cell phone rang as I settled into the chair. "Hello?"

"Hi. It's Logan." He sounded relieved, though I couldn't figure out why. "How are you doing today?"

"After two demon attacks, I'm still upright. Other than that, today has pretty much sucked. I did get to yell at the elf. That part was fun." My lips tried to smile, but it hurt, so I made them give the idea up. "How about you?"

"Not nearly as exciting. I wanted to talk to you about your car, but it doesn't sound like it's a good time." There was noise on his end, voices and other sounds. "Are you all right?"

"I'll live." I wanted to see him, which had to be wrong, considering that the guy I was sleeping with had saved my life less than an hour ago. "Um, I'll give you a call later, if that's okay? We have a meeting about to start."

"Sure. Talk to you then, and take care of yourself, Discord."

"I'm trying to. Bye." Ending the call, I wondered what the hell was going on with me. I'd never consciously drooled over another guy while involved. Nick stopped outside my door, and I forced a smile, shoving thoughts of Logan way into the back of my mind.

"Ronnie's doing her thing and Mr. Whitehaven is waiting on us." His eyes traced the burn on my face, and a slight frown appeared. "I still think you should go to the ER."

By morning, I'd be fine, as long as I had a huge dinner and time to concentrate on healing the rest of the damage. "I only go there when something's broken or there's spurting blood."

His frown turned into a lopsided grin, and the shifter put a hand over his eyes for just a second. "You're one of a kind." Rubbing his face, he said, "Burned Cordi doesn't smell as sexy. Just sayin'."

"Pervert." I left my seat and we walked down to the boss's office.

Mr. Whitehaven sat behind his desk. Elbows propped and fingers steepled, he gazed at me until I had to repress the urge to squirm. "What? I told you it wasn't my fault."

His lips parted, teeth flashing in a brief smile. "I'm merely thinking. You've had a vision and two demonic contact events."

"She's also had a contact event with vampires," Nick pointed out, from his position by the door. Kate was sitting in the chair next to mine, Percy at her shoulder.

Two, actually. Of course, he didn't know about the second one, because he hadn't called me back and there hadn't been a chance to tell him yet. "That may be personal."

Whitehaven leaned back, his chair creaking a faint protest. "Kate, what have you uncovered in regard to Derrick?"

"Damn little. He seems to be relatively unknown, which I find highly suspicious, if he's as powerful a telepath as Jones believes." She scowled, obviously miffed over the lack of information.

"Very well. I'll visit the Barrows myself as soon as possible, and attempt to meet with him concerning his interference."

I wondered how well that would go, while nodding in agreement. Eight feet of anything is impressive. If the boss could get the vamp off my back, that was cool by me. Then again, he was elderly, regardless of whatever he was. Plus, I wanted to know why Derrick was after me. It felt too determined to be just over a little spying. "As long as I sit in."

"Me too." The shifter crossed his arms. With a tiny smile playing over his lips, Whitehaven agreed. I got the impression he didn't really need any back up.

"Very well. Now, it's apparent that steps must be taken to provide Discordia the means to combat any future demonic encounters."

"Why? They'll leave her alone if she quits the case." Nick was scowling when I looked.

"I can't quit."

He dropped his arms. "Of course you can. Tell that damned elf to shove his book up his..."

"I can't stop hunting for the book. I have to find it." Raking a hand through my hair, I said, "I have to clear it out of my mental files or it'll interfere with every case I take from here on out."

Mr. Whitehaven spoke. "I am extremely sorry to have placed you in this situation, Discordia."

"It's not your fault. It's his - that damn elf's. He lied to you, to me, ooh!" Furious, I stood up and began pacing.

"He hired you. What if I kill him? Will that break this compulsion to find the book?" Nick's face was a mask of unconcealed rage when I spun around to look at him, mouth inviting flies by falling wide open in shock.

Kate waved his questions away with a calculated coolness. "Alive or dead, the elf has no bearing on her need to track down the book."

"I can't protect her from demons." He turned away, his hands clenching into tight fists and shoulders turning rigid. "If things had gone differently, we'd both be dead."

Though touched by his obvious distress, I felt a flutter of anger. How many times would it take before he realized I wasn't some weak little damsel in distress? "I'm not completely helpless, Nick."

"Cordi, Cordi, Cordi," Percy warbled, flicking his wings. "Blood shines through."

"What?" Kate turned a sharp look on her familiar. 'What do you mean, Percival?"

The parrot chuckled in response. Her frown promising a decrease in his cracker allowance, Kate continued regarding him while telling Nick, "She isn't helpless and she has us. My coven. We're not entirely impotent against demons, Maxwell. I believe we have provided proof of that."

Thank you, Kate. I was going to buy her a new pair of shoes for that vote of confidence.

"I can also help." Whitehaven rose, heading for the full-wall display case to the left of his desk. It was crowded with a collection of things I'd never quite had the time to peruse.

Nick turned back, expression grim and set. "How?"

"I've collected many unusual items." Our boss waved a hand over the lock, which clicked in response. Reaching inside, he informed us, "Some of them enjoy the taste of demon blood."

He removed a short sword, holding it out for our inspection. The hilt was a dragon's head, the wavy blade supposed to be the flame issuing from its open jaws. Whitehaven offered it to me. "I don't know how to use that."

"I do." Thorandryll's voice shocked us all for a moment, but then Nick snarled and went for him. They disappeared through the door and landed with a thump somewhere down the hallway outside.

"Wonderful!" Kate leaped up from her seat. Not sure if she was going to get popcorn or attempt to stop them wrecking the remains of the reception area, I rushed after her with our boss following on my heels.

The shifter and elf were trading blows. Not really thinking it through, I dove into them, but an elbow to the ribs knocked me away. Mr. Whitehaven stepped over me and pried them apart by means of one large hand around each neck. Dangling both a foot above the floor, he shook them and roared, "Enough!"

It went quiet, and Kate and I exchanged wide-eyed looks. I wondered what had happened to the sword while I climbed to my feet, gingerly testing my ribs with shaky fingers.

"You may fight later, once this threat is past," Whitehaven snapped, dropping them to their feet. Both men reeled away from him, and each other, gasping for air. "Now, come into my office, so that we may discuss this in a civilized manner."

No one argued. We filed back into his office, though Nick didn't take a seat. He stood behind my chair, glaring at the elf.

"I didn't realize you'd be compelled to complete this task. I'd planned to dismiss you once the location of the book was determined." Thorandryll seemed to have recovered his composure nicely.

"You don't give a damn about the danger you've put her in," Nick accused, his hands dropping to my shoulders.

"Hush." Kate shook a scarlet-tipped nail at him, and then pointed it at the elf. "You may speak. What's so important about this book?"

Thorandryll frowned, but answered. "It's Olven's grimoire, and contains the spell that separated the realms."

Mr. Whitehaven froze, his eyes slowly turning to blazing rubies. I tried not to stare, but it was a new and disturbing sight. "Someone wishes to work the spell again?"

"I believe someone wishes to alter it to meld the demon realm with this one," the elf corrected. "Why else would demons be attacking her?"

"All right, now I need a drink," Kate announced, sinking into a chair. Percy fluttered to her, an anxious croon attempting to erase her concern as he rubbed his feathered head on her cheek.

"I knew this was bad," I muttered, feeling a headache bloom behind my eyes. Just the topping to the rest of my aches and pains.

"It's worse than 'bad'. It's the end of this world we've only begun to build." Thorandryll glanced at Nick. "No sacrifice is too great to prevent it."

"Don't be too sure about that," the shifter growled back.

"He's right." I cleared my throat. "No one's that important, not with billions of lives at risk."

"He can find another psychic. Once someone finds the damn book, you'll be free."

"There isn't another available with her abilities. Other psychics can only claim one, or at the most, two talents." The elf shook his head, blonde hair waving. "I had no choice. Our magic can't penetrate the dark shroud of demon magic."

"Human magic can - at least to a certain extent." The witch sighed and stood up, one hand on Percy's side as the parrot continued crooning softly. "I'll call in the cavalry and see what we can come up with to keep Jones breathing."

"If you'll allow me to wield that blade, I'll guard her life with my own." The elf nodded at the dragon sword on Whitehaven's desk.

"No, you won't." Nick's voice was so cold that I twisted to look up at him, but he was glaring at Thorandryll. "You're going to stay away from Cordi. This is your fault."

"Yes, and I must do something to rectify that."

"I have a few other weapons that have proven effective against demons. One is a small dagger and you," my boss focused his newly bejeweled gaze on me. "Will carry it."

"No argument from me." No, I wanted something sharp and hungry for demon blood in hand when the next one appeared. Nick's hands tightened, so I looked up at him again. "And I'm with Nick. I don't think I want you at my back, Mr. Pants On Fire."

The elf's expression could have been carved from ice, when I checked to see how he'd taken that. "Would you accept another's help, should I bring it?"

"Maybe. I'd have to think about it. Trust issues? I have them where you're concerned." A grin fought for release, and I gave into it, even though it hurt. "When I find this damn grimoire of yours, I'm going to destroy it. It's dangerous."

He rose from his seat, eyes narrowing. "It is my possession."

"If I remember my dips into magical history correctly, Olven was a human warlock." Kate smiled. "Humans have the right to destroy dangers created by their own."

The elf transferred his glare to her, but didn't dent her Cloak of Smugness. "It was entrusted to my keeping."

I couldn't keep my mouth shut, not with an opportunity like that dangling in front of me. "And you lost it. Way to go. No wonder you specified 'discreet'. What are all the other elves going to think, if they hear how you lost such a major magical artifact?"

"You wouldn't dare." His face was beginning to flush dark rose. "We have a contract."

"Damn, things do slip out by accident. I'm only human, you know." From the smile Kate aimed in my direction, I'd just gained major brownie points.

Whitehaven spoke, his lips suggesting a smothered smile. "Though I'd have to reprimand her should something slip, I think you'd be far too busy with damage control to pursue any action against my agency."

There's nothing better than a boss who backs you up. I'd never hugged him before, but as soon as the elf was out of sight, it was so happening.

"Very well. I'll provide protection for her safety, in recompense for my mistake. Will that be acceptable to you?" Thorandryll's eyes were on Whitehaven, who nodded. "I'll return in the morn, then."

With that, the elf left the building, and Percy snickered. "Elf in the penalty box."

"I have a question." Everyone's eyes turned toward me. "A spell like this one, what kind of ingredients does it need?"

Kate shrugged, settling back into the chair she'd just vacated. "I don't know. We would never attempt one remotely like it."

"Spells of such world-changing power require quite a few ingredients," Whitehaven said. "Something like this will need the most powerful one of all: a sacrifice."

My breath caught. "Zoe."

Nick looked from the boss to me, eyes widening. "That was a jump I'm not quite following, Cordi."

"I'm not sure it's a good jump." My admission caused him to frown, but all I could offer was a shrug. "It's just a hunch. Kate, can you find out what the Mitchells do?"

"Mrs. Mitchell works for the mayor. She's in public relations." The witch frowned. "Her husband didn't give any work information, since she was the one writing the check."

"Mitchell and Associates, I'll ask her myself what his business is. It's about time I gave her a personal update."

"Not until you have the promised protection," Whitehaven said. "In fact, I think you should go home. Eat and rest, encourage your injuries to heal."

Touching my throat while checking the shimmer to assure myself Zoe was still among the living, I reluctantly agreed.

€ighteen

Ronnie wasn't certain how the demon had passed through the ward without causing the bell tone that was supposed to have occurred. That didn't send me home in a hopeful mood, and it wasn't a restful night.

Nick was out of bed, sword in hand, at every tiny sound. No cuddling. The only good point was he didn't think to ask about my car until we were driving to work the next morning. "Where's your little tin can?"

"It's a classic."

"A classic tin can. Where is it?"

"In the garage for some work. Can we stop and pick up some donuts?" With all the jumping up last night, we'd ended up sleeping through my alarm. There hadn't been time to make a real breakfast.

Slowing for a red light, he looked at me. "Yeah. What kind of work?"

Damn it, I'd forgotten to call Logan back, and hadn't even thought of calling the insurance company yet. "Some body work."

The light changed, and he let the truck roll slowly forward. "I thought you could drive blind-folded. You had an accident? When?"

"Night before last. There's a donut shop a block ahead. I hope they have the chocolate-and-nut-topped ones. Those are my favorite." He turned to pay attention to traffic, but didn't cooperate with my attempt to change the subject.

Hardly fair. I always cooperated when he did it.

"You went out after telling me you needed some alone time?" His knuckles were turning white, and I wondered if he'd rip the steering wheel loose or something. Checking the rearview mirror, he signaled a lane change, and asked, "Did you go to see Logan?"

No way to avoid it. "Not on purpose. I did try to call you, and left a message."

"I didn't have any messages last night. There weren't any calls."

My anger blazed to life. "Are you calling me a liar? I called you, damn it. Left a message telling you that I had to head into the Palisades again."

Nick didn't say another word until we were parked in the donut shop's lot. He turned off the engine and unbuckled his seatbelt. He leaned his head back and closed his eyes. "Let me guess. Your tracking sense blipped. What happened to your car, Cordi?"

"I pissed off some vampires, and they trashed it. Logan showed up, and he gave me a ride home. It's at his garage."

His jaw bunched. "That's twice he's shown up at the right time. Don't you think that's a little suspicious?"

Staring out the window at the shop, I decided it probably wasn't a good idea to tell him no. The only internal alarm Logan set off for me was my hotness radar. "He told me he likes taking walks at night. I didn't ask, but he probably heard it when I screamed."

Head snapping upright, Nick turned his murky gold eyes to me. "Why were you screaming?"

"Dude, I was fighting vampires. They're scary, and sometimes, there's screaming. It's like a reflex or something, okay? And then this big tiger showed up, except it wasn't a real tiger, but Logan."

"He saved you."

That stung. Man, did it sting. "For your information, I was holding my own. Even ashed two before it was all over, thank you very much. You and the boss think I'm totally helpless, and you can both kiss my ass for that. Now, I want some damn donuts."

Climbing out of the truck, I slammed the door shut and stomped my way into the shop. They had my favorite kind. With a half dozen of those, and a mixed dozen for everyone else, I returned to the truck.

Nick started the engine. It was a silent drive to the office, and there was a client present in the cleaned out reception area, so my donuts had to wait. She was a rich, elderly woman whose pedigreed cat had disappeared. She suspected foul play.

I suspected kitty hormones, but made arrangements to be at her place by three to look around. Nick stepped into my office the second she left. I'd just shoved half a donut into my mouth.

He shut the door and took a seat, lips twitching while taking in my temporary chipmunk cheeks. "I know that you don't like to talk personal business at work, but I have some things to say."

The best response I could manage was a nod.

"Maybe it's strange, but I care about you, even if we haven't known each other very long. I'm not human, Cordi." He paused, but I was still chewing. "I'm not going to act just like your previous boyfriend. Boyfriends. Whatever."

Finally able to swallow, I needed a gulp of coffee to help wash down donut. "Okay."

"I'm a shifter, and the elf is making my instincts boil. So is Logan. One's put you in serious danger, and the other keeps showing up when you're alone and in trouble." He took a deep breath, letting it out slowly.

"It's not like Logan has tried anything. We're just kind of friends. Having guy friends isn't against the law. David and Damian are my friends too."

"Right." He nodded, eyes leaving mine to survey the desk's top. "Did you really try to call me?"

"I did call you. There wasn't any trying to it. I left a message."

He offered his cell phone to me. I took it and scrolled down the list of received calls. None from me for the night in question. Frowning, I pulled out mine and showed him the outgoing call list. "See? I called you."

"Okay. Then something weird happened." We traded phones, and he sat back. "You called, but I didn't get it for some reason. Are we okay on that now?"

"Sure."

"Good. You have chocolate," he tapped one corner of his mouth. "Right there."

Licking it off, I picked the box up and held it out. "Donut?"

I was polishing off the last donut when someone knocked on the door. Nick was at the sideboard, pouring fresh coffee. "It's the elf."

"Yay." I didn't care if Thorandryll heard it or not, and went to answer the door. Wanting to make certain he realized I was still extremely pissed, I turned back to my desk instead of looking while opening it. "Come in."

Nick turned around, sounding a deep growl as his eyes flashed gold. Something in the hallway growled back. I turned for a look, only to scramble for cover behind my desk.

"What the hell is that?" I pointed at the huge dog following Thorandryll into my office once behind my desk. It bared its teeth at Nick, still growling.

"Quiet." The elf's order shut off the dog's growl. "The protection I promised. His name is Leglin."

"It's the breed they use to hunt us." Nick's eyes were on the beast.

My mouth fell open as I looked from him to the elf. "Are you serious? Get it out of here!"

Nick smirked at Thorandryll, who ignored him. "Leglin has never hunted shifters, Miss Jones."

"Yeah? Then why does it look like it wants to eat Nick?"

"Perhaps because he recognizes the unnatural when he sees it," the elf snapped.

"Get out." My voice didn't sound like mine. It was low and menacing. "Get out, or so help me, I'll teleport you into a wall and leave you there."

"I believe she means that." Kate appeared in the doorway and lofted Percy toward me. The parrot chortled, buzzing the dog's head before landing on my desk.

"Bad dog. Bad elf. *Vous troublez la petite déesse!*"

"Take this beast away. It's tainted." Kate was glaring at Thorandryll before he completed his turn toward her. "There's demon blood in its veins."

"Which is why I've brought him. He can protect her." The tips of his ears were flushing pink. "Don't you want her kept safe?"

Her red nail jabbed at him, just missing the tip of his nose. "Don't try the divide and conquer bit, old man."

Nick and I traded a confused look. I was the one who asked "What?"

"Don't be dense, Jones. He wants you, and you haven't swooned into his arms. He thinks that if he can make you doubt us, he'll be able to convince you that he's the only one capable of protecting you."

I was stunned. "Is that what you're trying to do?"

Thorandryll sighed, turning to me. "I'm responsible for the danger you face. It's my task, and honor, to see that you remained unharmed."

"She's not one of your people." Nick's hackles rose, at least figuratively. For once, Thorandryll looked directly at him. About to say something, probably incredibly snarky, he froze and stared at the shifter.

Kate chuckled. Crossing her arms and leaning a shoulder against the doorframe, she raised an eyebrow. "Ooh, bet that stings."

I was hopelessly lost. "What the hell is going on?"

"Mr. High-and-Mighty just realized how close you and I are," the shifter answered.

I watched the elf drag his gaze from Nick to me. There was something in his stony expression that sent dread sliding down my spine.

"It's true? You've shared yourself with him?" he asked. Struck dumb and unable to take my eyes off his, I nodded. "That was an incredibly stupid mistake."

My flaring anger returned my voice to me. "You arrogant prick."

"I merely state the truth."

"You're not winning any points insulting me."

Nick smiled. "I think that insult was aimed in my direction, Cordi."

"Either way, he can get the hell out of my office and stay away." I scowled, eyes going back to Thorandryll's. Anger seemed proof against the haze. "You don't get to be a jerk to my boyfriend. If you don't like it, then hop your happy ass back to your faerie mound and stay there."

"You're so young." The elf shook his head, blonde hair shimmering. "You don't know what he is."

I looked at Kate for help, but she shrugged, eyes narrowing to shoot daggers at the elf's back. "I know he's a shifter. It doesn't matter to me."

Mr. Whitehaven loomed into sight behind Kate. He must have overheard the conversation, because he said, "The hound is an acceptable guardian, if you bind it to Discordia."

"You have got to be kidding me." My eyes returned to the dog. It was tall, with a short, sleek, thick-looking black and tan coat. It rather looked like a cross between an Irish wolfhound and a Rottweiler. Just bigger and scarier.

"The breed was originally established to hunt demons, which slaughtered normal hunting hounds with ease. He will protect you until his last breath, and it would require quite a few demons to cause that."

"It wants to eat Nick," I protested. "And what do you mean by 'bind it to me'?"

The shifter carried my coffee cup over. "I'm okay with the hound if it's bound to you. We might even get some sleep tonight."

Which sounded good, and caused an elven frown, but I wanted more information about the binding deal. "If you're sure, but first, I want to know what the hell he meant by binding."

With a touch of Thorandryll's hand, the dog sat. "A drop of your blood placed on this jewel." The elf bent slightly, pointing to a large, pale blue stone set in the front of the dog's wide leather collar. "That's all that's needed. He will obey you faithfully, until this matter is settled and you return him to me."

Scanning my friends' faces, I discovered that Kate seemed to be the only one who still wasn't sold on the idea. "What do you think?"

"It's a perversion of Nature." The witch scowled. "Yet, it's perfectly capable of killing demons, so I suppose it's temporarily useful."

Damn. She was my last hope for refusing. "All right."

The witch insisted on handling the bloodletting once I left the safety of my desk. After jabbing my thumb with a needle, she gathered it and the alcohol wipe. "I'll dispose of these."

The blood I'd smeared over the dog's jewel was sinking in. Watching it turn lavender, I absently encouraged the pinprick to heal. Leglin's steady gaze left Nick, and the dog looked up at me.

He seemed to be waiting for something. "No attacking anything or anyone except demons unless I say different." To my surprise, the dog lifted and dropped his muzzle slightly. "Did he just nod yes?"

"He's quite intelligent." Thorandryll had returned to ignoring Nick, who wore a smug little smirk. "And he will not disobey you, even should it mean death."

That was a rather important fact, which required some clarification. "His or mine?"

"His." The elf's eyes bored into mine, his warning clear. I'd owe him if something other than a demon killed the dog.

"Right. What do I feed him?" Having never had more than the occasional goldfish or Betta floating through my life, I didn't know anything involving the care and feeding of demonic dogs.

"Meat and water are all that he requires. I expect to be kept informed of your progress, and will assist in the retrieval of the grimoire once you've located it." With that, the elf disappeared from sight. Quite rude of him to avoid giving me a chance to argue about destroying it.

"Now I know how people feel when I do that." Pointing to a corner of my office, I looked at the dog. "Go lie down."

Leglin obeyed. I focused on Whitehaven. "Is there anything else I need to know about him?"

The boss stepped close enough to engulf my shoulder in a gentle grip. "The hound has some magic of his own. He will come when called, whether near you or not. Treat him as an ally, but don't forget that he is a powerful weapon, Discordia."

"Fat chance of that happening."

Whitehaven smiled, patted my shoulder, and left.

Once alone with Nick and the dog, I realized that I'd forgotten to return Logan's call. "My car."

The shifter dropped into a chair. "Is that really important right now?"

"Yes." Pulling my cell phone out, I found the number and hit call. A strange male voice answered. "Hello, this is…"

Whoever he was interrupted me. "Yeah. Logan's washing his hands. Give him a minute."

"Oh, sure. Thanks." Listening to him setting the phone down, I leaned back. Less than a minute later, Logan picked it up. "Hey, I'm sorry about not calling back yesterday."

His chuckle rumbled through the phone. "You did seem to be having a busy day."

"You could say that." Nick was listening, eyes glued to my face. "I haven't even called my insurance company yet."

Something fell on his end, metal clanging on concrete. "They'll total it out. It's going to be expensive to repair, but it's not a lost cause, Discord."

I winced, thinking of the one, big-limit credit card in my wallet. Two weeks in Hawaii had been my plan for it, with my first vacation time approaching. My car was much more important than a couple of weeks on a beach were. "Are you set up for credit cards?"

"Yes."

Eyes closing, I grimaced. "I'll bring one you can use on it, so please go ahead with the work."

Nick moved. Eyes opening, I watched him point at the dog. "Oh, yeah. I sort of have an elf dog now."

Logan's voice dropped low, and I wondered if he'd turned away from whomever was around him as the noise level decreased slightly. "You have one of their hunting hounds?"

"Yeah, as protection against demons." Nick distracted me by making faces and pointing at his neck. "What? Oh. I had to smear blood on its collar, so the dog is stuck minding me right now. I mean, it's bound to me."

The tiger shifter was silent for a long moment. "I see. It'll be better if I meet you somewhere."

"Sure. Hey, if you can, why don't you come to my place for dinner?" Nick's eyebrows rose, but settled when I added, "Nick will be there too. Say about seven?"

"Ah...okay. I can do that."

"Cool. Bye."

"See you then, Discord."

Ending the call, I looked at Nick. "What?"

"Nothing, except now what?"

"Let's go to the Orb and see what's going on." We left my office, and were almost to the front doors when I remembered the dog. "Whoops. Leglin, come on."

Head and tail lowered, the dog slunk out of my office and to me.

"Nobody freak." It was the first thing I said, walking in while Nick held the door open.

Jo's familiar took one look at Leglin, and relocated from counter to the top of a bookcase, hissing and grumbling under her breath.

Copernicus raised his head from under one wing, blinked, and then went back to sleep. A couple of customers surveying tiny potion bottles decided the candles four aisles over were far more interesting.

"You sure can clear a room." Leglin's tail dipped to the floor at my comment. I felt sorry for him, and hooked my fingers through his collar. "It's okay. Come on."

David and Jo had both looked up from a pile of papers and books spread over the counter. The former's eyes popped wide. "Is that…"

"Elf-bred demon dog. He's mine until this case is over. His name is Leglin."

Jo's face lit up in a grin. "Guess you didn't piss off the elf too much. Hi, Nick."

"Hey." He added a smile. We crossed to the counter.

"Has Kate filled you guys in?"

"Olven's grimoire, demon attacks, and the two of you smacking down the elf, physically and verbally." Her grin widened, eyes appearing to twinkle. "Mr. Pants on Fire?"

"I have some thoughts." David straightened, hands flattening on the counter's marble top. "Do you still believe the demon in your vision saw you?"

A shiver of remembered horror struck. "It looked right at me."

He sighed, shoulders slumping. "I've done some research, and there's a possibility that demons don't move through time and space like everyone else."

"Okay, that totally clears everything up." My sarcasm fell flat.

"It's possible that their future selves are tied to their past and present selves." His expression was expectant.

The conversation was going to end in a headache for me. I just knew it. "Uh, aren't all of our selves actually the same self, just older or whatever?"

David buried his face in his hands. "Yes and no. Given a choice, you make a decision, but the other option still exists and…"

Jo poked him in the side. "Focus."

Dropping his hands, he said, "Right. Demons may be subconsciously aware of all the possibilities of their futures."

Lacking the proverbial clue, I glanced at Nick for help. The shifter didn't fail me. "So Cordi's vision, it saw her because," he paused, gaze rising to the ceiling. "She's a future threat to its plans?"

The thud of David's palm striking marble made me jump. He was grinning. "Yes. It's trying to remove her before she stops its scheme."

Damn, my abilities were stabbing me in the back. "If I hadn't had the vision, demons wouldn't be trying to kill me. That's what you're saying."

Jo snorted. "Don't underestimate your power to piss people off."

"Thanks a lot."

Nick donned his Master of Summing Up robe. "We've lost any element of surprise."

Score one for the demons. I patted Leglin's broad skull. He sat on my foot. "Ow. There's a problem."

David rolled his eyes. "You just have to stay alive and take the grimoire."

"Screw the book. I need to rescue the girl they're planning to sacrifice for the spell."

His eyes twinkled. "Stealing their sacrifice would be a fantastic disruption."

Mrs. Mitchell wasn't at work, and didn't answer when we stopped by her home, so we went to lunch.

Sitting at the outdoor patio of a Mexican restaurant, I fed Leglin strips of fajita meat. Though giant, he took each with careful delicacy. By then, my pleasure in figuring out why demons wanted to kill me had faded. "So I'm a big, fat demon target."

Nick swallowed a half-chewed bite. "You're not seeing the full picture."

"Nope, just painful death by clawed hands."

He laughed, and then leaned close. "You save the world."

I picked out another strip of meat. "That will look good on my resume. Much better than 'demon bait'. You know, if I live long enough to actually do it, and don't die during."

"Pessimist. You have me, him," he jerked his chin at the dog. "The coven and Mr. Whitehaven."

128

"Maybe the demons won't kill me since I come with such a delicious buffet of demon kibble." Sighing, I glanced across the parking lot. "Never thought I'd say this, but I prefer vampires. They're such simple creatures."

The dog nosed my leg. I fed him another strip. "Nick?"

"Yeah?"

"Is that guy in the yellow shirt watching us?" The man in question was across the street, leaning against a light post. Showing super sneaky form, the shifter took a bite of taco and let his gaze wander while chewing.

"Maybe." We both glanced over our shoulders, taking in the people eating their lunches. The restaurant teemed with cannon fodder, if another demon attack was imminent.

I patted Leglin. "We should go."

Nick grunted, cramming another bite into his mouth. Swallowing without any pretense at chewing, he rose from his seat. "I'll go grab some takeout containers. If he moves, sic Legs on him."

Left alone with the dog, I felt extremely vulnerable. "Don't you have, like, super demon sense or something?"

He poked my leg again, eyes on the platter of meat. Feeding him another strip, I peeked at Yellow Shirt. The man, or potential demon, was crossing the street and definitely looking right at me. "Leglin, is that a demon?"

Rising to his paws, the dog turned to have a look. His ears swept back, and he silently stalked away, through the patio's cactus-lined opening. Where the hell was Nick? I jumped when someone asked, "Is everything all right?"

The dog had disappeared from view. I forced a smile and looked up to reply, but my voice failed as solid black eyes speared mine. "Uh…"

I had seconds to shove away from the table before a clawed hand scythed air where my throat had been. Someone screamed.

It sucks to land on concrete. Grabbing my purse, I scrambled backwards while shoving a hand into it. The handle of the dagger was cool to the touch. Leglin howled from the parking lot, and that set off the panic stampede. Yanking out the dagger, I swiped at the demon's hand when he took another swing at me.

"Cordi!" My name was a roar, but Nick didn't appear. People were running through the patio's doorway, going inside for cover. Another frantic slash drew blood, and the demon snarled. Its human façade blackened, and began melting away as it grew taller, revealing a brown-scaled creature with yellow eyes.

I almost dropped the dagger as a wail of agony cut into my brain. Another roar of my name sounded, ending in a howl. There was an answering one from the parking lot. The demon's bat-like head turned, and I lunged up and forward, burying the dagger into its stomach.

The next thing I knew, I was several feet away, vision blurred, back aching, with something warm dripping down the side of my face. I had a front row seat to the demon's noisy contortions before it exploded in a cloud of ash and smoke.

Clattering to the concrete, the dagger glowed blood red. Leglin jumped the balustrade this time, landing in the remains of the demon cloud. Sneezing, the dog shook his head while walking to me. "Cordi?"

It took me far too long to realize it wasn't the dog speaking. "Huh?" Trying to turn my head hurt, so I stopped. Nick brought his face level to mine. "I'm okay."

Worry lines in sharp relief, he touched the side of my face and the back of my head at the same time. Displaying bloodstained fingers, he said, "No, you're not."

"Oh." The lights went out.

Nineteen

Quiet, cool dimness greeted my return to consciousness. I was in my own room, snuggled up to a large, fur-covered body. "Leglin?"

The bed shuddered under his response by tail: whump, whump, whump. After brief consideration, I decided against moving because of the sharp ache in my skull.

"Discordia?" Of all the people I expected to see after getting knocked on my ass, Mr. Whitehaven was the last. Especially in my apartment. My *bedroom.*

"Present." It caused a faint smile to cross his face. Ducking, he stepped into the room.

"Your injuries were rather severe. There was bruising to your spine, as well as puncture wounds and a scalp laceration." He paused beside the bed. "How do you feel?"

I took stock before answering. "Horrible. Where's Nick?"

"He went out to pick up a meal. Do you feel well enough to sit up?" A knock on the front door drew a quick frown from my boss. "Excuse me."

He left, and I heard the door opening, followed by low conversation. My mom came rushing into the room. "Cordi, are you all right?"

Aw, crap. "Just a little banged up, Mom. What are you doing here?"

Dropping a bag, she leaned over Leglin to pat me down with quick, light touches. "I brought your soap."

Every month, she made a huge batch of soap. Oatmeal, lavender, and other herbs went into it according to some recipe only she knew. It was fantastic stuff, and the center sold most of each batch in its gift store. "Thanks."

"What happened to you? And where did you get this pony?" Apparently satisfied nothing was broken, she turned to comparing her hand to one of Leglin's front paws. "Look at that. He'll eat you out of house and home."

"Yeah, maybe." My brain wasn't working well enough to form a plan that would end with her leaving. I wasn't exactly safe to be around at the moment, being demon bait and all.

"Let me put the soap away. Do you need anything? How about a cold cloth?" She was moving before I could answer. Leglin heaved a sigh, legs twitching, as she disappeared into the bathroom.

Things got even better a couple of minutes later. Nick returned, and came into the room. "I picked up Italian. Are you ready to get up?"

Mom popped out of the bathroom like a jack-in-the-box, her multi-hued gypsy skirts swirling and a bright smile on her face. "Well, hello. You must be Nick."

Confronted with a parent, he rose to the occasion with a smile. The fact my mom knew his name probably embedded his girlfriend designation deeper, but then again, I'd told Thorandryll Nick was my boyfriend this morning. "Yes, ma'am, and you must be Cordi's mother."

"Call me Sunny." She floated closer to him, extending her hand. "You should come to the center with her sometime."

That forced me upright as they shook hands. Leglin hefted himself into a sit, while I waited for the room to stop spinning. It quickly did, and I had to push his muzzle out of my face. Large paws on either side of my knees pinned the covers down. "Help. I'm stuck."

Nick grinned, releasing Mom's hand. "He's your hound. Tell him to move."

Slow on the uptake didn't quite cover my problem. I wondered if my brain was permanently scrambled. "Down, Leglin."

Thud. He was on the floor before I could blink, stretching and opening his maw in a cavernous yawn. We contemplated the sharpness of his exposed teeth in silence, until his jaws closed with a snap, and the dog shook himself. Leglin looked at me. "Uh, good boy."

His wagging tail smacked the shifter's thigh twice before a wincing Nick moved out of range. "Let me help you up, Cordi."

I tried to keep from limping or showing any other weakness as he guided me down the hallway. Mom was hovering and quiet, until she'd taken a seat at the table. "You didn't tell me what happened."

"A demon hit her," Nick said while placing an order of cannelloni in front of me. "After she stabbed it."

Mom's eyes bulged, her mouth opening into a silent O. I let an elbow fly, hitting Nick in the stomach. He looked from me to her, and back. The glare I was giving him had him hurrying to answer the door when someone rapped on it.

Mom closed her mouth, swallowing hard. "Why did you stab a demon? Didn't you know that would make it angry?"

Damn Nick and his big mouth. There wasn't a way to sugarcoat this. "It was trying to kill me, Mom."

Color drained from her face. She squeaked out, "Why?"

Oh, goody, there was an opening to sending her home. "Because of something I'm supposed to do, or keep from happening. It's not safe to be around me right now. You need to go home, Mom."

"Logan's here." Both shifters entered the kitchen, and Nick avoided my eyes while making introductions. "This is Cordi's mom, Sunny. Sunny, this is Logan."

She didn't look away from me to acknowledge the new arrival. "Hello."

He wasn't given a chance to respond, because Mr. Whitehaven, who'd been quietly observing, decided to speak up. "Please rest assured that we are taking all possible action to keep Discordia safe. I'll explain those measures while I see you to your car, if I may?"

With a slow nod, she rose from her seat. Before leaving, she paused by my chair for a hug and kiss, whispering, "Please be careful."

"I will, Mom. I love you." The shifters edged around to give her and Whitehaven room to leave the kitchen. She glanced back, eyes full of worry, before stepping out of sight. I managed to wait until the front door shut before saying anything. "I can't believe you just blurted that out. My mom's not good with stuff like people trying to kill me."

Hands up in surrender, Nick grimaced. "I'm sorry."

"Sorry doesn't cut it, Nick. She's worried about me enough for two lifetimes, and now she's going to be worried sick all the time again."

Nick seemed to shrink a little. After glancing at him, Logan spoke up. "It's not his fault, Discord."

"Excuse me?"

"If you didn't tell him you wanted her kept in the dark..." he trailed off, one shoulder rising and falling in a gentle shrug. Planting my elbows on the table, I dropped my head into my hands and fought for control.

Deep, slow breaths. One, two, three... "You're right. I'm sorry, Nick. It wasn't your fault and I shouldn't have blown up at you."

He had every right to jump all over me in return, but didn't. "It's okay, I understand. I really am sorry I said anything."

Lifting my head, I managed to smile through the cooling remnants of anger. "Not your fault. Did you pick up enough food for Logan too?"

Nick smiled back. "Yeah."

The boss re-joined us. My choice of a black iron dinette set proved its worth, the chair he sat in bearing his weight without a complaint.

Not only had Nick remembered my dinner invitation to Logan, he'd also stopped by a grocery store to pick up meat for Leglin. Once we'd demolished the various Italian offerings, he played house wife. Cleaned up the mess and then cut steaks into strips for the dog. A stainless steel mixing bowl was pressed into service as a water bowl.

Listening to Whitehaven fill Logan in, I had the distinct impression that a job offer might be forthcoming for the other shifter. There really wasn't any other reason the boss would be telling my mechanic what was going on.

Chair turned sideways, legs stretched out toward the dog's hind end, Logan had a forearm resting on the tabletop. He listened silently while watching me feed Leglin. Once they'd finished speaking, he said, "So Discord's going to destroy this grimoire."

"Or disrupt the spell by recovering the intended sacrifice." Whitehaven was enjoying a glass of red wine. I halfway expected the glass to break each time he picked it up.

Finishing his clean up duties, Nick pulled a couple of beers from the fridge and sat down. He'd certainly made himself at home in my apartment. Oh, wait. I had given him boyfriend status, hadn't I?

"Yellow Shirt was a demon. Where'd the other one come from?"

"I don't know. They freaking double-teamed us." I picked out another slice for the dog. "He made a move, so I set Linny on him. The other one showed up the second my new buddy was out of sight."

Nick's left eyebrow rose. "Linny?"

"It's better than Legs. How are we going to check out the other clubs? Did anyone reschedule my three o'clock? Did you try getting in touch with Mrs. Mitchell again?" The meat was almost gone. "Is this enough of a meal for him?"

The men exchanged glances, but I pretended not to notice, in spite of the sinking sensation in my stomach. Whitehaven cleared his throat. "Kate handled your appointment. The cat was found, locked in the pool house."

"Good. The client was really upset." Dangling the last strip, I forced a smile as Leglin delicately nibbled at it.

"I believe it will be safer for you to remain here…"

My sigh interrupted him. "I knew it. No offense to Kate, but I'm way sneakier at finding things out. She can't exactly pop a spell in a club without people noticing."

"True, but if another demon attack occurred in such a venue, many are likely to be injured. Alcohol consumption does tend to dull the survival instinct." He was using his fatherly tone. "Should your abilities choose to offer any enlightenment, I trust you'll make certain that Nicholas and the hound accompany you."

Great, I wasn't being completely benched. "Right."

"It seems the Palisades are part of this." Logan's fingers curled around his beer bottle. "I don't know why. Things still feel off there, but no one's talking."

Rising, I took the plate we'd used for the dog's dinner to the sink to rinse it off. "Maybe no one knows anything. Even humans can sometimes sense approaching danger. The book may still be there, somewhere."

Drying my hands, I dropped the towel onto the counter, and turned, straight into another vision. The same cavern surrounded me. My heart stuttered into a higher gear, eyes landing on the altar, and seeing the dried blood staining the dark stone.

Backing away, I smacked into the counter before Whitehaven whispered, "What do you see, Discordia?"

"It's the cavern where the cultists raised the demon. Empty right now." Something cold and wet touched my hand. Barely restraining a shriek, I realized that it was Leglin's nose. The dog seemed willing to be my anchor, and when I lifted my hand, he put his broad head under it.

My boss wasn't finished. "Is anything different?"

Obediently scanning the cavern, I didn't see anything. "Just the lack of cultists and blood stains on the altar."

"Describe the cavern to me." The combination of his calm voice and contact with Leglin's smooth fur was a steadying influence.

"All the stone is dark gray. I can't tell where the light is coming from, but it's just enough to be able to see by." I let my eyes slowly wander around. "There's a tunnel. I think that's where the cultists came in."

No one said anything, and my hand slid down the dog's neck, touching his collar. A loud sniff drew my gaze down. "How the hell did you get in here?"

"Discordia?" Whitehaven sounded worried.

"He's here with me. The dog is in the cavern with me." Nothing like it had ever happened before. Curious, I lifted my hand and he faded away. Dropping it back to his neck and collar caused the dog to reappear. "Dude, this is cool."

Swish, swish. Leglin's wagging tail moved the cool air. He drew in a deep breath, head turning as he looked around. I wondered if he'd remember the smell of the cavern, and what good it might be if he did.

Another thought struck, and I bent to act on it. Picking out a pebble from those at the altar's base, I held it up to the dog with a smile. "Can you hold this for me?"

He opened his mouth, carefully picking the pebble off the palm of my hand. I let go of his collar, and the dog faded from sight. "Drop it."

The distinct sound of rock striking ceramic tile made my smile widen into Joker territory. "Well, looky what we can do."

A second later, my kitchen replaced the cavern. The three men were staring, and the pebble lay at my feet.

Twenty

The rolling and bouncing sensations caused my stomach to shudder in protest. I set the pebble down. "I'm getting motion sickness."

"You should be immune to that, considering the way you drive." Nick grinned.

"Ha. Ha." Turning my attention to Whitehaven, I dove right in. "Explain how that was even possible. How did I bring something out from a vision of the past? I mean, how could Leglin do it for me?"

The dog's tail pounded tile a couple of times. Saying his name seemed to make him happy. Or maybe it was just being acknowledged. Whichever. I scratched him behind one ear. "You're a good boy."

"I have no idea." Whitehaven had to raise his voice a bit, over the increasing thunder of the dog's tail. "I've never seen even a mention of such a thing being possible." He rose, fingers tapping the table edge. "Further research is needed. I'll be at the office. Logan, may I speak with you?"

"Sure." The shifter stood up, meeting my eyes briefly before they left the kitchen. Nick and I shrugged at each other.

"Please tell me you grabbed my purse."

"I didn't, but your hound did. It's on the couch. Do you want me to get it for you?"

Still feeling a bit achy, my answer was yes. He went to collect it, and I dug through the zebra print bag to find the credit card promised to Logan. Maybe I could see Hawaii my next vacation. "Did you pick up the dagger?"

"Yeah. It's on your dresser." His gaze moved to the kitchen archway. "Wonder what he wanted to talk to Logan about?"

"If it's our business, one of them will tell us." Some things, you didn't poke at unless invited to. "Can I ask you a question?"

"Yeah." His attention was all mine. "What?"

"Do you jump into bed with strangers all the time?" It wasn't exactly the question I meant to ask, but close enough.

"I liked you before we were introduced."

Pause for thought, that was. "How can you like someone before you actually meet them?"

He shrugged. "I liked what Mr. Whitehaven had to say about you."

If that wasn't a response guaranteed to generate questions, I didn't know what was. "What did he say about me?"

"That you worked hard, were good at your job. He said that you were a good person, loyal to your friends, and determined to help those who needed it." A faint, teasing grin grew. "Of course, he also said that you have some difficulties with your abilities, and that that's why you sometimes panic."

All true, but was that really enough to predispose someone in my favor? To make a guy want to spend time with me, and jump my bones? Or had Whitehaven hired him with...

"I wasn't the first person he interviewed." Nick's comment drew my mind back from the unpleasant thought. "I don't know if it makes any difference to you, but I think part of the reason he hired me is because I'm a shifter. A wolf."

There was so much that I didn't know about shifters in general, much less about particular species, that I didn't know how to handle his comment. "Why do you say that?"

"We're pack animals. Loyal to those who become part of our pack. It's a little different when it comes to those who aren't pack by birth, but part of," he paused, eyes narrowing. "I guess part of like a chosen pack. One made of people who aren't blood, but important for other reasons."

Illuminating. "So Mr. Whitehaven, Kate, and I are this secondary pack for you because we work together?"

A nod. "Yeah."

That was a far more comforting reason than the thought I'd cut off in mid-growth. "Cool."

We smiled at each other, and heard the front door opening. Logan appeared just a second later. "I kind of need to head back, Discord."

"Oh, sure. Here's the card." He crossed, avoiding Leglin, to accept the rectangle of plastic. "Is everything okay?"

"Yeah, fine. I've begun making a list of parts, so I'll start looking for them," he promised, tucking it into a plain, black leather wallet. "You'll need to approve each purchase."

"Okay." Intending to see him to the door, I rose. Nick jumped up, hurrying around the table to take my arm. "What are you doing?"

"Helping." Since there wasn't a way to shake him off without hurting his feelings, I went along with it. The hound didn't see any need to play escort, though he watched us leave the kitchen.

At the door, we said our good byes, and Logan promised to be in touch soon after thanking us for dinner. Having waved him out, I shut the door and locked it before turning around. Leaning against it, I studied Nick's face. "You're acting kind of jealous."

His expression smoothed into complete blandness. "I don't understand what you mean."

"Not letting me walk Logan to the door alone?"

"You were hurt today. What kind of boyfriend would I be if I didn't try and take care of you?"

Good question. Another one was why did it irritate me when he did?

Letting it go with a sigh, I said, "I want a shower, and then sleep. Sound like a plan?"

Nick grinned. "Absolutely."

His help didn't end at the bathroom's door. The shifter insisted on showering with me, scrubbing me clean from head to toe, even washing my hair. Intense attention, combined with nakedness, resulted in his dashing out to retrieve a condom.

Shower sex wasn't exactly comfortable in my experience, especially if the guy was taller. After a few minutes of trying to find a position that wouldn't make us fall over, he growled impatiently. "Can I just pick you up?"

"Yeah." My back slid up the tiled wall when he bent, catching the backs of my knees in the bend of his arms. Halfway expecting help get my legs around his waist, I wasn't certain I liked finding myself wide open as he planted his hands against the wall.

Before I could say anything, he moved close to capture my mouth. There was an instant of slipping downward, and then he was pushing inside. Locking my hands behind his neck, I decided the position wasn't so bad after all.

Each slow thrust was punctuated by a kiss. His eyes swirled to gold, lips curved into a grin between kisses. Some found my lips, others my shoulders or neck. It felt good, building wonderful heat, but as usual, not really the kind I needed to come.

Which was fine, because the one time I'd tried to explain had resulted in a couple of episodes of semi-rough attention in an effort to get me off quickly. A lot of men didn't seem to realize that most women needed more stimulation than just their penis could provide. Not to mention more time. And that one had taken it as a personal insult, so I'd dumped him.

It would be silly to assume a shifter would know that, not being human. Sex felt good regardless, and if I really felt the need for an orgasm, I could take care of it myself. Later, when I was alone.

Relaxing and enjoying what was happening worked just fine. I traded kisses, let one hand move to his hair, concentrated on how his body felt against mine.

Several minutes passed, our bodies sliding against each other's, his skin growing hotter under my lips and hands. He came, face buried in my neck, and a deep, low rumble rising from his chest.

Lifting his head, he grinned again, golden eyes searching my face. A tiny line appeared between his brows. Before I could ask what was wrong, we both went sliding down. He went farther than me, slipping free, and kneeling with his arms still braced under my legs. "What are you…"

His mouth interrupted the question, landing directly between my legs. Both my hands found his hair as my eyes closed and he began licking. After a few minutes, I had to resist the urge to squirm while wishing I didn't sound so damn needy, moaning like a deranged woman.

Tongue stroking, swirling, he found the perfect combination. Another few minutes, and I came, biting back a shriek. Nick straightened, hands dropping down the wall, and fastened his lips to mine the second we were face to face.

I responded whole-heartedly, riding the high for all it was worth.

This relationship might work out all right.

Twenty-one

First to wake the next morning, I almost tripped over Leglin when climbing out of bed. "Ooh. Sorry."

The hound blinked, head still resting on his legs. After bending to give him a pet in further apology, I discovered Nick's eyes were open. "Morning. Coffee?"

"Mm." He rolled onto his back and stretched, the sheet sliding down his chest. Rubbing both hands over his face, he smiled. "Sure."

Twenty minutes later, I was cooking breakfast. The faint emotions emanating from him made it clear Nick was pleased as hell with himself. It was pretty awesome, having a guy who'd not only noticed, but decided to do something about my lack of orgasms. Hopefully, he'd keep doing something about that.

Nick came into the kitchen, humming under his breath. He hugged me from behind and rested his chin on my shoulder. "What are we having?"

"Pancakes. Unless you don't like them?"

"I don't know. Haven't had them before. You've been introducing me to a wide world of new food." He released me and moved to the side, pulling a couple of mugs from the cabinet.

"If you're used to hunting for most of your meals, please don't tell me." There were a lot of things that I could deal with as long as no descriptions were offered. "I mean, if you do, that's cool and all, I just don't want to hear any particulars."

"No problem." Nick began pouring coffee for us.

"Except, you've had other jobs, so how can you not have had pancakes at some point?" I poured out batter.

"I worked night jobs. Breakfast and lunch were at home, so dinner was the only meal off our territory. Do you want milk?"

Watching bubbles rise and pop, I nodded. He collected the milk and kept talking while doctoring my coffee. "Usually, the only places open when I got off work were fast food places. Not great, but it fills you up."

"You never took a date to a restaurant before?" I flipped the pancake over.

After sniffing at the air, he moved to the table, out of easy view. "I thought women didn't like to hear about others from guys' pasts."

"No, women don't like to hear about how amazing old girlfriends were. Talking about past relationships is fine, as long as you leave that part out." *Butter. Need the butter.* Leaving the stove for the fridge, I looked at him.

His expression reminded me of one of my little brothers caught doing something they'd been told not to a thousand or so times. "If you don't want to talk about it, it's okay."

Relief peeked out, only to quickly fade. He shook his head. "I know how that one goes."

"Excuse me?" Returning to the stove, I switched done pancake for new batter after putting the butter down.

"Ask about something, say it's okay if I don't want to talk about it, and then you're going to get mad because I don't share."

I had to hide a grin, ducking my head over the pancake I was buttering. What had he been doing, reading women's magazines as research? "I'll try not to, but that's what people in a relationship are supposed to do, Nick. Share stuff."

"Yeah, I know. Okay." His breath huffed out. "No, I didn't take anyone to a restaurant before, because the girls I...it wasn't dating, Cordi. I was working in clubs. It was just sex."

Great. He was a slut puppy who'd targeted drunk girls. "Working that bouncer mojo, huh?"

"More like there were a few who wanted to screw a shifter, just so that they could say they had." He didn't hesitate to meet my eyes when I glanced over my shoulder. "It was fun, for a while, but then it started to get boring."

Hurriedly flipping the pancake, I asked, "Boring?"

"Yeah." He changed the subject. "Anything I can do to help?"

Clamping down on the question *How many?* I said, "If you want bacon, bring me the package."

"Okay." He did so, and studied my profile. "You're mad at me now."

"No, I'm not. What you did before is your business." Transferring the pancake, I oiled the griddle and poured out more batter. Anger wasn't the emotion poking its nose in his business. "Can you butter that one for me?"

"Sure." Nick moved around to handle the task. Though focusing on the bubbles popping to the surface of the cooking batter, I caught his sideways glance. "There were only three, Cordi. I wasn't going home with a different girl every night or anything like that."

"Not my business."

"Is it not your business because you're mad, or because you don't want me asking any questions about the guys you've dated?"

A demon attack would've been welcome about then, because I sucked at the relationship conversations. All I had were pancakes. "I'm not mad at you. But you did use a condom each time, right?"

"Yes. My Alpha has been quite clear we're not to run around creating half-breeds." A pause. "That's not why you were asking, is it?"

Flipping the pancake, I shook my head. "No, it wasn't. You know, I don't usually jump into bed with guys, no matter how sexy they are. There's a getting-to-know-each-other period, and even though talking about it embarrasses me, I know they're clean before getting to the point of sex with someone. I didn't ask you about any of that stuff."

"I'm clean. Shifters are immune to human diseases, and we aren't carriers of any of them either."

The tight, uneasy feeling that had been building in my stomach eased. "Really? You can't even catch a cold?"

He smiled. "We're disgustingly healthy. Or that's what the doctors who checked our pack said, after running all of their tests."

"Great." Yes, that was relief pouring through mind and body. At least my leap of lust hadn't exposed me to anything potentially lethal. Condoms weren't foolproof. Maybe my healing ability could handle anything, but that was a theory probably better not to test. "Will you get the small skillet out? Second door there."

Retrieving it, he moved around to place it on a burner. "Do I get to ask you questions?"

Fair was fair, damn it. "Sure."

"Why were you single?" His hand stroked down my back.

"Ah...just was. It's not like I'm ready for the white picket fence and one point four kids, or whatever, right now." There was also my job, my nutty mother, and being psychic just to top the list of roadblocks to long-term relationships.

Nick had no problem asking the question I'd resisted. "How many boyfriends have you had?"

"Counting you?" At his nod, I busied my hands laying bacon in the skillet. "Six. But if you mean ones I went to bed with, four."

"That's not very many." His fingers walked up my spine, and moved to stroke my hair. "Some of the regulars in the clubs I worked at were with new guys every week."

"I'm picky. Usually. Oh, I mean..." Foot, meet mouth. Eyes wide, I looked at him. "Forget that I just said that."

He laughed, and planted a kiss on my lips. "I'm going to take the fact you made up your mind that fast as a compliment."

That, I could live with. "Your pancakes are ready. The syrup's in the pantry."

"Thanks." Another kiss, and he carried off the offered plate as though it were a prize. Heaving a silent sigh of relief, I was proud at having gotten through the conversation without making more than one dumb comment.

Noticing Leglin sitting in the archway, I cooked extra bacon and a third stack of pancakes before joining Nick at the table. Setting the extra plate on the floor, I called the hound over. "Here, Linny. Try this on for size."

For such a large animal, he moved silently, not even a tap of his nails on the tile. Sniffing at the food, Leglin began eating before I had my first bite. "I think he likes it. Crap, you're not supposed to feed dogs table food, are you?"

Nick shrugged, chewing and swallowing before answering. "It won't hurt him. He's not an ordinary dog, Cordi."

Right, he was part demon. Funny how that had slipped my mind. Maybe it was because the dog was the only demon around that hadn't tried to kill me.

Breakfast over, and both of us dressed, we met back at the kitchen table with legal pads and pens to work on the case reports, which we had neglected woefully. "Okay, first off is order of events."

"Right. Meeting the Mitchells, Kate's locator spell placing Zoe in the Barrows." Nick wrote that down then paused. "What about the episodes with the vampires while we were there?"

"Skip the one I head-butted. He was on the prowl for sex. Write Derrick down."

He nodded, pen beginning to move again. "He came along after the hi-jacking by elf. Thorandryll met with Mr. Whitehaven, and had the first meeting with you."

"Yeah. Next was the visions I had handling the scarf, second try with the locating spell, and then was the first hit with my tracking sense. The construction site, vampire ashes, and Fake Elf Guy." Tapping the pen against my chin, I scowled while recalling it before dropping the pen to paper to write down what had happened.

Nick waited until I was finished. "What happened next?"

"Second client meeting with Thorandryll, trip to the morgue, and retro-cognition of a demon raising." While he added those events to his list, I wrote down brief descriptions of each. "And then the trip to Thorandryll's library. Another kick of tracking, which led to the magic string."

Pens scratched paper. Leglin slurped water in the corner. "Trip to the Orb to find out the magic string was a concealment spell. Research into Goth clubs to look for cultists." More scratching noises. "And then another tracking insight. Had a brief vision, met Logan, fell into underground tunnels, and we were attacked by Derrick and his goons."

Scritch, scratch. "Third show of Thorandryll, and then you and I drove around the Palisades. More tracking, which led to recovering the scrap from the grimoire and another attack by vampires."

Nick interrupted. "Do you think that was Derrick?"

"Has to be. He's not the first vampire I've pissed off, but it's too much of a coincidence." Watching him write that all down, I lined up the next events.

"Took the scrap to David for a look…"

He looked up from the pad. "Does the boss pay them for doing stuff like that?"

"Yep. Monthly consultation fee. Anyway, that's when we found out it was a grimoire. I went with Damian to the construction site, and that's where the first demon run-in occurred."

"Human in appearance?"

"No. It wasn't making any attempt to fit in. All scaly demon on display." Since that hadn't worked out so great, it was logical to me that they had resorted to human facades since. "Then the second demon attack, at the office."

"I've been meaning to ask how you knew it was a demon."

Train of thought interrupted, I stared at the top of his head. "Its eyes."

"What about them?" He looked up.

"They were solid black, no whites, no distinguishable pupils."

Nick leaned back. "It had blue eyes, Cordi."

"They were black. So were the ones of the demon I stabbed at the restaurant."

He shook his head. "I didn't get a good look at that one, but the first one I saw had blue eyes."

Wasn't that interesting? "Put a mark by that one. We'll come back to it."

He did so, and I continued. "The elf showed up after that, and said the grimoire had the Melding spell, which someone wanted to alter in order to meld the demonic realm with ours. And so far, the last thing was the attack at the restaurant – two demons." After a pause, I said, "Need to get Kate to try again with the locator bit."

Surveying the list he'd made, Nick scowled. "Three demon attacks, and two attacks by vampires. Which might be all Derrick-related."

"There was the ash pile. You really didn't see that his eyes were solid black?" Something was nibbling at the edge of my mind. "Because his and the one's at the restaurant were black."

"The only time his eyes looked black to me was after Percy bombed him, and the demon went black all over, Cordi."

Black. What was it… "Fake Elf Guy. His face was covered in like this swirl of darkness." We stared at each other. "Can you smell demons, Nick?"

"Those smelled like humans, at least until they began smoking." He paused. "You think…"

"The reason the one at the office didn't set off the ward was because he was wearing a human body? Yeah, that's what I think. Where's my phone? I need to call Kate." Pushing away from the table and grabbing my purse from the catchall near the archway, I dug out the phone.

<hr>

Kate wasn't happy. She detested having to visit the morgue. "Put the body in the middle of the room."

Damian and Nick obeyed, moving hastily back while I began placing candles at the four compass points around the corpse. Making use of a black wax marking pen, the witch created a circle on the linoleum. "Percival?"

"Bad magic." The parrot wasn't impressed with the scene, squawking his opinion through a beakful of feathers he was busily preening.

"Noted, but get over here and help. This is for Cordi, remember?"

"Is bad magic," the parrot insisted, flapping his wings violently. Leglin barked, the deep sound reverberating off steel surfaces. Huffing, Percy launched off the desk he'd been perched on. "Bad dog."

He landed at Kate's feet, feathers puffing. She rolled her eyes, gesturing for us to move further back. Once we'd complied, the witch began a soft chant. The candles popped, their wicks catching fire.

Kate's chant continued, her familiar rustling his feathers in irritation. A final word sent the room plunging into almost complete darkness. I blinked, noticing the lights in the hallway outside were still working.

Nick shuddered, sliding an arm around my waist. "Did it just move?"

"Hush." Kate's order was crisply delivered.

Squinting, I could see a faint outline beginning to rise above the corpse. It was grotesque in shape, twisted and streaked with sickly green. "Please tell me that's not what our souls look like."

"No, that's definitely a demonic aura. Congratulations, Jones. You were right. He was possessed."

Damian muttered something then spoke in his normal tone. "The others disappeared as smoke and ash. Why didn't this one?"

"Ooh, I know." Everyone looked at me. "I didn't puncture this guy, or use a banishing potion on him. Or maybe, since there was already black escaping, the demon was vacating the premises, and finished before I uh…sealed him up."

"Feasible," Damian decided. "But there hasn't been a true case of demon possession ever recorded."

Kate snorted. "That we know of. You're forgetting that we're running a couple of thousands of years behind in the learning department."

That statement confirmed my opinion that no one was an expert on anything. "Well, now what?"

"Now, we do heavy research on demonic possession." At her answer, Percy began cursing in French.

Mr. Whitehaven didn't appear all that pleased, seeing us entering the office. "You've been attacked here, so this isn't a safe place."

"Neither is my apartment. Not from demon possessed humans." His worried expression became one of surprise. "Kate's calling Ronnie to see what she can come up with by way of new wards."

"Possession." The boss heaved a long, mournful sigh. "Are you certain?"

"She did a spell on Dead Guy. Damian's been questioning the dude's known contacts – not that anyone's admitting to being involved in a cult. But yes, we're sure." I was looking around the reception area, which was repaired and even the furniture replaced. "Looks like nothing happened here."

Whitehaven ignored the remark. "This presents a rather large problem, Discordia. Demon possession isn't possible, unless there are already portals opened between our realm and theirs."

Nick sat on the new sofa, a deep pine green, overstuffed and comfortable-looking thing. "If they've already got portals available to them, why would they need the grimoire?"

Good question. I sat next to him, waiting for the boss's reply. Leglin followed, sitting so that he could rest his head across my thighs. Having saved my life, among other things, the hound was gaining points with me, so I petted him.

"It's a matter of…I suppose 'magic saturation' is as good a term as any. You and I have always lived in a realm with magic, whereas Discordia has not. Without that magic saturating our melded realms, we would not be able to exist here." Whitehaven paused. "Demonic magic is different, and portals won't supply enough saturation for more than a small number of demons to be present in this realm."

He gave us a few minutes to let that soak in. Glancing down at Leglin, I asked, "How does it work for him, then?"

It was as though I'd thrown some switch, and both men were suddenly holding their breath. "What?"

Nick growled, jumped to his feet and moved several steps away before turning around to stare at the hound. "So the rumor's true. It has to be, doesn't it?"

I looked at my boss. "What rumor?"

Sinking into a chair, Whitehaven focused on Leglin, his face displaying an expression I hadn't seen on it before. "I'm afraid so, Nicholas."

Whatever it was, it had to be bad news. "Hello, this is Cordi. She's still here, and would like to know what rumor you two are referring to."

"Their hounds aren't just part demon, but part shifter. Wolf shifter." Nick's lips peeled back, baring his teeth. "The original breed was normal canines. Forerunners of the breed humans have named Irish wolfhound."

Oh, my. Hand stilling, I looked down at Leglin, who moved his head just enough to meet my eyes. For a long, silent moment, another pair of eyes lay superimposed over his in my mind.

Clear, green eyes with flecks of gold dancing in their depths. Logan's eyes, when he was his tiger shape. The same intelligence was present in the hound's gaze. "Oh, my god. That's… How did they even…"

Mr. Whitehaven answered, still staring at the hound. "The elves recorded their development of the breed. A demon, captured and forced into hound shape, bred to selected bitches from their hunting packs. At that time, all the realms were one, and demons were a continuing threat to human existence."

Dropping into another chair, Nick clenched his hands into fists. "But it's said that the first litters weren't controllable. That the elves slaughtered most of the pups, keeping only a few males for breeding." He took a deep breath. "And around the same time, there were several disappearances. Female shifters. Wolves."

I couldn't seem to keep from staring at Leglin. "If he's part shifter, why can't he shift? Why is he stuck as a dog?"

"Not all who hold shifter bloodlines are able to change their forms, Discordia." My boss's voice was hushed. "The second litters were controllable and intelligent, exactly as this hound is. The elves claimed they'd simply bred the kept males back to normal dogs, to dilute the demonic blood further."

"That's why my Alpha doesn't want half breeds. The pack would be responsible for them, and those who can't shift shape sometimes go insane." Nick forced his hands to uncurl, and leaned forward, elbows resting on his knees. "When that happens, we have to kill them."

Sometimes, there were things about the supernatural types that I could go all my life and be happy not knowing. I'd now added two more to that list. My mouth opened, a question tumbling out before my brain could catch up and put the brakes on. "Does that mean that he could be *related* to you?"

Without looking up, the shifter nodded. His voice was soft. "Yeah, it does. Our pack is one of the oldest, and two women went missing during the time the elves were experimenting. Or so say our historical records. My family's bloodline traces back to both."

"And they've used them to hunt shifters." I shuddered hard enough to make the hound lift his head. He whined, looking up at my face. Forcing a smile, I touched his shoulder. "It's not your fault, bub."

Scratch the surface of any supernatural, and you'd discover unpleasant secrets. Dig deep enough, and *unpleasant* could become *horrible*. There was a question to ask, but I didn't want to find out anything horrible about my boss.

Not knowing more about him than what he'd presented had always worked for me. However, the question had to be asked. "How did you know that about demons?"

"The advantage of being rather advanced in years. One can learn many things, as long as one makes the effort to pay attention." He sounded like a schoolteacher.

Leglin dropped his head back onto my lap. Petting him calmed me enough to clarify another question I needed to ask in conjunction with that scream I remembered.

Killing vampires was one thing. They were walking corpses; a piece of wood was all it took to turn them to ash. At least as long as they'd passed the natural length of decomposition. But a human taken over by a demon?

That was something entirely different. Taking a deep breath, I asked, "Can possessed humans be saved?"

Whitehaven's smile was mournful. "No. The possession requires tearing the host's soul free of its physical housing, and leaves the body too polluted for that soul to return home."

My eyes closed as I leaned my head back, air sighing out between my slack lips. Knocking a punk unconscious here and there was something I had no problem doing. Staking vampires? No problem. But killing humans? That wasn't what the good guys did, and being a good guy was definitely my agenda. "Well, that's a relief."

Nick's cell phone went off, and I listened to him jump up. "My Alpha. I'll be back in a minute."

Opening my eyes, I watched him hurry down the hall toward Kate's office and wondered what to do if he was needed at home. There hadn't been any calls for him since the second vampire attack. Maybe he'd told his Alpha what was going on, and the guy was just checking on him.

I needed a lot more information, so that I'd have a better idea of what to expect, dating a shifter. Maybe we could talk about it once things were settled with the cases.

"If you have any reason to visit the Palisades, I want you to call ahead and inform Logan. Do you know where his business is located?"

"Not really. I mean, he told me the address, and we went there the other night, but I don't remember where it is." Studying my boss's face, my curiosity about his origins rose again. Old, strong, and able to do some magic. Calm even when everyone else was freaking out. Apparently not afraid of anything or anyone. He was kind of like a giant elf, just not arrogant or as pretty. Though not exactly affectionate, he always came across as warm and caring.

Shoving the curiosity back into its box, I smiled. "So, are you hiring him?"

151

"At least for this case. The Palisades appear to be involved, so it's best to have someone available who is familiar with the environs. His place of business is located on West Haymill." After my nod, Whitehaven asked, "You do trust him?"

"Yes, I do. He's been nothing but helpful since we met."

The boss smiled, but if he had anything to say, Nick's return kept him silent.

"Problem?" I asked, and the shifter shook his head.

"Nothing important. We should probably go back to your place."

"Sure." Rising, I petted Leglin's head and remembered a final question. "Has anyone found out what Mr. Mitchell does?"

"He's an architect."

Architect. Wasn't that interesting? "Is it okay if I borrow one of the laptops?" They had all the search software installed.

Whitehaven inclined his head in permission. "Certainly."

A few minutes later, just about to leave, I remembered something else. "Did anyone talk to Mrs. Mitchell yet?"

"No, she hasn't returned Kate's phone call. I'll place another call," Whitehaven assured me.

"All right. Thanks."

Twenty-two

Nick's hand dropped from the steering wheel to my thigh. With the previous revelation, the urge to scan the dog's mind was growing, but I was resisting it. If Leglin was part shifter, he was more of a person than some people considered their pets. It would be rude to pry.

Not to mention, one hell of a shock if the hound thought like a person. Normal animals thought mostly in pictures, sounds, and smells, using only a few words each assigned importance to. Their minds were confusing, so I usually relied on my empathic ability and gauged their moods instead.

There were a few psychics who specialized in animal communication. They'd blown several animal whisperers out of the water, establishing lucrative careers for themselves. Not me. I preferred people, whose minds were easier for me to understand.

I needed a distraction before the urge overwhelmed me. "Did your pack's territory come through during the Melding?"

Nick smiled, his eyes flicking to the review mirror to check traffic behind us. "Yeah. Not everyone's did, which I guess you know. Some think it has to do with blood and ties, for those that did."

"Come again?"

"Our pack was first formed over four thousand years ago. We've held the same territory for most of that time. Our dead are buried there." He paused, signaling a lane change to pass a slower moving car.

"Most of those that did come through are ancient territories. Newer packs with less established ones lost theirs."

Listening, I suddenly realized I had no clue which of the four faerie mounds that had appeared in Santo Trueno was Thorandryll's. That was another thing to remedy as soon as possible.

To the east, in San Antonio, I knew there were a dozen. Larger cities had received bigger influxes of supernaturals. "How many packs are here?"

"Two larger and about a dozen smaller ones. Ours is one of the larger ones."

"How many is 'large'?"

His answer astounded me. "Around twelve hundred or so, last count."

Census time was going to see a huge jump in population, if everyone was honest about their numbers. I knew that there were at least a few thousand vampires in the Barrows, possibly a lot more. "Wow."

His face dissolved into a proud smile. "We've been lucky."

Maybe not entirely lucky. Glancing over my shoulder at Leglin, I wondered if he had understood our conversation about him earlier.

The hound's head turned, his eyes briefly meeting mine before going back to watching the scenery. It was the work of three seconds to convince myself it was important to know what his mood was.

Opening a tiny crack in my shield, I peeked at his emotional state.

Interested. Content.

Before my curiosity led to delving deeper, I closed my mental shield tight. His emotions weren't as complex as a human's, but more so than any true dog's that I'd scanned.

A true dog usually had just one emotion uppermost. Not so the hound.

Did he dislike being treated like a dog? Was he aware that he couldn't shift? Several other questions buffeted my brain, but fell aside as a blazing line of silvery red flashed into existence in my mind.

"I have a trail. Turn around."

Twenty-three

"You wouldn't let me drive, so you're going to have to go faster." I was getting extremely impatient with our slow pace.

Nick tossed an exasperated look at me, but increased the truck's speed. The thread shimmered down the highway, fading in the distance. *Are we heading toward the Palisades?* I dug out my phone, just in case.

A sign flashed past, and the truck slowed. "I'll let you know if there are any cops around, Nick. Keep going."

Nick increased the truck's speed again. Almost certain of our destination, I began pulling up Logan's number.

"Who are you calling?"

"Logan. Whitehaven said to call him if the Palisades came into play again. He hired him as a local liaison."

The tiger shifter answered on the second ring. "Hello, Discord."

Just the sound of his voice woke my smile. "Hey, I think we're heading your way. My tracking sense is wide awake."

"All right. Drop by here, and I'll be ready to go."

"Cool. I'll call back if I'm wrong." We traded good-byes and ended the call.

Logan was waiting in front of an opened garage door, and waved us toward it. The truck stopped before entering, Nick rolling the window down.

"We'll take my truck. Yours is too new. Someone might mess with it," Logan said. A single jerk of his head signified Nick's acceptance of the idea, and we rolled through.

Two other men were present, and they stayed well back while we exited the truck, their gazes glued to Leglin. Nick grudgingly accepted Logan's offer to shake, before the tiger turned to me. "Still have your trail?"

"Yeah. It's a good one."

"Let's load up and go, then." He led the way to the other truck. Leglin had to jump into the bed, since it was a regular cab. I sat between the two shifters.

"Open the back window, and he can stick his head inside," Logan suggested while starting the engine. I did so, twisting around as he guided the truck out of the garage.

Still afternoon, the streets were crowded, and I wondered if the trail would continue to hold. "Left up at the next light, please."

My directions were the only conversation for the next twenty minutes.

Eventually, buildings and crowded streets gave way to actual houses, all old and in dire need of repair or razing. Those dribbled off until Logan stopped the truck at the end of a road, between two that were slowly collapsing in on themselves. "We're out of road. Now what?"

"I guess we walk." I slid out through the driver's door, following him to the tailgate. He lowered it, and Leglin jumped down. He spun around, head held high, tail whacking Logan in the leg.

Taking a step sideways to keep his balance, Logan said, "Ow."

"Sorry. I'm going to have to register his tail as a dangerous weapon."

He rubbed his thigh. "Let me know if you need an affidavit."

Nick joined us, sliding an arm around my waist and scanning our surroundings. "Which way, Cordi?"

"Straight on. Let's go, Leglin." The hound bounded ahead, ranging side to side with his nose to the ground and tail waving like a banner. At least he was enjoying the outing. It didn't take long for me to begin to feel cranky, with the heat, bugs, and vegetation all seeming to be out to get me.

Trees seemed determined to catch and pull my hair. Scratches opened up all over my legs, thanks to the lower-lying weeds and brush. Shorts had been a huge mistake.

"I wish we'd brought some water." Slapping a bug off my arm, I grimaced at the streak of blood left behind. "The country life, it ain't for me."

"I can carry you," Nick offered, wiping sweat off his brow with the back of one hand.

"Thanks, but I'd just sweat and bleed all over you."

Logan spoke up. "Is this the longest your tracking sense has stayed active?"

"No." The question was enough to cause a mini-flashback. A blade held up, blood dripping black in moonlight. Pushing it away, I realized that I'd stopped, and both men were watching me. "What?"

"Maybe we should take a breather. You're pale." Nick reached for my hand. "And cold."

"I'm fine. Bad memory." Pulling free and walking, I explained. "The first time my tracking sense popped up, the trail lasted for four days."

Batting aside a tumbleweed, Nick caught up. "Four days? What did it lead to?"

"Well, the first day I spent trying to convince someone to listen. The trail led to California, and a serial killer who liked to do his victims with a straight razor." Mom hadn't known how to handle it, so had called Dad. He'd convinced the right people to listen, and then accompanied the two Feds and me.

Afterwards, he'd taken me to Disneyland to try and offset some of the horror. Come to think of it, that sort of set the tone for how each parent handled my decision to join Arcane Solutions.

"How old were you?"

"Nineteen. I was just getting a decent handle on my abilities." Hopping over a branch, I pointed ahead. "It ends up there. Can either of you see anything?"

No, because trees and heavy undergrowth obscured the view. We kept going until Nick pulled me to a halt. "What?"

He sniffed the air, glancing at Logan before answering. "There's a dead body in there. Stay here and I'll take a look."

It was tempting to agree, but no. "I've seen dead bodies before."

As the stench hit my nose, my decision wavered, but turning chicken in front of them didn't sit well. Upon reaching the body, my first reaction was to move away. I knew not to contaminate a crime scene, so vomited the remains of breakfast a good distance from it.

Neither shifter felt the need to unload their stomachs, or remarked on my doing so. Dragging a hand across my mouth, I fumbled for the phone and called Damian while telling them, "Don't touch anything or go any closer."

The warlock answered on the first ring. "We found the woman who was sacrificed in my vision."

"Where?"

Looking around, I gave up before even attempting an answer. "Do your GPS tracking magic on my phone. We're out in the hills, way past the edge of the Palisades, pretty much BFE. Oh, and bring some water."

"All right, give us a moment to locate you." He spoke to someone before asking, "How bad is it?"

"Bad. Demons eat their sacrifices." Much of her was missing, bones marked with gouges from large teeth. The hanks of dark hair still attached to strips of scalp were my evidence she was the sacrifice. Part of her face was still present.

"Damn." He breathed the word. "All right, we have your location. We're on the way."

"Don't forget the water." Call ended, I looked around for somewhere to sit that didn't include a view of the corpse. "Cops are on the way. Leglin, here boy."

He obeyed, sitting next to the rock I picked as a seat. Thanks to the trees, there was plenty of shade available. The men crouched down, exchanging mutters while pointing out things to each other.

It wasn't long before they finished, walking over to pick shady spots. Nick vented a gusty sigh. "There's some faint tracks left, and a torn piece of plastic under her left shoulder."

"Looks like those cheap plastic painter's drop cloths you can buy at a hardware store," Logan clarified.

"Wrapped her up. I guess even cultists don't like getting their cars messy." Digging my fingers into Leglin's ruff, I gave his neck and chest a good scratching.

No one really had anything else to say, so we waited quietly for the law. It took a while, with the faint sound of sirens heralding their arrival. Those were shut off, indicating they'd found Logan's truck.

Damian appeared first, Schumacher on his heels, a couple of uniforms following behind. More people appeared a minute or two later.

Nick jumped up to talk to them, and I let him, catching the bottle of water the warlock tossed my way. First rinsing out my mouth meant I could enjoy the long drink that followed. "Ah."

Everyone received a bottle of water, and Damian conjured up a bowl so that Leglin could have a drink too.

We waited. Crime scenes take a while to process. The sun was dipping toward the horizon before Damian came over. "Cordi, do you think you could try and see if there are any other bodies out here?"

Nick was objecting before he'd finished. "I can look, if no one has a problem with my shifting to do it."

More than happy to hand off that job, I nodded when the warlock glanced my way. "Faster his way. My way might not work."

"All right. If you'll step over here," he led Nick off a ways, until a waist-high tangle of grass and weeds partially blocked sight of him, protecting the modesty of the one uniformed female. She looked disappointed.

I smothered a giggle, which faded further on its own, buried under the beginning of a vision. "Damian!"

"Just a min…"

"Vision." I heard him running toward me, and stuck out a hand.

Grabbing it, he asked, "What do you see?"

"The cavern again. Cultists and," I needed to take a hard swallow. "A whole bunch of demons."

"Geeze, I hate when she does this," Schumacher muttered.

There was a struggle, two cultists dragging a shrouded figure toward the altar. "This sacrifice isn't so willing."

A couple of other cultists broke rank to help, and the four simply picked up their victim. She struggled, and even got in a few good kicks and elbowings, but the cultists won. They chained her face up and some of the covering moved enough to show she was dressed in something flowing and dark crimson in color. Another figure entered the cavern, dressed in a red robe with ornate black and gold embroidery. "I think the leader just showed up. Damn it, I can't see his face. " The shadow cast by his hood was too dark.

He lifted something high, held in both hands. "He has the book."

"What are they doing with it?" Damian asked.

Cultists moved about, lighting candles and drawing symbols on the base of the rock altar. "It looks like they're doing the spell."

Dread curled inside when the leader picked up a knife and began intoning a chant. This couldn't have happened yet. Zoe's shimmer was still shining gold, and she was their sacrifice, wasn't she? Demons weren't running loose in the streets either. "I don't understand."

Five cultists arranged themselves around the altar, kneeling with bowls of some sort in their hands. One at each hand and foot, and the last at the head. The leader moved around, making shallow cuts on Zoe's wrists and the soles of her feet. I felt the sting of each. At another gesture from the leader, the cultist at her head yanked off the material covering her head, and I forgot how to breathe.

"It's not Zoe."

"Then who is it, Cordi?" Damian asked.

I didn't answer. Seeing yourself chained, about to be sacrificed, is an interesting, voice-stealing experience.

Watching a knife plunge deep into your chest and rip you wide open? Not so much.

A scream burst from between my lips when the pain blasted through my chest, my body stiffening while everything went black. Convulsions followed, and barely felt hands caught hold, lowering me to the ground.

There was shouting, muffled by my frantic attempts to breathe. My body was full of lava, and there was blood in my mouth, filling my throat.

A tiny spark of light broke the darkness, growing larger to become a small, bent, wrinkled man. Deep brown eyes gazed into mine, lips pursing in disapproval. With weathered, walnut brown skin, he appeared to be Native American. He shook his head, long silver gray hair rustling. "You're not following the right path."

"Excuse me?" My voice sounded normal, even though I was choking on my own blood. "Who are you?"

"Eh, call me an interested bystander. You're on a course filled with danger, Discordia Angel Jones." His lips curved slightly. "Give your mother my compliments on that name. It suits."

"I'm sort of dying here, so I doubt there'll be a chance to pass that on." Awareness of what was going on with my body was fading fast. A voice seemed to be whispering to me.

"Giving up that easy, are you?" The old man shook his head. "Maybe I'm backing the wrong horse."

"I have no clue what you're talking about. Can you help me?"

He smiled, revealing strong white teeth that belied his apparent age. "Silly girl, what do you think I've been doing? Not that you ever thank me or anything."

Great, I was dying, and stuck listening to a crazy delusion in the process. "And you are...?"

A scowl moved his wrinkles in odd directions. "That, you'll have to figure out for yourself. Now, can you hear him?"

That lone voice was still whispering to me. Quiet desperation seeped from it. "Yes, but who..."

"Shush the questions." He rolled his eyes, one hand rising in an impatient gesture. "Listen to him, and let him guide you back. I'm far from done with you, young lady."

He turned, beginning to walk away, and then stopped to look back at me. "Pay closer attention to those colors."

With that, he disappeared, leaving me alone in the darkness. Well, not completely alone. The voice was still there, though even fainter.

It was hard to reach for. I couldn't feel anything, didn't know what was happening to my body. Making one last, panicked effort, I reached out and caught hold of the whisper.

Light blazed, burning my eyes. Hot air rushed deep into my lungs, and I retched, bloody drool spilling out. Sound returned, but I couldn't make sense of it at first. Someone had my hands. Someone else was supporting me in a semi-recline.

My first clear image was Nick's face. He was shirtless, face pale and drawn. "Cordi."

"Hey." My voice cracked. Someone laughed in sharp relief, probably Schumacher. Nick squeezed my hands, head dipping over them to press his lips against my knuckles. I rolled my head enough to find out who was holding me.

Dark green eyes, flecked with bright gold. Logan also looked a bit pale. He smiled. "Gave us a scare."

"Sorry."

"Somebody owes me a shirt." Sitting on my rock, I held the front of my tank top closed with one hand. The material was tacky with drying blood, and ripped open from neck to hem.

Everything but my shoes was covered or at the very least, splattered. Not that any of it had been my first concern. Checking the shimmer had been. Zoe was still alive.

So was I, which could only mean one thing: a new ability.

Damian had dragged Nick away to do the promised searching after one of the EMTs checked my vitals and announced they were normal.

Logan removed the work shirt he wore, revealing a snug white tee, and silently offered it to me. His forearms had smears of dried blood, and his left hand was coated in it, because he'd cleared the blood out of my mouth.

"Thanks." After a glance around, I decided everyone had already gotten a look at the lacy, once lilac bra under my tank. Yanking off the ruined top, I quickly slipped the shirt on.

"I'll replace that," the shifter said, nodding at the wadded remains.

"You tore my shirt up?"

He offered a sheepish grin. "When the blood soaked through, I thought you'd been shot or something. But there wasn't a wound."

Yet. My future wasn't looking bright enough to wear shades for. "Oh. Don't worry about it."

"No, she seems fine now." Phone glued to his ear, Damian paused a few feet away, his gaze raking over us before looking around. "I don't know. Yes, that's correct. Four minutes."

Fingers busy with buttons, I asked, "Four minutes what?"

Logan's eyes widened. "You were dead for a little while, Discord."

"No I wasn't. I could hear someone saying my name." At least, it had felt like my name being whispered, over and over again.

A slight pucker appeared between his brows. "I think that was Nick. But seriously, you weren't breathing, didn't have a pulse. I checked."

"Cordi, can you..." Damian paused when I held up a hand.

"I saw myself being killed." Taking a deep breath, I added, "Guess I have precognition, since I'm still here." For now.

The warlock grimaced. "Sorry. Mr. Whitehaven is worried."

"Tell him I'm fine." I hoped the boss didn't ask us to come in, because I'd have to relive the whole thing. It was too soon for that. Logan dropped down beside me, an arm hesitantly sliding around my shoulders.

Letting go, bawling my eyes out and yelling about how unfair everything was seemed like a potentially good idea. I was terrified.

How often were precogs wrong? Were visions of the future only one possibility of what could happen?

Or was I definitely going to end up on that altar with a knife sticking out of my chest?

I didn't know any psychics with precognition to ask. Hell, I didn't know any other psychics at all.

"It won't happen." The shifter's quiet assurance poked at my barely established resolve not to break down. Rapid blinking didn't keep the building tears from falling.

I buried my face against his shoulder, failing miserably at stopping the flood. Logan's response was an embrace as a soft rasp jump-started his purr. At least my sobbing wasn't too loud. I could hear Damian over it.

"She needs rest. He's helping to search for more bodies. Yes, he's here. All right." A pause. "Logan, is it possible for you to take her somewhere quiet until Nick's finished?"

"I'll take her home. Someone will have to give him a lift, because his truck's at the garage I work at."

"I'll bring him along. Cordi, you get some rest and calm down." Damian patted my shoulder. "We'll figure it all out."

Without further ado, Logan adjusted his hold and stood, sweeping me up. "I can walk."

"You died. That takes a bite out. Grab your purse and call your hound."

Obeying seemed my best bet, and really, being carried off by a hunk of a guy, like some heroine on a romance cover, felt kind of cool.

Way cooler than getting stabbed.

Twenty-four

He carried me the whole way back, not setting me down until we were beside his truck. After retrieving the keys from a front pocket and unlocking the door, he stepped back while opening it. Leglin jumped inside.

"Guess he didn't like riding in back," I said, scratching at my chin. There were dried flakes of blood under my fingernails when I checked. A rub of a finger under one eye showed dark with damp mascara.

I climbed in, wanting a shower to wash away the visible marks of the whole horrible situation. "I need something from Nick's truck."

"We'll swing by," Logan promised, sliding behind the wheel and starting the engine. He eased the truck free of the crowd of vehicles surrounding us, and pointed the nose toward the Palisades.

Leglin tentatively licked my right hand. When I didn't push him away, the hound settled in to wash both. Closing my eyes, I leaned my head back. "This has been one hell of a bad day."

"I was wondering about something. Do you think that tunnel we fell into might lead to this cavern you keep having visions of?"

"I don't know. Can you smell demons?" Eyes opening, I turned my head just enough to view Logan's profile.

"Yeah, they smell bitter and smoky." The corner of his mouth quirked. "Guess I just answered my own question."

I grinned briefly. "You'll make an investigator yet."

"So location still unknown." His fingers drummed the steering wheel. "Feel like talking about it?"

"No. Oh crap. I'd better call my mom." She'd be worried, not having heard from me since last night's shocker. Freeing one hand from Leglin's ardent attentions, I found my cell phone.

"Hey, Mom."

"Cordi." She sounded relieved, which added to the burden of guilt I was carrying.

"I'm sorry I didn't call earlier, but I'm fine."

"Just as long as you have, and you're safe. Is Nick there?"

"Uh, no. He's busy. But I have Leglin and we're with Logan right now, heading home." I made a note to grab the sword out of Nick's truck too, just in case.

"All right. I'll call your father and let him know you're safe."

She'd called Dad? Betty probably loved that. "Okay, thanks, Mom. Love you."

"Love you too. Be careful."

"I will. I'll try to call earlier tomorrow too. Bye."

"Bye, honey."

Ending the call with a sigh, I dropped the phone back into my purse. "There."

"We'll be at the garage in a few minutes. What did you need out of Nick's truck?" Logan slowed and stopped at a red light. Music pounded the atmosphere from the low rider next to us. The driver stared at me.

I stuck my tongue out at him before answering Logan. "Laptop and sword."

Head turning, he raised an eyebrow. "Sword?"

"Kills demons."

"Oh. All right, I'll grab both. Do me a favor, and keep your hound in the truck. Some of the guys have been hunted before." The light changed, and he let off the brake.

"Did you know the hounds are part shifter?"

"There's always been rumors."

"They are. Being part demon, Leglin couldn't be here unless he's also part something else that doesn't need demonic magic. He's like," I'm no scientist, so went with what seemed logical. "One third each demon, shifter, and regular dog."

Logan glanced at the hound. "Are you keeping him?"

"He's on loan."

"He's bound to you by blood. If the elf's at fault for the danger you're in, you can demand the hound as," he hesitated. "As hazard pay."

"But that would make me his owner, and he's kind of a person."

"Elves consider hounds little more than possessions, Discord. Not pets or people."

"Well, that doesn't mean I have to go with the flow." The hound was a thorny issue for me.

"He'd be an asset," the shifter remarked. "Vampires are demonic."

"They are?" No one had told me that. "Really demonic, not just act like demons?"

Logan chuckled. "According to legend, the first vampire was a child of Lilith. She was a succubus, impregnated by a human. Which is almost unheard of, since it usually takes a combination of humans, succubus, and incubus to produce a child."

After a minute of trying to puzzle that one out, I just asked. "Explanation, please."

"The succubus has sex with a male human, then with an incubus to pass the collected," he hesitated, shooting me a glance. "Sperm. The incubus turns around and uses that sperm to impregnate a human female."

My first reaction was "Eww, gross!"

He laughed again. "Here's the weird part: those children aren't vampires. Sometimes they're hybrid succubi or incubi. Other times, they're dhampyrs."

"Wait. Dhampyrs are for real?"

"Most things are, or were."

"Fan-freaking-tastic. Vampires that can walk in the sun." We reached the garage, and Logan honked. The door rolled up almost instantly. He drove inside, and parked.

"Be right back."

"Sure." I seriously needed to re-think the whole private investigator career. Fast food or retail sounded far less dangerous, and even downright relaxing.

Logan returned, handing both sword and laptop case over. I realized that I felt a little better. "Thanks."

"No problem."

"No, I mean, well, yeah, for getting these, but mostly for the distraction by vampire info."

He smiled. "You're welcome."

Logan sat at the table, nursing a beer. The sword lay within easy reach.

I'd had a shower and was preparing dinner. Nick hadn't called yet. "If you need to go after you eat, it's okay."

"No plans for the evening. I'm good."

The potatoes were almost ready for draining. "I'm going to make a wild guess that you called Whitehaven while I was in the shower."

"You're a natural at this private investigating thing." He grinned when I looked over my shoulder. "I thought someone should update him."

"Thanks. The boss does like knowing we're still in one piece."

"He cares about his people. What are we having?"

"Chicken-fried steaks." I laid one in the waiting skillet, and after the crackling become less deafening, heard someone sniffing. "Is that you, or Leglin?"

"Both," Logan admitted. "Do you feel like talking about it yet?"

"There's not much to say. I have to find Zoe, destroy that book, and not get killed doing either." Watching the oil bubble around the edges, I sighed. "And yeah, I'm freaking scared to death. If I'm the sacrifice now, where does that leave Zoe?"

"Probably safe. Have any of you considered the fact her case might be a set up?"

"What?" I turned around, shaking my head. "No, it can't be. I'm empathic, Logan. Her mother was a hair away from being completely frantic when I met with them."

He studied the condensation on his beer bottle. "Maybe she's not part of it."

About to naysay that, I paused. "You may be onto something. Her husband certainly didn't seem to care that Zoe was missing. But that opens up more questions."

"Such as?"

"Why the hell go through such a convoluted mess to get me, and why would I be a sacrificial choice?"

Logan seemed fascinated by the beer bottle, the tip of one finger chasing drops across the label. "I think you may have answered that second one the night we met. You're a psychic with more than one or two abilities. You're powerful. Power fuels a lot of things, and this spell is a huge thing, Discord."

"Okay, let's work with your take. Can you get out the laptop and boot it up? I want to check something before we go any further with that."

"Sure." I continued cooking while instructing the shifter how to access programs and run the search I wanted. By the time I had three plates loaded up, Logan had the answer. "He's listed as the architect for that hotel's blue prints."

He pushed the laptop out of the way, and I set a plate down for him. "Damn, this looks good."

"Thanks. Okay, so it's way more possible Mitchell is involved. I still don't know why a vampire would've been there. Zoe had already been missing for days by then." I put a plate down for Leglin, and waved my hand. "Let's forget the vampire parts for a minute."

Logan made a sound of agreement, and watched me sit down with my own plate. "Mitchell arranged for Zoe to disappear, in order to have a reason to establish contact with me. Thorandryll said the book had gone missing three days before our meeting. The second meeting."

"Okay. This is really good." He'd begun eating.

"Thanks. Would elves want the demon realm brought into this one?"

The shifter shook his head. "I doubt it. Demons can kill elves. One of the few things that can."

So Thorandryll's interest in me probably wasn't murderous. Good to know. "You know, I've avoided the press, and vampires aren't exactly media darlings. They're the ones that know the most about me, since most of my cases have dealt with them. So how did the cultists figure out I'd make such an awesome sacrifice?"

Logan chewed, eyes slowly scanning the kitchen. After swallowing, he set the fork down, had a drink of beer, and then met my eyes. "Rumors and gossip. Word of mouth by satisfied clients."

"You are getting good at this." I reached to pat his shoulder. "Must be that, because Thorandryll knew I had more than one ability. He said as much after that demon showed up at the office. Plus, the first time he mentioned being told that I work alone."

We ate quietly for a few minutes, and then Logan asked, "So what would happen if you disappeared? Took a vacation to Tahiti or something?"

Boy, did that idea sound amazingly tempting. "I don't know. But it would probably mean someone else ending up with their guts spilled all over the place."

The shifter sighed. "Yeah, guess so."

"A totally selfish part of me liked the idea." We traded a grin.

"But you're not going to go with it," he said, and I shook my head.

"Good guys don't hide from trouble. I try to be one of the good guys." My cell phone rang. "Let me get that."

The second I answered, Jo's worried voice sounded. "Cordi, Kate's here and she's been in one hell of a fight. Percy's screeching his damn head off about demons, and says he has to talk to you."

My stomach dropped. "I'll be right there."

Logan was already rising, sword in hand. "Where?"

"Let me call Nick, leave him a message. It'll be faster to teleport."

Twenty-five

Kate lay under a thick coating of David's healing salve, her skin blistered and raw. Hunks of melted hair guaranteed to piss her off were clumped around her face.

David sat at the bedside, eyes closed and hands up, maintaining a thin bubble of blue over her. Magical life support.

"Is she going to be all right?" My whisper turned Percy's head, and with a squawk, he launched himself from the headboard to land on my shoulder.

"Found girl. Demons!"

The parrot was shaking, his nails digging through my jacket. Jo herded us into the hallway, shutting the door. "She's pretty bad off. Ronnie and Damian are on their way. David's keeping her asleep until they get here. We're going to have to move her to the hospital."

It was really bad, if the coven thought the hospital was a good idea. I felt useless, which made me angry. "Okay. Percy, where did you see the girl?"

"Club. 'Stay in car, Percy'," he mimicked Kate's voice perfectly. "Demons attack my witch. I feel, go. We fight demons, Cordi. My witch..." the parrot choked, stretching his neck and lifting his wings. "I bring her here."

He settled when I stroked his feathers, beak open and one eye focused on the bedroom's door. "Which club, Percy?"

With a chirp, he burst out singing 'Bodies'. It was no help at all, but in a pinch, I thought he could stand in for Drowning Pool's lead singer. It took a few minutes to calm him down enough to pass the parrot over to Jo. "We're going to try and find her car. Call Mr. Whitehaven, tell him what happened."

"He was next on my list," she said, cuddling Percy. "Be careful, Cordi."

"That's my plan." I led the way downstairs, trying to hold in anger, worry, and fear. Crystals murmured when I halted in the middle aisle, shivering in their velvet nests.

Logan moved around me, his gaze on one large, deep blue crystal as it began to chime discordantly. "You'd better calm down before they explode."

Taking a deep breath, I spent a few moments clearing my head, forcing away those three emotions. Calm determination was what I needed. "Okay. I know what Kate's car looks like, so I'll try teleporting us to it."

Eyes narrowing, he didn't immediately take hold of the hand I offered. "Wait a minute. Don't you need to see where you're going when you teleport?"

"It's a car, Logan. It's going to be in a parking lot, and those all pretty much look alike." Leglin bumped my other hand, pressing against my leg as I took hold of his collar. Wiggling my fingers, I told the shifter, "Trust me."

"All right." His hand closed around mine.

Closing my eyes, I visualized the silver rear end of her car. "Here we go."

Logan spoke before I opened my eyes. "This doesn't look like a parking lot, and I smell elves."

"What the…" Leglin's bark cut me off, and elves seemed to pour from the woodwork in response. Every single one of them armed with swords or bows, and all the weapons were pointing at us. Logan stood extremely still, sword held point down, and grip on my hand tightening. Massive confusion filled me. "This hasn't happened before."

"Miss Jones?" Thorandryll appeared, people clearing a path for him. "What are you doing here?"

"I have no idea. But I'm, uh, on the clock." How discreet was that?

"Ah. It's all right. Return to your pursuits, these are guests of mine," the elf ordered, and the others quickly cleared out. As soon as the last was out of sight, Thorandryll spoke again. "What's happened?"

Where to start? If he'd kept the damn grimoire in a more secure place, or destroyed it the second it came into his hands, none of this would have happened. Letting go of Logan's hand and the hound's collar, I swung a punch. "You bastard!"

It didn't land, smacking into Thorandryll's palm. That was fine, because his hand closed around it, and the elf yanked me closer. My knee hit the real target while he glared at me, and I stepped back as Thorandryll bent over, skin a yellowish white as he gasped for air. Logan grabbed me around the waist, swinging me away before I kicked the elf in his arrogant face. "Okay, Discord. We have to be here for a reason, and I don't think it's for you to beat on him."

He did have a point, and I had gotten one good shot in. The elf was still trying to catch his breath, and warily watching us. "If you stop me next time, we can't be friends anymore."

"I won't stop you," the shifter promised, arm loosening. "But tonight's not the right time, Discord."

"Yeah, I hear you. I'm done - for now." He let go, and I was thrilled when the elf retreated slightly. "Kate was attacked by demons tonight. She might not make it. They kidnapped a teenaged girl. I found the woman they sacrificed in that vision, and had another where I get ripped wide open as the sacrifice for the spell in the damn book you lost."

"I didn't…"

"Shut up. Logan's right, we're here for a reason. The demons that took Kate down might still be there. You," I'd stalked close enough to jab a finger in the elf's chest. "Are going to help us."

"Of course." Thorandryll straightened, trying to regain his composure. I bet no one had ever kneed him in the family jewels before, and was damn proud to have been the first. "Give me just a minute to arm myself, Miss Jones."

"I was thinking more of you being a distraction. Like dinner."

Logan touched my shoulder. "Discord."

"Oh, all right. Go get your sword, or bow, or whatever." Waving the elf off, I turned to face the shifter. "I was joking."

He grinned. "Sure you were."

Standing on the lawn, I surveyed Thorandryll and the milling pack of hounds. "I can't teleport everyone, and if they turn on Logan, I'll be using something sharper than my knee next time."

The elf flinched. "They won't, Miss Jones. Handle the transport of yourself and those two. The other hounds will follow Leglin, and I will travel with them."

"Fine." I hoped my teleportation ability didn't malfunction a second time while grabbing hold of both shifter and hound. "Take two."

Chilly night air caressed my face, and Kate's car waited in vain, the lone occupant of a smallish parking lot. "The Velvet Razor. There's a name for a Goth club."

Thorandryll and his hounds appeared. Logan held me back when I took a step toward the club's entrance. "Let him go first."

"But…"

"But, nothing. I smell death." He refused to release my hand. Hounds ran into the club, Thorandryll shooting us an arrogant look before following after them.

Leglin was the only one who stayed, his eyes focused on the entrance. I slung my purse strap over one shoulder and my head, digging out the dagger before zipping it shut and pushing it toward my back.

Danger oozed from every shadow. Logan let go, hefting the sword and taking a few steps forward. Leglin growled, his hackles rising. Thorandryll's yell, and the sudden tumult of snarling hounds, jolted me into motion.

Avoiding Logan's grasp, I skidded to a halt as a demon popped into existence directly in my path. The dagger caught it in the stomach.

Leglin rushed by, lunging into another one. I spun around, teleporting away from the demon behind me and buried the dagger between its ragged, green-tinged black wings.

Logan was swinging the sword as if he knew how to use it. A scaly arm went flying, the sword keening something vicious and eager. The fight inside the club spilled out, and things become too confusing to keep close track of.

It didn't take long for my head to start pounding with the teleporting and use of TK to toss demons away. Claws cut through the sleeve of my jacket, leaving bleeding furrows in my left forearm. Leglin jumped that one, and was back instantly with two more hounds. They circled, holding the demons back and creating a path through the mess toward Logan.

I went down practically at his feet, and swiped at scaly legs while the sword whistled overhead. The dagger didn't make any sound, just glowed brighter red with each trip through demon flesh.

A really large, dusky black demon flew through the air, landing on Kate's car. The hood dented under one cloven hoof, the windshield cracking under the other. I hoped her insurance had a trashed–by-demon clause. "Leglin, sic that sucker!"

The hound raced off, but Logan grunted and blood splattered down. Grabbing hold of his leg, I looked up to see how badly he was hurt, and the green shield suddenly appeared around us. A demon ran into it, striking with a thud and bouncing off. "Logan?"

He was panting. Dropping to one knee, he planted the sword's tip on asphalt and grinned. "Already healing. How are you holding up?"

"I'd kill for my bed and two days' sleep." Not to mention a shot of something that would kill the pain in my head. My brain was screaming in protest. "Not sure how long I can hold this shield thing."

"You're bleeding." His fingers hovered over the dark, wet rents in my jacket sleeve.

"Yeah, that's not helping." I spotted Leglin's return. The hound tore into another demon, chunks flying and hitting the shield. "Ugh. Can you see Thorandryll?"

"He's fine. Looks like he's enjoying himself."

Thunder lanced from temple to temple, and I dropped the dagger to grab my head. "Ahh!"

"Discord?" The shifter touched my hair.

"I'm about out of juice." Gray seeped into my vision, and I squeezed my eyes shut, hoping to remain conscious.

"All right." Logan rose, swinging a leg over mine so that he stood over me. "Just trust me and the hounds."

Like I had a choice, as agony smothered me. The shield faded, and the sword began keening again, its song cutting my eardrums to shreds. I stayed put, eyes closed, and my hands sliding over my ears to try to muffle the noise. I did trust him. Something about Logan inspired trust.

Silence dropped a sudden blanket. Cracking my eyes open, I asked, "What happened?"

Logan knelt, straddling my legs, and laid the sword down. "I don't know. They just left. Let me see your arm."

He shucked out of his t-shirt after helping take my jacket off. My head was full of thunder, multi-colored sparkles shooting across my vision. Hounds milled around us, sniffing the demon grit left behind.

Thorandryll walked up while Logan was wrapping his tee around my arm. "Rather rousing skirmish."

"Did you find a girl in there?"

A trail of pink glimmered, hiding the elf's face. "There are several bodies inside."

Crap didn't quite cover the situation. "Damn it all to hell."

Logan overrode my protests, accepting the elf's offer of his healer and home. The healer turned out to be Mr. Nosy who'd assumed I was the new flavor of the moment.

"Aren't you the little warrior?" Alleryn asked while surveying me after Thorandryll left to return to the scene. He'd promised to handle things, calling the cops and speaking with them. I wondered how much lying he planned to do, while Alleryn continued rattling.

"You're filthy, so it's the bath for you before I can tend to your wounds." He peeled the bloody tee up to peek at my arm. "Where all do you hurt?"

Logan answered. He was holding me up with an arm around my waist. "Her head. Mind. Whichever. She said she was tapped out and in pain."

My stomach chose that moment to punctuate the statement by heaving. I almost passed out, bending over to vomit all over Thorandryll's marble floor.

"Lovely. In here."

The shifter didn't move. "That's your prince's room."

Alleryn snorted. "She's his lover, so is allowed inside. Move it, kitty, so that I can tend to your mistress."

"My name is Logan." The shifter's voice was a silky growl. I managed to open my eyes and focus on the elf.

"Yeah, use it, or I'll throw up on you next time. He's not a pet."

Alleryn rolled his eyes. "As you wish. Inside."

I balked at either helping me undress or giving me a bath, so Logan removed my boots before settling me at the edge of an enormous tub. "Thanks."

"Yell if you need help. Don't pass out and drown, Discord." He touched my cheek, glancing at the doorway. Voice lowered, he asked, "Why does he think you and Thorandryll…"

"Cover story."

"Oh, right." Standing up, he smiled and left me to it.

I somehow managed to undress, slip into warm water, and attempt to scrub myself. The tub didn't have a faucet, but two tiny slits at either end. Warm water poured from one, and the cloud of demon grit, stained pink with blood, flowed into the other to disappear.

Elven plumbing was pretty nifty.

Crawling out of the tub, I sat on a thick bathmat and slowly dried off. It took a few minutes of looking before I realized my clothing was gone, and that a sleeveless white nightgown had replaced it. No one had come in, unless he or she was invisible and silent. After putting it on, I levered myself to my feet and used the wall as support. The door stymied me. "Hello?"

"I'm here. What do you need?" Logan sounded anxious.

"Help getting out of here. Can you open the door for me?"

He did, and carefully picked me up. A moment later, he was tucking me into the bed that dominated the outer room. "The elf left this for you to drink."

I eyed the golden goblet he showed me. "What's in it?"

"Wine with herbs for pain. They're safe, Discord. I watched him mix it up."

"Okay." I drank it down with his assistance. "Where's Leglin?"

"He had some wounds. The healer decided to stitch them while you cleaned up."

The doctored wine left a bitter aftertaste, but worked quickly. Cotton seemed to insulate my mind, cushioning it against reality. "He can't heal like you do?"

"Not as fast. He'll be fine within a day or less."

"You're dirty too. Why don't you take a bath?"

Logan collected a chair, settling beside the bed. "I'm not leaving you alone here. I told that elf that I'm your bodyguard, when he made noises about moving me down the hall to a guest room."

Realizing I was actually in Thorandryll's bed, gratitude spilled over. "Good, thank you. Yeah, I don't want to be alone with either of them."

"You won't be." He patted the chair's arm. "I'll stay right here until you wake up, Discord."

"You can't," My eyes drifted shut, and it took effort to open them again. "Sleep in a chair."

"Don't worry about me. Get some rest. That girl is counting on you."

"Right." When my eyes shut, I left them that way. More cotton muffling, but sleep was in the mood for a slow dance. I was vaguely aware of voices, and someone messing with my arm.

The bed gave, something warm and wet sliding over my cheek. Fur brushed my arm as a large body settled beside me. My hound had returned. More voices then a quiet click. After a little bit, someone lay down on my other side, and a hand slipped over mine.

My smile grew just before sleep ended its teasing dance.

Twenty-six

Soft, silvery light shone through the windows when my eyes opened. I stood beside the massive bed.

Thorandryll lay on his back, asleep with an arm around the dark-haired woman cuddled to his side. Peering at what I could see of her face, I knew she was the one from the vision I'd had when I'd first handled the red silk.

Climbing onto the bed for a better look, I froze when the elf moved. His free hand slid up the arm she'd rested upon his chest. Eyes opening, he stroked hair from her face and laid a kiss on her forehead.

A chill shivered through me. She was the woman whose body we'd found earlier. The sacrifice.

I'll be damned, Thorandryll had been led around by his gonads. No wonder he wanted discretion.

My curiosity flared, watching her tilt her head back and smile. Why had she volunteered for such a horrible death? Thorandryll was a prick, sure, but I wouldn't trade him for a demon.

Without thinking it through, I reached over Thorandryll and touched her shoulder. My hand went through it, and silvery red light blazed, obliterating the scene.

A few blinks, and the soft moonlight returned. Same room, only now, I was in the bed with the elf spooned against my back. His hand slipped from my stomach to my breasts, and forged a warm trail upwards to settle his fingertips against my jaw. Head turning at his gentle urging, I received a kiss on the corner of my lips.

The resulting tingles made every little hair on my arms stand at attention.

No, not my arms. I was definitely in her place, from the strands of black hair visible from the corner of my eye.

Pure terror sank claws deep into my soul. The only other time I'd found myself taking someone's place in a vision, I'd lived through hours of torture. Watched and suffered as a straight razor sliced skin away in thin strips. This one might not be a painful experience now, but I didn't trust the vision not to time-warp, and drop me right into the middle of being sacrificed on that stone altar.

While I tried to no avail to wake up or break the vision, it continued. Thorandryll shifted to recline, moving me onto my back. Her back. Whatever.

He murmured something and began kissing my neck.

Head tilting, eyes half closed, a movement caught my attention. Thomas Merricott, AKA Dead Fake Elf Guy, stood just outside one window.

Fingers in Thorandryll's hair, which was as soft as I'd imagined, my eyes opened wide. Merricott held up the grimoire, the concealment spell a thin, black line around his left wrist.

I felt a smile grow on my face. I mean, her face. Mission accomplished.

With a nod, Merricott disappeared from sight, and all of my – her!- attention returned to the elf. I suppose she couldn't just get up and leave with an "It's been fun, see you around".

Thorandryll proved no slouch when it came to foreplay, and seemed more than happy to draw it out as long as possible. Trapped, I was along for the ride.

Not the most painful vision I'd ever had. He kissed me and I noticed that he didn't taste like I remembered.

No sunshine or spring breezes. Instead, he tasted of copper-flavored pine, laced with something both sweet and faintly nutty.

The vision flickered as I buried my hands in his hair. It didn't feel as soft as before, and I was relatively certain that elves didn't purr.

"I don't allow animals in my bed, Miss Jones." That icy statement broke the vision to a thousand pieces, leaving me staring into a pair of wide, clear green, gold-flecked eyes.

Logan's purr cut off as though a switch flipped, dark green flooding over the pale. "The hell?"

My response was utterly brilliant. "Ah…"

"You are taking far too much advantage of my hospitality." Thorandryll had reached the side of the bed. "I believe it's time…"

Logan slid off me and sat up. I followed suit, mouth already running to put the awkward situation behind us. "What was her name? The woman you were seeing? She had black hair."

The elf's angry expression became one of confusion. "Why do you need that information?"

"Oh, come on. She took you for a ride. Distracted you with sex while the dead guy stole your damn book." I barely paused for breath. "Another lie. You said you had no idea who took it."

Logan had made the edge of the bed by then. Looking over his shoulder at Thorandryll while settling the sword across his lap, he chuckled. "Thanks for the loan of your bed. It was an illuminating experience."

Thorandryll flinched and took a step backwards before gritting out, "Carole Bronson."

Offering a hand to Logan and grabbing Leglin's collar, I said, "She's dead."

The elf's eyes widened, but I missed anything else by teleporting us back to my place. My bedroom, to be exact. Logan frowned, quickly standing up. "You didn't give me time to grab my boots."

"Damn. I forgot my purse too." Waving that aside, I said, "Okay, the first thing we need to do…"

Logan interrupted me. "Is take showers. I've got a change of clothes in my truck."

"We don't have time for…"

He cut in again. "Do you care about Nick, Discord? He's going to be really unhappy when he smells my scent on you."

"Oh." Yeah, personal problems that could be avoided should be, especially right now. I needed to be somewhere. "Okay. You go first, while I make coffee and get online. I need to find her address."

The shifter nodded. "I have to run out to my truck."

He was out of the shower by the time I'd figured out which of three Carol Bronsons listed in the Santo Trueno phone book was the right one, and had written down the address. "Hey, coffee's ready."

"Do you want a cup?"

"Please." I reached for my purse, only to remember. "Damn it. Do you have your phone?"

Logan deposited a cup on the table. "No, it's sitting on the elf's dresser, right next to your purse."

"Crap." I wasn't quite able to meet his eyes. "I should go back and get our stuff."

"I would like to have my boots," he agreed, glancing down at the brand new-looking running shoes he had on. "These don't feel like mine yet."

"Okay, let me take a shower. I want to return this." I plucked at the lace edging the square neckline of the gown. "Um, I guess the vision stuff is changing. I'm sorry you were dragged in like that."

His coffee cup seemed to become immensely fascinating when I finally managed to look up. Logan stared into it. "No harm done. It might be better if we didn't tell Nick about it though."

I winced. "He'll go ballistic, huh?"

"Probably."

"Okay. Wait. Thorandryll might open his big mouth. That would be worse."

Logan frowned. "True. Awkward situation."

"Tell me about it." I hesitated before I took a drink of coffee, because I could still taste him, sweet and weirdly familiar. The coffee washed it away.

"I'm not seeing anyone, so I don't know if Nick will believe nothing really happened."

"Why would whether you're seeing someone or not have anything to do with it?"

"Because he's a wolf, and I'm a tiger."

I had to put a hand over my mouth to control the urge to laugh. Voice muffled, I said, "This is a dog and cat thing? Really?"

"It sounds dumb, I know, but yeah, it's a cat and dog thing, and a territorial thing."

"Okay, I'm not anyone's 'territory'." Rising from my seat, I had another swallow of coffee before setting the cup down. "Nick can either believe the truth, or not. If he doesn't, that means he doesn't trust me."

Logan seemed about to say something, but didn't. He nodded instead. "All right."

"I'm going to take a shower. Be back in a few." Leaving the kitchen, I ran over the last week. Aside from the lie about the elf kissing me – which wasn't my fault anyway – I hadn't done anything horrible enough to make Nick not trust me.

But if he didn't, well, our relationship was over just as it was beginning to be one to me.

Twenty-seven

My plan was simple: get in, get our things, and get out.

To my relief, no one was present when I popped into Thorandryll's bedroom to leave the gown and retrieve our things. While Logan exchanged running shoes for boots, I called the office. "It's me. Any word on Kate?"

"Good morning. She is awake and demanding a hair regrowth spell." Whitehaven's response conveyed a smile.

"Great. Did Nick find anything last night?" I collected the laptop and my purse when Logan stood up. He pointed at the door, and when I nodded in response, led the way outside.

"No."

"Is he there?"

"Yes."

"Would you ask him to meet us at 2214 East Belvedere, Apt 16 B? I have a lead I want to check out." Locking the front door, I turned in time to see Logan letting the hound in on the passenger side of his truck.

"He'll be there," Whitehaven replied after a moment. "Logan and the hound are still with you?"

"Yeah, and we're heading there now." I glanced around while walking toward the truck. "We're all fine."

"Excellent." We ended the call as I slid to the middle of the seat, and after promising to report the results of my new lead. I'd already checked the Zoe shimmer several times, but did again while wondering what sort of horrors the girl had suffered.

My decision to call Mitchell was met by his secretary informing me that he'd yet to arrive at the office. There was no answer at the Mitchell house. Uneasiness caused a case of the internal squirms, so I called the Detective Division. Schumacher answered. "It's probably nothing, but can you go check an address for me? I have a client we haven't been able to get in touch with."

"This client involved with last night's dead body?"

"I think so, but not as a suspect."

He grunted. "All right. I'll let you know what I find."

"Thanks." Ending the call, I dropped the phone in my purse and sighed. Leglin snuffled my hair. "Are you all better now?"

"He's fine." Logan signaled a turn. "Had a look while you were showering."

"Thanks." Petting the hound, I tried to ignore my growing uneasiness, and the weird spikes of urgency that punctuated it. Rushing seldom helped anything.

We arrived before Nick, and I remembered to call my mom. Reassuring her that I was fine, followed by a promise to call again later, calmed her anxiety to a dull roar.

"There's Nick." I left my purse in the truck. He was out of his before we reached it and half-crushed me with a hug.

He kissed me, a grin followed on its heels. "Cordi."

"Hi." Returning the grin, I basked in his relieved happiness. "Ready for some work?"

"Sure." He nodded a greeting to Logan, who returned the gesture.

"Number 16 B," I said, and we began searching.

Less than five minutes passed before Logan called, "Here."

We met in front of the dark gray door trimmed in white. The complex's color scheme of choice was subdued and tasteful, with each building painted a soft, pale gray with white accents. A small, brushed-nickel plate beside the door was engraved with 16 B in flowing script. I bet the rent was twice as high as mine.

"Let me check." I used telepathy to determine the apartment was empty, as were those around it, aside from pets. "All clear."

Just a second of concentration and the lock clicked. I grabbed Nick's wrist as he reached for the doorknob. "Don't touch anything."

"Let me go in."

"Sure." Stepping back and using TK to push the door wide open, I said, "Take a really good sniff."

He nodded. "What am I sniffing for?"

"Dead Guy and Mitchell."

Nick went inside, and we watched him sniff the air. Once he disappeared through a door, I studied the living room. No signs of any struggle. He reappeared. "Dead Guy, no. Mitchell, yes. His scent's all over the bed, mixed with hers."

"Okay. They were involved. Our new question is whether Mitchell knew about her being a member of the cult or not." Frowning, I used my abilities to shut and lock the door once Nick was outside. "We're going to his office."

My cell phone rang while we walked back to the vehicles. "Jones here."

"Hope you already got paid." Schumacher paused. "Woman, age about forty, apparent suicide at the address you sent me to."

Failure washed over me. Poor Mrs. Mitchell. "I'll bet five it wasn't suicide. Her husband may be involved in her daughter's disappearance."

"I'll pay him a visit."

"We're about to do that. If he's involved, demons could show up."

The detective cursed for a whole minute. "Fine. You handle him, but I want full disclosure, Jones."

"That's my middle name."

He snorted. "Your middle name's Angel. Go, and call me after."

Ending the call, I marshaled my troops. "Nick and I will go talk to Mitchell. Logan, will you go to the office and fill Whitehaven in?"

"Sure." Opening his truck, he pulled out the sword to hand it over to Nick. My purse followed. "Laptop?"

"It can go with you."

"All right. You three be careful."

"We will." Nick was putting the sword in the backseat of his truck. Leglin came at my call, and we piled in. I waved at the other shifter as he pulled out of the parking lot.

A moment later, we were doing the same. Nick glanced at me. "So what happened last night?"

I filled him in, including the vision and how Logan was pulled into it. "Before you say anything, he was dressed and on top of the covers. It wasn't his fault."

Jaw clenched, he stared ahead. "Nick?"

"What the hell was he doing in bed with you?"

I winced. "Protecting me. It was Thorandryll's bedroom, and I didn't want to be left alone."

Another glance, this one more searching. Nick growled. "You lied to me about the elf. He kissed you that day."

Crap. "Yeah, I did, and he did. It wasn't any of your business and I handled it."

"We're sleeping together. How the hell can it not be my business?" He hit the brakes, narrowly avoiding the rear end of a car ahead of us that was stopping for a light.

My seatbelt tightened as I jerked forward. "Ouch. It wasn't your business because I didn't know what we were doing then. I didn't ask him to kiss me or flirt with him."

Nick was grinding his teeth, so I kept talking. "That vision I had handling the red silk? It appeared again, from a different perspective when I was checking out the crime scene. Thorandryll took advantage of the moment."

He was glaring at the light, and his eyes had changed colors. "I'm sorry I didn't tell you, okay? But personal life can't be a consideration on the job." No response. Piqued, I added, "Just so you know, if I did ever decide to do something with another guy, I'd break up with you first. I don't cheat, Nick."

Expelling a hard sigh, he relaxed. "You told him we were involved. Are we, or did you say it because you were mad?"

"Well, we didn't start out the way I'm used to doing this kind of thing, but...." The light changed, so I paused until the truck was moving again. "Yeah. You're my boyfriend."

"Which is why you told me about Logan." It wasn't a question. "If the elf pulls something else...?"

"I'll tell you ASAP," I promised.

"Okay."

"You're not mad at Logan, are you? It really wasn't his fault. He didn't do anything on purpose."

Nick half-smiled. "Yeah, I am, but I'll get over it."

His eyes were brown again. I smiled back. "Okay. Good."

He patted the empty space next to him, and I unbuckled the seatbelt to scoot over.

Twenty-eight

"You can't go in there." Mitchell's secretary, a short, gray-haired woman with a stern face, tried to block the doors to the conference room.

"Move, or I'll move you." Nick's growl bared his teeth, and his eyes changed to gold. She flinched, meeting them, and then slowly eased right, clearing our path. I pushed the double doors wide open, immediately spotting Mitchell, who sat at the head of a long, rectangular table. There were about a dozen other people present, sitting on each side of it.

They all stared as we walked into the room.

"Miss Jones." Mitchell frowned. "This isn't a good time."

"Too bad. Your wife's dead, but I'm betting you already know that." Shield down, I watched him closely.

"What?" Perfect shock appeared on his face, but his uppermost emotions were anger and worry.

"You do surprised well, and I'd be convinced if empathy wasn't one of my abilities."

Mitchell held the façade, offering wide eyes and a tremble in his voice. "I don't understand."

"Do you have any idea how hard it is to lie to a psychic?" Giving Nick a nudge, I smiled. "It's extremely hard. Where is Zoe?"

He flushed as eyes turned his way. "We hired you to find her."

"Your wife hired me. As I recall, you didn't seem to give a damn about the girl." By then, Nick was in place behind him. "Where is Zoe?"

I hoped he'd think something about her location, but instead, gibberish rose in his mind. Nick snarled, grabbing Mitchell's shoulders. "He's casting a spell."

Shifters could feel or smell magic? News to me. The warning was a trigger, sending those at the table scurrying for the doorway. Jostled as they retreated, I lost focus and contact with Mitchell's mind. What I couldn't miss was his eyes turning inky black. "Nick, he's poss...."

Mitchell lunged to his feet, and the shifter hit the plate glass window behind the head of the conference table. It shattered, and I screamed as he fell out of sight.

We were four stories up.

"Now we're alone," the newly arrived demon wearing Mitchell said. He smirked while straightening his jacket. "Let's make a deal, little girl. You for the other one."

"No way." Shoving my hand into my purse, I dug for the dagger but didn't locate it. Instead, I got a clear image of it lying on my kitchen table. "Crap."

"You really don't have a choice." The demon began walking down the left side of the table.

"Oh, yeah? That's what you think." I waited until he was only a few feet away before teleporting to the window. Then I jumped.

I'd planned and my panic wasn't strong enough to interfere with my abilities. A cushion of thick air broke my fall, and I landed next to Nick's sprawled body. Blood spread from underneath his head in a widening pool. "Oh God. Nick?"

"How touching," Mitchell drawled from behind me. Twisting around, falling on my ass, I gaped at him, unable to figure out how he'd gotten there. "The wolf's dying, just as you will."

With his first step, a grin stretched across his face. I scrambled away, trying to make it to my feet, and fell again as Leglin appeared from nowhere. The hound growled, his head lowered and hackles raised. It was my turn to grin. "Meet my friend. He eats demons for breakfast."

Mitchell wasn't eager to stick around, and with a ferocious scowl, faded from view.

"Oh, you are the best boy. Steak for dinner." I praised the hound while crawling back to Nick's side. "Come here. We have to get him to the hospital."

With a hand on each, I teleported us to the ER of Santo Trueno General. "I need help now!"

Good luck was finally on my side, because Dr. Jamison was at the nurses' station. He'd been one of my doctors during and after my coma. "What happened?"

"A demon threw him through a fourth-floor window. He's a shifter."

"All right. Are you hurt?" Jamison checked Nick's pulse.

"No."

"Then get the dog out of my ER. Is he an associate?"

"Yeah, Nick works with me." I bent to kiss the shifter's forehead. "The boss will take care of the paperwork. Don't let him die."

"Don't intend to. Dog, out." He began calling out orders, and grabbing Leglin's collar, I teleported to the office.

Right into Whitehaven's office, in front of his desk. He frowned. "Discordia. Are you injured?"

There was blood on my jeans. The warmth of it made my stomach roil. "Nick is. Mitchell called a demon and it possessed him. He threw Nick out of the window. Four stories. I got him to the hospital," I was babbling, and stopped to calm down. "He was unconscious and bleeding really bad."

The boss already had his phone in hand, and I squeaked as someone touched my arm. It was Logan. "You all right?"

"He'll be okay, won't he?"

His smile was reassuring. "He's a shifter. We're pretty tough. Sit down and give yourself a few minutes."

Hand still clamped around Leglin's collar, I shook my head. "The sword's still in his truck, and I left the damn dagger at home. We need them."

Before he could respond, I teleported.

There were police on the scene, but no one saw us when we appeared next to Nick's truck. Using telekinesis to unlock it, I decided it shouldn't be left there. Leglin jumped in, and I began searching for an extra set of keys the second my butt touched the seat.

There weren't any. "Crap."

Digging out my cell phone, I called Schumacher. "Hey."

"Damn it all, Jones. What the hell happened over there?" He sounded relieved.

"Aw, were you worried about me?" I grinned as he sputtered, leaning forward to rest my head against the steering wheel. "If you'll shut up, I'll tell you."

He mumbled under his breath when I finished. "All right. Now tell me what all of this shit means."

"It means big trouble."

Sarcasm dripped from his response. "I realize that much, Jones."

"Mitchell's possessed. My boss said that means his soul is gone, and can't return to his body. If you see him, shoot him."

Schumacher grunted. "Will that work?"

"Probably not, but it might give you time to run." That earned a brief laugh. "Where's Damian? He can banish demons."

"He's," the detective paused. "Oh shit. He's here."

I sat up. "Damian?"

"Mitchell."

"Get out of there. Everyone out now." Before I finished, the connection went dead. Punching redial resulted in three rings and shunting to voicemail. Leglin whined.

"We're going." I found the sword, took hold of his collar, and teleported to the lawn of the Mitchell house.

Two cops were down, EMTs bent over them. Shots sounded from inside the house. I released the hound and let my purse fall to the grass. Hefting the sword, I said, "Let's go."

We ran inside, and I yelled at the hound to stay the instant we reached the living room.

"Drop the sword, witch, or one of the humans will die." Mitchell sneered over Schumacher's shoulder. His hand was wrapped around the detective's neck.

There were three other cops, each held by a demon. I could get out, teleport. They couldn't. I bent and laid the sword on the thick beige carpet. "All right. Let them go."

"You don't make the demands. Send the hound away."

"No."

Schumacher gagged as the demon's hand tightened. "I will kill him. Send the hound away."

"You must think I'm pretty damn stupid. They'll all die anyway, if you work the spell. You have Zoe, so why are you screwing around here?"

Mitchell laughed, a broken sound that grated the air. "Trying to gather information?"

Demons weren't stupid. I added that tidbit to my list. "I know that I can mess everything up, and that's why you want to kill me."

"Send the hound away, and the humans go free. Otherwise," Schumacher's face began turning red and a rasping wheeze escaped him. "They die now."

"Leglin, go to Mr. Whitehaven." The hound looked up and whined. "Go to him right now." He looked at Mitchell, silently baring his teeth, and then disappeared. "Okay, now let them go."

The four men were released, and the detective stumbled towards me, gasping for breath. "Jones..."

"Get out." Until they were clear, I was stuck. "Hurry the hell up."

He hesitated for a second longer, and then went. Mitchell was smiling. "How fortunate that you have some sense."

"Depends on your point of view." The door shut behind me. I dropped and grabbed for the sword, intending to teleport the hell out of there, but a clawed foot stomped down on the blade.

Its mate kicked, hitting me in the shoulder as I rolled away. Before I could leave, another demon had a handful of my hair, and we were suddenly elsewhere. I tried to teleport, and fire raked my brain, causing me to squeal in pain.

"This is our realm, Miss Jones. Your magic won't work here."

Blinking away tears, I managed to glare at him. "Lucky for you."

"And not for you. Put her with the girl," Mitchell ordered, and the green gargoyle began to drag me away.

The only bright spot I could find was that I'd finally found Zoe.

Twenty-nine

The tunnel it was dragging me through was made of the same dark gray stone of the sacrificial cavern. I winced as one of the demon's claws poked into my arm. "Hey, watch it."

"Hold silent, witch." Its voice sounded like gravel sliding downhill.

"I'm not a witch, or you'd be toast. I'm a psychic." Arguing what I was wouldn't really help, but might distract it a little. "It's not magic, but brainpower, lizard face."

It grunted, a particularly unhelpful response. You can't argue with something that's not going to argue back. I pretended to trip, but the demon just tightened its grip and we both stayed upright.

"Ow. Let go, your claws are sticking me." It was holding most of my weight, so I kicked backwards and landed a blow on its shin. The demon growled, released one shoulder, and hit me in the back of the head.

Dazed, knees giving out, I dangled from his other hand. With a huffing sound, it transferred its grip to my arm and dragged me along behind it. Moments later, it opened a door and tossed me on a pile of blankets. The door clanged shut almost immediately.

Blinking in the near darkness, I resisted the urge to gasp when a pale face swam into view. "Are you all right?"

"Zoe?"

She backed away, eyes narrowing. "How do you know my name?"

Sitting up, I checked the back of my skull and found a small lump. "My name's Cordi. Your mom hired me to find you, and hey, I found you."

"Well, great job there. Now we're both trapped in this stinking cell." Zoe crossed her arms, attempting to sneer, but her lips were trembling too much. Pressing them firmly together, she asked, "Now what?"

"Well, that's a really good question. The good news is that you're no longer choice *numero uno* for the sacrifice." I managed to stand up, and stood wavering until she jumped up to grab my arm. "Thanks."

"What's the bad news?"

"I can't use my abilities here. I'm a psychic." Pointing to where I thought the door was, I said, "I need to check out the door."

The girl led me over. "A psychic? Mom hired a psychic?"

"I'm also a private investigator." The door was solid metal, no handle, no opening whatsoever. "Crap."

"That man she married did this. Did you find that out?" Zoe helped me back over to the pile of blankets.

"Yeah." I didn't bother mentioning that I'd just figured that part out. "Let me think for a minute."

"Sure." She sat down next to me, pulling her legs up to hug her knees to her chest.

I didn't want to be the one to break the news her mother was dead. There had to be something I could do to at least get her out. "Wait."

What had the boss told me the day Thorandryll brought the hound to me? Something important. "There's...oh. I remember."

"Remember what?" Head turning, the girl looked at me with eyebrows raised.

"I'm going to get you out of here. Promise. But I need you to do something for me. Tell the people who'll be there when you arrive that I can't use my abilities because I'm in the demon realm."

"If you know a way out, why aren't you coming with me?"

The smile I offered felt crooked. "Believe me, I'd rather do that, but I have to destroy the book first, and we don't know how to get here. Where here actually is. So I have to stay."

Zoe slowly nodded, brows drawing together. "Is that all you want me to tell them?"

"No. These are the really important parts, okay? Tell them to ask the elf when the spell has to be done, and to have him bring some of his hounds so that they can all come when I need them. They need to load up for demon killing."

She nodded. "I can remember that, but I know when they're planning to do the spell."

"You do? When?"

My heart dropped to stomach level when she answered. "Tonight."

Not much time for preparing. "Okay, tell them that and then the rest of what I said. Repeat it back to me."

Zoe did so without forgetting anything. Giving in to a sudden impulse, I hugged her. "Great. Now I'm going to call a friend who will take you to my other friends. Don't be afraid of him."

"Are you kidding me? If he's taking me out of here, I don't care if he's a snake." The girl grinned, and I felt about two inches tall for not having broken the news about her mother. After being a prisoner, surely she needed a little bit before that newsflash whacked her over the head.

"He's a dog. A big dog." About to call the hound, I added, "And do me another favor: make sure someone feeds him some steak."

"Okay."

Closing my eyes and breathing a silent prayer, I called the hound. "Leglin."

Zoe's "Holy shit" was followed by a wet tongue dragging across my face. "Oh, you are a good boy." I hugged the hound's neck, and then grabbed his muzzle with both hands. "I need you to take her to Mr. Whitehaven."

Leglin sat down, tail stilling. Baring his teeth, he sneezed in my face. "Are you telling me no? Don't tell me no. I have a plan."

Lips dropping, he cocked his head to the right with ears perked. "That's better. If it doesn't work, I'll call for you again, to get me out of here. Okay?"

Gazing into my eyes, the hound thought about it briefly before dipping his muzzle in agreement. I hugged him again. "Thank you."

Zoe licked her lips before asking, "What do I do?"

"Grab hold of his collar. He'll take you directly to my boss, and that's who you need to talk to. Do you remember everything I need you to tell him?" She nodded, moving to her knees and setting a hand on Leglin's collar. "Good. Leglin, get her out of here."

"Wait. Are you sure you'll be okay?"

"Yeah, don't worry about me." My reassurance held every bit of confidence I could scrape up. Zoe smiled.

"Okay."

With a final lick across my face, the hound lifted his head. Both he and the girl disappeared. I sighed, and carefully lay down on the blankets. My head was pounding.

I'd done everything I could for the moment. Eyes closing, I dozed off.

"You don't listen very well." The old man was back.

"Excuse me?" I couldn't tell if I was asleep or awake. My surroundings were the same, and the blankets smelled.

"I warned you." He was scowling. "Yet, here you are. From frying pan to fire."

"I have a plan."

"You're in the demon realm, girl."

Sitting up, I scowled back. "Not news, already knew that. Even know I can't use my abilities here."

The old Indian snorted. "Of course you can."

Okay, that was news. "I tried and it set my brain on fire."

"Because you aren't properly shielded. With just a little help, you can use your talents in this realm. However," he held up a gnarled finger. "This realm will seek to drain you. It hungers for power, specifically, power from other realms."

"How do I shield properly?"

"You'll need a bit of demon blood." He shrugged. "Ingested."

I tried to think that through. What exactly would drinking demon blood do to me? Assuming nothing horrible, like turn me into a scaly thing with horns, how the hell was I supposed to get my hands on any?

"Their throats are the softest, most convenient spots," the old man said.

"Oh well then, no problem. I'll just fuss until one comes to check on me, and then try and bite its throat. Yeah, great plan. I think I like mine better."

He snorted again, the sound ripe with derision. "The place they'll take you rests between this realm and the one you're accustomed to. Your abilities may work there without the demon blood."

Because I'd seen human cultists in my visions about the cavern, I'd hoped it was part of my world. "What if I'm surrounded by a pack of elf hounds?"

He gave a slow blink, mouth working as though he were chewing a tough piece of meat. "Aren't you the smart one?"

"So it'll work? That would be enough of a shield for me to be able to use my abilities?"

"The hounds are of mixed blood, and their presence should fully lock that chamber into your realm." His wrinkles moved, revealing white teeth. "Quite impressive thinking for a child."

I let him think I'd planned that, even though the thought hadn't crossed my mind until just a few seconds before. "Who are you? My fairy god-father or something?"

The old Indian laughed, a surprisingly robust sound. "Something like that. You may call me Sal."

Sal seemed like a super dumb name for a fairy god-father, but at least I'd gotten that much from him. "What else can you tell me?"

He shrugged. "Not much. There are rules."

"Rules?"

"Don't get too nosy, kiddo. Telling you much more would land you in a field of trouble you'd never escape from." Hair rustling, he turned his head to survey the rock walls. "What a dump."

"Tell me about it." I was willing to stop asking questions about him, being in quite enough trouble already. "Can you tell me if Zoe passed on everything I asked her to?"

Sal's teeth showed again. "Those who care will be ready to answer your call."

"Thanks." I rubbed a hand over the lump on my skull. "Am I going to be seeing you every time I sleep now, or what?"

"No, just when the rules allow me to contact you." He raised a hand. "No more questions, Discordia. You should take what rest you can before the time for action arrives. Sleep."

Darkness swirled and he faded away.

Thirty

A creak woke me, and opening my eyes, I found the demon wearing Mitchell and the green gargoyle walking into the cell. "Morning already?"

"Get up. You need to be prepared." Demon Mitchell was wearing the hooded robe I'd seen in my getting sacrificed vision. "Where's the girl?"

"Your buddy whacked me over the head. I didn't see any girl." I did sit up, but made no move to stand. "Prepared?"

He gestured, and Green Boy pounced, hauling me to my feet. "Bring her."

Turning, Demon Mitchell swept out with an impressive swing of his robes. Walking alongside the other, I glanced at its throat. Tiny scales covered it, and they did look softer than the larger ones everywhere else. For a minute, an attack seemed like a really good idea. But then I wondered if they'd just knock me out. Being unconscious would ruin the plan I'd come up with.

I'd just be dead. Maybe a better opportunity would come along.

We arrived at another rocky opening, but the room beyond it looked as though it had been lifted from a palace. There was a bathing pool in the middle of it, surrounded by marble floor and walls. "Nice place."

"Shut up, witch. Remove your clothing and bathe."

No way in hell I was getting naked while they watched. "Sure, as long as you both turn your backs. I don't do audience participation when nude."

Demon Mitchell sneered. "I can have him undress and bathe you."

Modesty was elbowed out of the way by panicky disgust. "Guess there's a first time for everything."

He laughed. Trudging toward the pool, I began undressing with my back to them. The water was pleasantly warm, but smelled of rotten eggs. High sulfur content. How appropriate.

I scrubbed, washed my hair with stuff from a bottle Demon Mitchell tossed at me, and then rinsed. "Need a towel."

He pointed, and a stack of thick, blood-red towels appeared on the pool's wide ledge. Wading over, I grabbed one to wrap around me while climbing out.

By the time I'd finished drying, he'd conjured up a long, sleeveless crimson gown and a black, hooded robe. "These aren't really my best colors."

"Put them on."

Grumbling under my breath about demonic lack of fashion sense and color palettes, I obeyed. A woman entered the room, carrying a tray with a brush and some other things on it. She was possessed, so no hope of help there.

"Sit."

"You are one bossy son of a bitch, you know that? Most people use a little courtesy. You should try it. More flies with honey than vinegar."

Demon Mitchell snarled, his teeth showing points. "I am not most people. I am a prince of the demonic realm. Now sit."

I sat, wondering if that meant he would be more difficult to kill than the demons we'd fought so far. The possessed woman began messing with my hair. She even trimmed the ends and my bangs. After that, she rubbed some sort of oil around my wrists and ankles. It seemed no time at all had passed before she was finished, and was placing a pair of red slippers on the floor for me to wear. Sliding my feet into them, I stood up and turned around. "So how do I look?"

"Like the perfect sacrifice."

I pretended dizziness, leaning back against the table where the tray sat. "That's not very gentlemanly."

Another sneer appeared on the demon's face, and my hand closed around the scissors. "Shut up, witch, and come."

"I'm not a witch. I'm a psychic. Now, I do know some witches, and I'll tell you, I can't do the things they can. There's this spell they can do that makes a net drop around demons, and squishes them out of existence. It goes like this…"

Green Boy lunged, evidently convinced I knew the spell. Arm swinging, I slashed at his throat. Blood sprayed, but not a damn bit of it landed on me because Demon Mitchell shoved him aside.

He knocked the scissors out of my hand and caught hold of both my wrists. Before I could yank myself free, I was cuffed with manacles that had a short length of silver chain between them.

"Enough from you. Forward to your destiny, witch," he ordered, yanking on the chain. Green Boy's throat sealed shut, and I shuddered at the nasty glare it gave me.

Forward we went, toward what I sincerely hoped was the destiny I wanted, and not the one they were imagining for me.

Just like in my vision, I fought while being led into the cavern and toward the altar. I didn't see the book anywhere. The cultists who'd taken over leading me lifted me onto it. That's when my nerve broke. Ready or not, I needed the cavalry. "Leglin!"

All hell broke loose. Cultists screamed as hounds appeared and began attacking everyone in reach. I kicked Demon Mitchell in the stomach, and to my relief, my TK worked. The lock on the manacles clicked. Yanking them away and rolling off the altar, I crouched down. Where was that damn book?

"Cordi! Behind you!" It sounded like David. Turning, I peeked over the altar, and yes, there it was. The book lay open on a short stone pillar on the other side of the altar.

It seemed close, but a red glow of magic lay thick around it, Demon Mitchell was waiting, and the witches were too busy to try breaking it out.

Flames, lightning and bodies flew around the cavern. Dropping back down, I took in the situation as well as possible in the crush. Leglin and four other hounds were keeping demons away from me.

Nick and Thorandryll stood back-to-back thirty feet away, each swinging demon-blood-hungry blades that keened in delight. Percy was screaming obscenities in French as he buzzed demons to distract them so that Kate could cast spells.

Trixie yowled, and I glimpsed Jo throwing a potion bomb and the demon it shattered against disappearing in an explosion of smoke. To her left, David had found some high ground. He was grinning like a mad man, throwing bottles and loading Copernicus each time the raven returned from dive bombing demons like a fighter jet.

Surrounded by blue-green lightning, Damian netted demons too stupid to avoid him. Illusion stood pressed tightly against his leg, barking rapidly. I spotted Ronnie, safe within a circle. Saki, her ferret familiar, sat upon her shoulder, apparently pointing out targets as the blonde witch threw potion bombs.

Whitehaven had made it close to the middle of the cavern, but stalled out, swords flashing as he whirled in a circle. He was wearing a leather outfit that left his arms bare, and didn't look nearly as gaunt as usual.

A black tiger burst through the demons nearby, and then Logan snarled at my left, huge paws slapping away one demon, claws raking through the flesh of another like scythes. On my right, Leglin echoed the sound, his fangs dripping fiery blood as he dropped an arm he'd ripped off another demon.

I got busy using my TK to toss demons away, but it became obvious that no matter how many we downed, more were steadily arriving to replace them. We weren't gaining any ground and in truth, were barely holding our own against the horde.

Something had to be done before we ran out of steam. Before someone was killed.

I didn't have a friggin' clue what, though. Just realized how incredibly stupid it was to have thought we were enough to take on a whole realm of demons.

Spotting two demons trying to take advantage of Thorandryll and Nick's intense concentration on others, I used my cryo kinetic ability to freeze them. Thorandryll's blade leapt sideways, striking one, and frost-rimmed black fragments flew everywhere.

The sight encouraged me. Concentrating, I began freezing all those within view until David yelled my name. "Cordi!"

He was waving frantically toward a spot I couldn't see. "The tunnel! Cordi, the tunnel!"

Oh. I moved closer to Leglin, desperately trying to spot the tunnel. The stream of demons arriving through it helped. Focusing, I pushed my CK to its limits and froze a huge chunk of the demonic reinforcements, effectively plugging the tunnel up.

"Thatta girl!" Jo yelled, still throwing bottles.

There were hundreds of demons trapped in the cavern with us. I blasted a few more to frozen stillness, but Mitchell called out something in a sibilant language that made my skin want to crawl away and hide. Flames sparked and spilled like liquid over mottled skin, instantly thawing out frozen demons. My CK had just become useless.

Panting, I felt panic strike.

Damian and Kate were both retreating to Ronnie's circle, pale faces creased in concentration and their magic barely crackling about them.

A yell from Nick jerked my head around in time to see a demon drawing a clawed hand back and blood spurting from his neck and chest. A curse from Kate had me looking back, just as a clawed hand batted Percy out of the air. The parrot struck her back, sending the witch stumbling forward. Damian turned to confront the demon responsible.

Whitehaven roared something that sounded like a challenge to the demons surrounding him. I saw Thorandryll grab the second sword before shoving Nick toward me. Spinning to put his back to us, the elf had both blades dancing to keep the demons at bay.

I couldn't see David because I was reaching for Nick, who was falling at my feet.

We were all going to die, and everyone who might have been able to break the demon's circle of magic was no longer in any condition to do so. Kneeling beside Nick, my hands warmed by blood as I pressed the slashes in his throat and chest closed, I felt the first cold flutter of defeat.

"Cordi." Nick stared, an unspoken plea on his face as he grabbed my wrist. I looked away, my eyes beginning to burn and my lips trembling. This was my fault. They were here because of me. Logan roared, leaping onto a tall demon with wickedly pointed horns. "Run. Get away from here."

"I can't." There was no way I could leave any of them. Anger fluttered in my belly, only to die as he pressed his cheek to the palm of my hand. "I can't, Nick."

He released my wrist and I rose, flinging away a demon rushing toward Thorandryll's back. The elf had been injured. Blood flowed down his arm from the slashes, but he continued fighting without seeming to notice. Looking at the book, I had a wild idea.

"Leglin!" At my call, the hound released the demon throat he was chewing on and rushed to my side.

"Cordi!" Nick said, but I was digging my hand under the wide leather collar and concentrating.

It was quiet behind the red haze of demonic magic. I looked at Leglin. "It worked. You were my key."

The dog's long tail swept once from side to side. Letting go of his collar, I reached for the book before changing my mind. Instead of touching it, I set it on fire, and it exploded.

Demon Mitchell spun around, his expression shifting from glee to shock. Rage followed quickly on shock's heels and the magic shattered when he charged through it. I threw myself backward. Claws erupted from his fingers as he took another swipe, narrowly missing my throat thanks to Leglin's timely jump. The dog's teeth dug into the possessed man's arm, his weight carrying them both several feet away.

Someone screamed my name, but I couldn't tell who. It didn't matter; all that did was leaving this place. Getting everyone out.

Teleporting was a series of blinks. Jo and Trixie. David and Copernicus. Whitehaven. Damian, Kate, and their familiars had already reached the safety of Ronnie's circle, and the pack of hounds was forming another circle around them.

Nick tried to keep me there. Peeling his hands away, I teleported to Thorandryll. The elf avoided my grasping hands. "Logan's down!"

My heart dropped when I couldn't see the tiger. Thorandryll twisted to sheer off a clawed hand, and then I was stumbling after him while he cleared a path towards a knot of the evil beasts.

The elf fought them away, revealing a torn, still figure. Falling to my knees, I touched the tiger, aware of Thorandryll standing behind me. I couldn't tell if Logan were still alive. A scream that sounded like a baby's cut through the din, and the elf called out. "Leglin!"

As Thorandryll turned, I grabbed his calf and a handful of thick fur. We landed in the midst of the others and my vision went black for a second, but taking a deep breath, I teleported one more time, determined to leave no one behind.

"Grab on!" I yelled once back among them. Hands obeyed, some latching onto my arms, others onto those I had hold of. I put every last ounce of energy into the effort, but darkness struck before I knew if I was successful.

<hr />

When I awoke, it was to the certainty I'd lost several friends. Losing consciousness while teleporting had to have consequences. Ones that I wasn't ready to face yet - if ever.

Instead, I tried to guess where I was at without opening my eyes. The lack of cinnamon in the air said I wasn't home and the bed was too soft to be hospital issue. From somewhere close by, I sensed movement and heard a soft sigh. Dreading it, but needing to know who'd survived, I turned my head and opened my eyes.

Logan's face was marred by fresh, angry, red furrows from his left jawbone to right temple. How the demon that left them had missed his eyes was beyond me.

"Cordi?" Jo's quiet voice led my gaze to her. She sat in a chair and looked exhausted.

"Is," I choked on the question, but tried again. "Did..."

She smiled. "Everyone's in one piece. We're over the shop, and a little cramped, so we put both of you in here. He was the most injured and we couldn't wake you up."

"Oh." I swallowed, eyes closing in pure relief. "What about Leglin?"

Jo chuckled. "He made it too, along with the rest of the hounds."

Knowing everyone was safe freed me to look at Logan again. "Is he going to be okay?"

"Nick says yes, that he'll wake up when he's healed enough to."
Her smile was reassuring.

"How long will that be?"

"He wasn't certain. Some of those gashes are really deep. Are
you hungry?" She stood up.

"No. Just tired." I wanted to curl up and sleep, despite
wondering if Logan would want anything to do with me once he was
awake. It was my fault that he was hurt. I'd left without warning. Had
just gone, leaving Nick bleeding out and him without any back-up.

"Okay." Jo nodded. "I'll go let everyone know you're all right."

"Thanks." As soon as the door shut behind her, I used my TK to
put the twin bed I was on against the side of his. Lifting the sheet
that was covering him, I saw what seemed to be miles of bandages.
After gently replacing the covers, I found his limp hand and picked it
up to hold it.

<hr>

"Discord, wake up." The urgency in Logan's voice brought me
blinking awake. I was lying half on him and hastily moved off, afraid
I'd hurt him. The shifter tossed the sheet off and disappeared into the
bathroom. Rolling over, I stared at the wall and wondered what he'd
say when he returned. It was a few minutes before he did.

Sitting on the bed, Logan's first words were, "Looks like I got a
hell of a beat down. Is everyone else all right?"

"Yeah. I'm sorry." My lips were trembling.

"For what?" He sniffed. "Are you crying?"

A tear had slipped from one eye. Before I could wipe it away,
Logan twisted around to roll me onto my back and brushed it off.
"Why are you crying?"

"I just went." He didn't look angry. "Why aren't you mad at
me?"

"Is that why you're crying?" Brow creasing, he wiped away
another escaped tear. "Fights are usually pretty chaotic and someone
always gets hurt, Discord."

"But I just left."

He tilted his head a bit. "What, you thought I'd think you had
cut and run? Is that it? That's not who you are."

"How do you know that? I didn't say anything, just left."

Logan smiled. "I know because I trust you."

Thirty-one

Thorandryll sat at his desk, head bent over whatever he was writing. Peeking around the door's corner, I watched for a minute, noticing there was only one chair opposite his seat at his desk.

The elf had left once he'd been told I was all right. Coming here hadn't been something I was completely sure about, but I was on a special mission. Taking a step into the room, I said, "Hey."

"Welcome, and come in, Miss Jones." It was clear I hadn't been nearly as quiet as I'd hoped. Walking in, I sat and Leglin appeared from behind the desk, tail sweeping from side to side.

Bandages covered most of the hound's torso, and he was limping. When I held my hand out, he came to me. "He saved me from Demon Mitchell."

"Then he completed his task with honor." Thorandryll put his pen down and finally looked up. "You're fully recovered?"

"Yeah. You?" I couldn't see any marks, though I knew he'd been injured.

"I suffered nothing more than minor wounds, all healing well." After a hesitation, he asked, "How goes Logan's convalescence?"

The question surprised me. "He's fine. Still has some marks from the worst ones, but shifters don't scar."

"Nor do elves." He glanced down at the paper.

Carefully picking my words, I said, "If you'd destroyed that book, none of this would have happened."

"The grimoire was placed into my keeping for a reason. That spell wasn't the only one it held, and destroying it wasn't allowed." He glared across the desk.

"A lot of people died because of it, and some of them were innocent. Your people have enough magic at their disposal."

The elf stopped glaring to simply frown. "No one ever has enough power."

With that attitude, this conversation wasn't going to go well. "You only need enough to keep people from attacking you, and I think elves have that completely covered."

"I'm seeing to it that all burial expenses are taken care of for those killed by demons."

Not having expected that, my mouth fell open. Thorandryll continued: "The child they held will be given compensation."

"You think money's going to replace her mother?" I had to hold myself back from leaning across the desk to slap him.

"Of course not, but I can't raise the dead, Miss Jones. What reparation can be made, will be made."

There it was: my opening. "What about reparation to me?"

His eyes narrowing, he gazed back. "I paid double your fee, as well as certain expenses for those who required medical care."

"I know that, I'm talking about personal reparation." Leglin laid his head across my knees, but I didn't pet him. "I spilled blood in your service, Lord Thorandryll, yet I am not one of your own."

The formal statement stiffened the elf's back. "What would you have of me, Miss Jones?"

"Not only did I spill blood, several times, but your actions have placed me in future danger from the demon realm." Mr. Whitehaven had told me to point that out. He wasn't certain it was completely true, but with my luck, there would be demons bearing grudges popping up from time to time.

Instead of frowning, Thorandryll smiled. It was a small one, but there. "You wish the hound."

"Yes, I do." Now I let a hand rest on Leglin's head, and the hound rolled his eyes enough to look up at my face. One eyelid dropped down into a wink.

"Will releasing Leglin, the finest of my hounds, permanently into your service be enough compensation?"

It was tempting to respond with a no and go for more, but I resisted. Whitehaven was giving me the second fee as a bonus. "Yes."

The elf gave that elegant inclination of head, as though he were granting a favor. "Then he is yours."

"Thank you." My fingers slid around the collar, and I grinned down at the hound. "Let's blow this pop stand, boy."

Teleporting no longer worried me. I wasn't afraid anymore, not after safely delivering everyone to the Orb despite losing consciousness. Whitehaven had once told me that I needed to learn to trust my subconscious more, and he'd been proven right.

The first thing I did was make Leglin comfortable on the giant doggy bed waiting in the corner of my office. Sitting down after that, I checked for messages before beginning to type up the case report.

No one bothered us for several hours, but then, only three of us were around. Kate and Nick were still recovering. They'd refused to be left out of the fight.

I'd left my office door open, and looked up just as Zoe Mitchell and a man came through the front door and into the waiting area. "Hey."

She joined me, but the man stayed back by the front doors. "Who's he?"

"Bodyguard. Derrick hired him. My dad's on his way back." The girl noticed Leglin. "You made the elf give him to you."

"Yeah. How are you doing?" I'd been surprised to discover that Derrick was one of her father's business partners. The vampire's attempts to nab me had been with the intention of hiring me to find Zoe. He'd knocked me out so that I wouldn't set him on fire, like I'd done to those two goons of his.

Since I had found and rescued her, Derrick had offered to pay for the repairs to my car. He'd also sent an open invitation to dinner, but so far, I wasn't taking him up on it. After all, he could have just freaking made an appointment instead of sending his goons after me.

"I guess okay. Everything's changed so much, you know?"

"I know." I didn't apologize for her mother's death again. The teen had told me that I was stupid for thinking it was my fault, and that the only person to blame was Hugh Mitchell – her deceased stepfather.

"Dad's going to take me with him from now on. Guess I'll be a world traveler." The faintest smile touched her lips, which were painted pale rose. Zoe had ditched the heavy makeup, and without it, was a truly beautiful young woman.

"Well, there's a bright side. Right?"

"Right. Anyway, I just came by to tell you thank you again. You saved my life. You and Leglin." She sent a smile over her shoulder, and the hound's tail thumped the floor once in response.

"You're welcome." I stood up and walked around the desk to hug her. "Take care of yourself."

"You too. Bye." Smiling, she left. I watched until she slid into the backseat of a waiting limo and heaved a sigh.

Two more cases successfully closed. I hoped the next wouldn't involve demons.

My cell phone rang, so I hurried back into my office to answer it. "Jones here."

"Hi." It was Logan. He'd been right about the Palisades playing a part, aside from being the location where Carole's body had been dumped. Turned out the cavern was under an outer section of the area. I'd been right about even humans sensing supernatural danger.

"Hey. What's up?"

He sounded embarrassed. "Well, I found something under the passenger seat of your car."

"Something?"

"It's pink, and it kind of looks like a crystal...."

Oh yeah, my life was definitely back to normal.

About the Author

A sword-toting alien with a fetish for fur and four-legged creatures, she writes fiction and spends entirely too much time distracted by shiny things online, like Twitter.

She prefers Netflix because there aren't any commercials and she can ignore all the reality series. As a voracious reader, she enjoys both ebooks and physical books, though her ebook collection doesn't require regular dusting.

She writes scifi as G. L. Drummond, fantasy as Gayla Drummond, and other things as Louise Drummond.

If you're interested in news and future releases, you can find her on Facebook (http://www.facebook.com/G.L.Drummond), Twitter (@Scath), or visit her author web site at http://gldrummond.com.

The Discord Jones urban fantasy series has its own web site at http://discordjones.com.

Free Ebook Copy!

Thank you for purchasing Arcane Solutions. You can claim a free copy of the ebook by going to http://katarrkanticlespress.com and clicking on 'Claim Your Free Ebook Copy'. Please read the information on that page before logging in.

The login information is as follows:
Username: ArcaneSolutionsPB
Password: xHI5x6Za

Printed in Great Britain
by Amazon.co.uk, Ltd.,
Marston Gate.